WORTH THE WAIT

A CLOVERLEAF NOVEL

JESSICA PRINCE

DISCOVER OTHER BOOKS BY JESSICA

THE PICKING UP THE PIECES SERIES:

Picking up the Pieces

Rising from the Ashes

Pushing the Boundaries

Worth the Wait

THE COLORS NOVELS:

Scattered Colors

Shrinking Violet

Love Hate Relationship

Wildflower

THE LOCKLAINE BOYS (a LOVE HATE RELATIONSHIP spinoff):

Fire & Ice

Opposites Attract

Almost Perfect

THE PEMBROOKE SERIES (a WILDFLOWER spinoff):

Sweet Sunshine

Coming Full Circle

A Broken Soul

To my mom, who did everything she could to give me and my sister a happy life.
You took on single-motherhood like a total badass!
If Kenzie comes across even half as amazing as you are, then I know I created a wonderful character.

PROLOGUE

KENZIE

PAST

MY POUNDING HEART felt like it was about to come right through my chest at any moment. This was it. I had been planning for this moment for months. Everything had fallen into place earlier that morning, and we were finally on the move. But despite the euphoria of being free, I still held on to a strong sense of fear that, despite all my best efforts, Lance would refuse to ever let us go. I'd lost track of how long I'd been building up everything I needed to ensure he'd never come after us, but I knew I wouldn't feel completely safe until the phone call. The phone call that would hopefully be the very last time I ever heard from Lance.

"Mommy, I'm tired," Callie called from the backseat. A quick glance in my rearview mirror showed my babies both fighting to keep their eyes open. Thankfully, a neon sign ahead showed a motel only two exits away. Truthfully, I was also having trouble keeping my eyes open.

I'd been driving for the past twelve hours straight, only stopping long enough for bathroom breaks and to grab something we could all eat on the road. But traveling long distances nonstop with two four-year-olds in the back seat wasn't humanly possible. And I'd have given my left arm for a bed right at that moment. No doubt about it, sitting in a car for half the day was a literal pain in the ass.

"Okay, guys, we're here," I said over my shoulder as I pushed the gearshift into park and unbuckled my seatbelt.

"Are we going home, Mommy?" Callie asked as her wide eyes stared out the window toward the lights of the motel parking lot.

I reached back and stroked her tiny leg. "No, baby, I told you. We're moving somewhere very special. A place Mommy hasn't been to since she was a little girl."

"Cloberfield?" Cameron asked.

"Clover*leaf*," I answered with a smile at my two little reasons for living. Nothing about my life had ever been easy, but giving birth to these two perfect little hellions was the very best thing I'd ever done. And I'd do absolutely *anything* I could to protect them.

"Yeah, Clober*leaf*," Callie repeated in her little toddler voice before sticking her tongue out at her twin brother.

"Mommy," Cameron whined. "Callie stuckeded her tongue out at me! Tell her that's ugly."

The anxiety induced migraine churned behind my eyes as the two of them went at it. "Play nice, the both of you, or I won't let you sleep in a super cool motel room tonight."

Yeah, so a Super 6 motel wasn't exactly what I'd consider high end, but to two toddlers, sleeping anywhere other than their own beds was an adventure, so I was successfully able to con them into thinking the motel was a five-star resort.

"Sorry, Mommy," both of them told me with sullen expressions.

"It's okay. Now, how about we go get a room so we can get some sleep. Tomorrow's a big day!" I exclaimed, hoping my enthusiasm would rub off. Thank god, it did. "Tomorrow, we start our new lives in Cloverleaf. You guys are going to love it so much."

Or at least that was what I hoped. To be honest, I'd only been to Cloverleaf once in my life, and it had been when I was just a little girl. My father had grown up in the small Texas town before moving away to Ohio for college where he met my mother, an Ohioan, born and raised. Dad had all too happily shucked his roots and stayed in Ohio so he and my mom could start a life together.

When I was six, my dad's mother passed away and he'd taken us back to his hometown to attend the funeral. I still remember the sheer wonder when I saw the view from her tiny house on the lake. It was mesmerizing, and at that very moment, I'd fallen in love with the town. Growing up, I'd created fantastical images of how wonderful life in Cloverleaf could be. Those fantasies helped me through some very lonely, cold times in my life.

Even though we never went back, I still held such fond memories of the little town that when I made the decision to leave Lance, it was the only place I ever considered going, made even more perfect due to the fact that Lance knew nothing about it.

"Mommy, how come Daddy's not coming to Cloberleaf with us?" Callie asked sleepily.

"Because, baby, Daddy had to stay back home for his job, remember?"

"Oh, yeah."

Desperate for a subject change that didn't include discussion of Lance, I pasted a cheerful smile on my face and asked, "Who's ready to sleep in a super special motel bed tonight?"

As hoped, my little guys cheered enthusiastically, all prior thoughts forgotten. As I wrangled everyone from the car and into the lobby, I made a promise to myself that everything I did from there on out would be for the two little people hanging off my arms. I'd messed up a lot in my life, made some unbelievably bad decisions, but this was my second chance to make things right. And so help me god, I was going to do just that.

———————

AFTER TUCKING THEM IN SNUGGLY, I pulled out their favorite book. I hadn't even managed one full reading of *Goodnight Moon* before they'd both passed out from exhaustion. With one last peek over my shoulder, I confirmed that Cameron and Callie were both sound asleep on the king-sized bed before stepping from the room and pulling the door to, leaving it cracked open just enough that I could hear if they woke up and needed anything.

The room I'd managed to rent in cash for one night wasn't swanky by any stretch of the imagination, but at least it was clean. I'd gathered the kids' blankets and pillows from the trunk of the car and, dumping the motel pillows on the floor, I made a pallet for them to lay on top of the comforter, just to be on the safe side. I didn't care if it was a five star hotel or a rundown, side-of-the-road place like this, you wouldn't catch me or my twins sleeping in the sheets.

Allowing myself one brief smile over the fact I'd given birth to two of the best kids on the planet, I lowered myself to the sidewalk outside the hotel room door and pulled my phone from my pocket.

It'd been turned off since Lance left for work early that morning, and although I knew I had to do it, a ball of dread plummeted low in my belly with the knowledge I had to turn it back on.

As expected, alerts for numerous texts and voicemails sounded as soon as I had a signal. They could only be from one person. Deleting everything without listening or reading, I quickly scrolled for his number and hit the call button, willing myself not to get sick as the phone rang.

"About fucking time, Kenz," Lance's seething tone broke through the line.

"I take it you got my note," was my only response.

"Yeah, I got your note, you stupid bitch. If you actually think this is going to work, you've lost your goddamned mind!"

Sucking in a breath and squeezing my eyes closed, I gave myself a mental pep talk. I wouldn't let him intimidate or frighten me. For once, in the ten years we'd been together, *I* had the upper hand. And I was keeping it.

"It's already done, Lance. The kids and I are gone and we aren't coming back."

"Listen here you stupid piece of—"

"If you come after us, I'll leak every single piece of information I have on you. I'll make sure you go down for every sick, twisted, illegal thing you've done. You already know I've got the proof, Lance. Just be smart about this. Leave me and the kids alone, *for good*, and no one will ever know."

"You're nothing without me, Mackenzie, and you know it. You won't last a fucking week without me," he spat out menacingly.

"Yeah, well, I'm willing to take that chance. Now, do we have a deal?"

A bone-chilling chuckle rumbled through the line. "Fine, you got a deal. I'm better off without a dumb cunt like you anyway. And I bet those little brats aren't even mine."

It took every ounce of energy in me not to respond. That

was typical Lance; he was needling me, trying to get a rise out of me because he got off on my anguish. He knew damn good and well there had been no man before or during him. He just thrived on being cruel.

"Goodbye, Lance," I said before disconnecting the call and shutting the phone off once again. I wasn't worried about him tracking me. Even if he were able to figure out a way, we had a twelve-hour head start; he'd never get to us before I woke the kids up and hightailed it out. And I had no intentions of leaving the motel with that phone anyway.

It was over.

Finally.

With a relieved sigh, I stood from the ground, dusted off the back of my jeans, and headed inside our little room. I climbed onto the bed between my sleeping angels and pulled them tightly against me, relishing the warmth of their tiny bodies. Ease settled over me knowing that, when we woke it would be the first day of our new lives.

Better lives.

I kissed Cameron and Callie on the tops of their heads and burrowed down beneath their blankets, letting sleep pull me under. It was the first peaceful sleep I'd had in almost ten years. The weight sitting immobile on my chest all those years was finally gone.

And I couldn't wait for what the morning would bring.

CHAPTER ONE

KENZIE

"OH, come on, the guy's been staring at you all morning like you're a freaking popsicle and he wants to lick you all over. You can't tell me you aren't interested. He's hot!"

God, I loved my boss. The kids and I had been in Cloverleaf for eight months and I'd been lucky enough to score a job working for Lizzy at Elegant Nails within our first week. She was one of the best people I'd ever met, but it had taken a while for me to finally warm up to her. I'd spent so many years having to hide the evidence of what Lance was doing behind closed doors from my friends that it finally became too tiresome, leading to me eventually cutting out any relationships outside of my home, so as not to risk anyone finding out the truth.

Not that Lance was at all disappointed with that development. He'd been thrilled to have me even more under his thumb. Over the years, it grew to the point that the only time I was ever allowed out in public in a social setting was when Lance dragged me to whatever functions his firm was throwing.

I'd be his arm candy for the night and always had strict instructions to keep my mouth shut at all times, unless absolutely necessary. A life without substantial friendships was a lonely and depressing one, but it gave Lance one less reason to lash out, so I swallowed down my misery and bore it.

When I started working for Lizzy, I quickly discovered the woman was a powerhouse of energy. As the days passed, it became evident that she refused to allow me to stay tucked inside the tiny shell that I'd grown accustomed to. She wormed, and poked, and prodded until I had no choice but to finally accept that there was now a person in my life who genuinely wanted to be my friend.

Slowly but surely, I let her in. We'd go to lunch together, and occasionally meet for drinks at Colt 45's when I was able to find a sitter. She also introduced me to her close circle of friends who were some of the most accepting, loyal people I'd ever had the pleasure of meeting. Eventually, I invited her over to my tiny two-bedroom apartment and did the one thing I'd been avoiding since moving to Cloverleaf—I introduced her to Cameron and Callie.

My little bundles of excitement immediately took to the fiery redhead and instant bonds were formed. I even reached the point where I trusted her enough to babysit on the rare occasion I felt like getting out by myself for a movie or dinner.

Forming a friendship with Lizzy had been exactly what I needed to feel like I was finally putting down some stable roots for me and my kids. For the first time in as long as I could remember, I was actually *happy*. It was a foreign emotion and took some getting used to, but I'd grown to love it.

Over time, our friendship grew to the point where I found myself opening up to her about my past. I told her about my childhood, and how my tumultuous relationship with my parents led to an even worse relationship with Lance. I trusted her whole heartedly to keep my secrets to herself, and she'd yet to prove herself unworthy of that trust. I'd grown closer to her girlfriends, Emmy, Savannah, Mickey and Stacia, and could even consider them to be close acquaintances. I was thrilled to finally be filling my life with so many wonderful people.

But there was still one aspect of my life that I refused to change anytime in the foreseeable future. I would *not* allow a man into my and my children's lives. I was happily single and determined to stay that way. It had been beaten into me from a very young age not to trust men, and I didn't see that mentality changing any time soon.

Lizzy was fully aware of that, which was why it surprised me to see her pushing this so hard.

"Liz, honey. Just because you went off and married yourself one fine piece of man doesn't mean I'm on the market. No relationships," I insisted as my friend stared at me, her shiny green eyes filled with mischief.

She let out a dreamy sigh, "Trevor is one outstanding specimen, isn't he?"

I laughed in agreement. I didn't know the man all that well, and just because I didn't trust the male species didn't mean I was blind. I could still appreciate a fantastic piece of eye candy when I saw one. And Trevor Devareau was certainly that.

He and Liz had been close friends since he moved to Cloverleaf a while back. One weekend took them from BFFs to husband and wife in the blink of an eye, and even though she was hesitant at the beginning, I could see it written all over her face, she loved that man something fierce. I was happy for her. Truly, I was. My past relationship might have been a nightmare, but I refused to allow myself to be so disillusioned that I believed all relationships out there were just as bad off as mine was. Trevor really did seem genuine, and he never bothered to hide his love for Liz whenever he looked at her. There were even times when I saw him watching her like she was his universe and I'd feel almost...envious. I used to be naïve enough to think that was how Lance looked at me.

Never in my life had I been so wrong.

"You know," Lizzy started casually. "He asked about you the other day..."

I knew she was hoping to capture my interest, but fear immediately took hold of me as I spun around to look at her. "What did you tell him?"

Her eyes widened in understanding as she grabbed each of my hands in hers. "Nothing, I swear! I'd never do that, honey. Everything you told me was in the strictest of confidence. I'd never repeat that."

At her assurance, I released the breath I hadn't realized I'd been holding.

"He just wanted to know about you. He's interested in you, Kenz. And I promise you, Brett's one of the good ones."

"It's not that I don't believe you," I explained. "I'm sure he's great, but you know how I feel about getting involved with a guy. It's just not something I'm capable of doing."

Lizzy's face grew soft with understanding and—God help me—pity. I hated the pity most of all. "I understand, love," she said quietly. "Please, just promise me you won't close yourself off from the idea of a relationship for the rest of your life. You deserve to have someone who'll treat you like you're his world."

I offered a placating smile and answered, "Maybe one day, just not today, all right?"

With a definitive nod of her head, I knew the subject was dropped. "Okay."

The rest of the day went off without any problems...well, except for the fact that I couldn't stop thinking of my earlier conversation with Lizzy. And I couldn't seem to keep my gaze from darting over to the man in question.

Brett Halstead, or as I'd begun to think of him since he started working on Lizzy's expansion a week and a half ago, Mr. Hotty in a Tool Belt. Mr. HTB for short. The full nickname was too much of a mouthful.

If I had been honest with Lizzy, I would have admitted that yes, I was, in fact, *extremely* attracted to Brett. But admitting that to her, let alone aloud would have led to a panic attack, and I'd blessedly been without one of those crippling attacks for months. I didn't want that to change.

Unfortunately, despite the fact that getting involved with another man made me want to run screaming for the hills, I couldn't get my mind off of Mr. HTB in all his sexy, rugged glory.

Since he started construction on Lizzy's salon, every waking moment seemed to have been dedicated to thinking about him. The previous night, he'd oh so stealthily snuck his way into my dreams where the images of what he could do with those amazingly strong hands of his woke me up in a panting, sweaty mess. The dream had been so damn vivid. His brown hair tousled from my fingers running through it, his warm brown eyes staring into mine, that delicious stubble that always graced his cheeks rubbing against my skin, that hard, tight body pressed against me...

Gah! Get a hold of yourself, Kenz!

A spontaneous orgasm in the work place was not ideal, especially with the star of all my fantasies only a few feet away.

And all of this was without the two of us having spoken a word to each other! Knowing he'd been asking Lizzy about me, and that he was interested sent me into a tailspin.

I needed to get my shit together. And fast.

There was no place for a man in my life. I neither wanted nor needed one. I had no doubt Brett was a nice guy, but it became evident at a very early age that something about me brought out the worst in the men in my life. There wasn't a doubt in my mind that if I stupidly allowed something to come of Brett and me, I'd turn him from a good, kind man into a mean, hateful bastard in no time.

It was a gift. My very own special brand of fucked-up.

I wouldn't allow myself or my children to be hurt again.

I also refused to allow a good man to be sucked down into my vortex of drama, only to come out worse for wear. It was best to just ignore our supposed mutual attraction and go about my new life as I had been.

I was making the smart choice—the *right* choice—for once in my life.

CHAPTER TWO

―――――――――

KENZIE

I PUSHED through the door of the daycare, silently counting down the seconds until I could get home, cook dinner, bathe my rugrats, put them to bed, and collapse on the couch for an hour or two of mindless TV before I finally crashed myself. Doing people's nails for a living wasn't the most strenuous job on the planet, but sitting hunched over for ten hours a day then having to wrangle two toddler tornados for hours on end, day after day, still left me exhausted.

"Hey, Ms. Webster. You have a good day?"

I looked up to see Lori, the daycare director, sitting at the front desk with a pleasant smile on her face.

"Hey there, Lori. It was good, how was yours?"

"Good, good. Just one more day closer to the weekend."

I let out a small giggle as I hit the touch screen in front of me and began checking my kids out. "Preaching to the choir, girl. I'm counting down the seconds until my next day off."

"Any big plans?"

"Other than sleeping later than seven a.m.? Not one."

We exchanged goodbyes before I headed down the hall to the twins' classroom.

Peeking through the tiny window in the door, I took a second to watch Cameron and Callie before pushing it open and making myself known.

"Hi, Ms. Webster."

I looked to the side to see their teacher, a pretty high school senior, wringing her hands in front of her.

"Hey, Megan, what's up?"

"Well...we, um, had some...issues today with Cameron and Callie."

Not good.

"What happened?"

Just as I asked the question, Callie released a war cry that would have made a Viking proud and went charging straight at her brother, plowing into him and taking them both to the ground. It all happened so fast; there was no time to react. Cameron screamed out as Callie planted herself on his stomach and shoved her foot is his face.

"Kiss it. *Kiss it!*" she yelled at him as Megan and I ran into the chaotic fray.

"Callie Anne Webster! What on earth do you think you're doing?" I reached down and scooped her up while Megan picked up a wailing Cameron and held him to her chest.

"Explain *now*, little girl," I warned as I stared into my daughter's face, unmoved by the big hazel doe eyes she was giving me.

"I wasn't doin' nothin' wrong," she pouted. "Ms. Lizzy told me boys is stupider than girls. That they'd be lucky to kiss our feet. That's jus what I was doin'."

"She put her stinky toes in my mouf, Mommy!" Cameron cried, not to be one-upped by his sister when it came to dramatics.

"Yeah, it's kind of been like this all day," Megan informed me with an apologetic smile.

"I'm so sorry—"

She raised her hands to stop me. "It's okay, Ms. Webster, really. Some days are just more tense than others. But we all know Cameron and Callie are good kids. And trust me, they're far from the worst," she added in a conspiratorial whisper.

I looked down at Callie in my arms with the sternest expression I could muster. "Well, I appreciate that, Megan. But violence against another person is *never* okay. We'll still be having a talk about this behavior when we get home. Won't we, Callie?"

At least she had the good grace to look apologetic. "Yes, ma'am," she answered with her little bottom lip poking out.

AFTER MAKING THE KIDS' dinner later that evening and getting them bathed and de-stickified, I dressed them in their jammies and tucked then into their twin beds in the second room of our tiny apartment.

"Now, you remember what I told you?" I asked Callie as I pulled the covers up to her chin and tucked them tightly around her body, making her into the little bedtime burrito that she liked so much.

"Never put your hands...or feet on oder people."

"And?"

"Never listen to anyfing Ms. Lizzy says," she repeated.

"And?"

"And no more puttin' my toes in bubby's mouf," she stated matter-of-factly.

I smiled and placed a kiss on her forehead. "That's right, baby. Now, give Mommy night night kisses."

She tilted her face up to me and planted a smacking kiss on

my lips before I climbed from the side of her bed and went over to Cameron.

"Mommy, will you make me into a burrito, too?" I smiled down at him, brushing his sandy brown hair from his forehead. "You got it, bub." I pulled his covers up and tucked them tightly around his body, just like I'd done to his sister, before giving him a kiss goodnight.

I reached up to turn off the bedroom light when Callie asked, "Will you read *Goodnight Moon*? Jus one more time? *Pleeeeeease*?"

"I already read it three times, baby. Go to sleep now."

I flipped the switch and pulled the door to, leaving it open just a crack. Walking into the kitchen, I poured myself a glass of iced tea, and curled up on the couch. My DVR was calling my name. I had about a million episodes of *The Mindy Project* and *New Girl* just waiting to give me a much needed hour or so of enjoyment.

My life was chaotic and every hour of my day seemed to be full, but I had my little ones, a job I loved, and new friends. Best of all, I was doing it all on my own, just me taking care of my kids and building a happy life for all of us.

Shooting up a quick prayer of thanks, I sipped my tea and queued up a mindless sitcom.

This was what life was all about.

"GOOD MORNING, SUNSHINE," Lizzy called as I walked through the door of Elegant Nails. She was in a chipper mood. I wasn't sure if it had to do with the cup of coffee in her hand—no doubt her second or third by now—or the fact that she had that sexy man warming her bed, but I was still planning to rip her a new one after the little scene at the daycare.

"You have a good night?"

"You tell me," I told her dryly as I propped my hands on my hips and stared her down. "First, I had to deal with Callie pile driving her brother into the ground like she was Xena the freaking Warrior Princess. Does that sound good to you?"

Lizzy choked on a surprised laugh.

"Or how about when she planted her little ass on his chest and tried to shove her foot down his throat, all because *you* told her boys are stupider than girls and should be kissing our feet?"

Her eyes grew wide in that *oh, shit, my bad* kind of way. I opened my mouth to lay into her when a deep, amused laugh from the front door caught my attention. I turned around to see Brett standing there, his gorgeous face alight with humor as he chuckled. That devastating smile of his momentarily short-circuited my brain.

"Sounds like your girl's being raised right, if you ask me," he joked as he took a step closer to Lizzy and me.

Giving my head a quick shake, I pulled myself from my lustful haze and narrowed my eyes at him. "I'm glad you find this funny." It dawned on me in that second that those few words were the first we'd ever spoken to each other.

"Oh, come on, beauty. You have to admit, there are worse things than your little girl being tough."

The first thought I had was how him calling me "beauty" caused a flutter deep in my belly—a flutter I hadn't felt in more years than I cared to count. The second thought was how that flutter was *not* a good thing. I needed to stay away from this guy. Everything about him was just too tempting. I couldn't risk letting myself feel any more for him than I already did.

Turning my back on Brett, I faced Lizzy and shoved my finger in her face.

"You," I scolded. "No more teaching my kids bad habits or

I'll make sure to feed each of them a pound of candy before your next babysitting gig."

Without another word to either of them, I walked away and started preparing for my first appointment.

CHAPTER THREE

BRETT

DAMN, that was one prickly woman. No matter how I went about it, I couldn't get so much as a civilized conversation out of her.

And damn it, that just pissed me off. I knew she was interested. I caught her staring at me when she thought I wouldn't notice enough times to know that much. And if that hadn't been enough to go off of, how those expressive hazel eyes of hers darkened as they scanned over my body was a pretty damn strong tell.

She wanted me. I was convinced of it. And I wanted her like I couldn't recall ever wanting another woman before. Female companionship was never something I lacked. I'd just never really wanted anything longer than a few nights. But I could see something more with this woman. She'd piqued my interests the moment I walked into Lizzy's salon and caught sight of her. There was just something in those eyes, something that ran so deep in those jade pools I couldn't decipher what it was.

Lizzy told me she had some baggage and an asshole of an ex, but other than that I had no real clue who the woman was. She was a complete mystery, one I was desperate to unravel. I found myself wanting something I'd never wanted with another woman before.

I wanted to *know* her. Not just bang her, but actually find out what made this woman tick.

I was tired of tiptoeing around, waiting for something to magically happen. I was a man used to going after what I wanted and that was exactly what I planned to do. But I was going to have to go about it in a different way. Something told me that waltzing up to her and flirting my ass off before asking her if she wanted to go home with me was definitely out of the question. Everything about Kenzie's demeanor indicated she wasn't a one-night stand sort of woman, and for once in my life, that actually worked for me, seeing as I was pretty sure I wanted *way* more than one night.

Pursuing Kenzie was out of my comfort zone, but there was a pull every time I was in her presence that I just couldn't ignore. I wanted to take that darkness, that sadness I saw deep in her eyes, and make it disappear. Comfort zone or not, I was going after this woman with everything I had.

Taking the opportunity to catch her unaware while she rummaged through a drawer for whatever it was she needed, I walked over to her little table.

"I didn't mean to offend you a minute ago."

Her head shot up as a startled gasp escaped her lips. "Jesus, you scared the crap out of me. You can't just wander up on a person like that."

She looked so damn cute when she was all ruffled and repri-manding me like I was one of her kids; I couldn't help but laugh.

Her eyes narrowed in a fierce glare causing me to hold my hands up in surrender. "Sorry, beauty. Didn't mean to scare you. I just wanted to come over and apologize for earlier. I didn't mean to upset you. I just meant that it's good your little girl's already so strong willed."

The anger slowly crept out of her gaze as she eyed me cautiously. "Thanks," she said, sounding somewhat hesitant.

"You're very welcome, beauty."

"Why do you keep calling me that?"

The corner of my mouth tipped up in a smirk that most women found irresistible, and I answered her with complete honesty. "Because I think you're beautiful. You're one of the most stunning women I've ever laid eyes on. I'm just calling it like I see it."

Usually, a woman would have melted if I told her something like that, but Kenzie's demeanor didn't shift, except to grow a tad icier.

"Thanks," she repeated. Her tone as she spat out that one word was anything but thankful. She clipped out that syllable so sharply I was surprised she didn't cut her tongue.

I was floundering, and to make matters worse, Trevor and the rest of my crew had just come waltzing into the salon to get to work. And by work, I meant they were hovering around, pretending they weren't eavesdropping on every freaking word between Kenzie and me.

"Look..." I took a step closer and leaned in so no one could hear. I realized my mistake instantly. The moment the smell of her perfume hit me, my mind blanked. Inhaling deeply, I sucked in as much of that clean floral scent as possible, wanting to keep it with me for as long as I could. I couldn't remember a time when just the simple scent of a woman turned me on so much.

Her lips parted on a gasp at my close proximity, drawing my gaze down to her luscious pink mouth. Her bottom lip was just a hint plumper than the top, and images of sucking it into my mouth as she moaned my name had my dick pressing painfully against the zipper of my jeans.

Great, just what I needed...a fucking semi in front of my crew.

"What?" Her soft voice pulled my gaze from her mouth to her intense eyes. Christ, everything about her did it for me. Her eyes, her mouth, that adorable little button nose. Everything about her looked sweet and wholesome, and damn if I didn't want to spend days dirtying her up in all the best ways possible.

"Huh?"

She blinked slowly as our eyes locked on one another. If I hadn't been so close, no doubt I would have missed the sweet way her pulse thrummed in her neck as she drew in a deep breath.

"Uh," she stuttered, and I couldn't contain my grin. I *knew* I got to her. She acted distant and abrasive, but the attraction was definitely there. I could see it clear as day. She cleared her throat and started again, "You, um, started to say something, but then you just stopped."

What was I about to say? Hell, I couldn't even remember my last name with Kenzie's soft skin so close that I could almost touch it. She was the best kind of distraction.

"Go out with me," I blurted, unable to control myself when it came to her. I wanted her so damn bad I couldn't think straight. I got within inches of that lush body and all thought of going slow flew right out the goddamned window.

Her eyes bugged out in complete shock. "What?"

The damage was already done so I figured I might as well just roll with it. "Let me take you out."

"Like a date?"

Jesus, even her cluelessness was irresistible.

"Not *like* a date. I was thinking about an *actual* date."

One second she was staring at me with wide-eyed bewilderment and the next the shutters came slamming down, closing her off from any emotion at all.

"No."

Just like that. She answered with one simple word in a voice as flat as a soda that had been left open for a week. She didn't even take the time to think about her response.

"Why not?" I asked like the idiot I was beginning to turn in to when it came to this woman. "Are you seeing someone?"

"Well," she hesitated, "no."

"Are you a lesbian?"

Two things rushed through my head as soon as that asinine question came out. One, I was a fucking idiot. Two, please dear sweet Lord in heaven, don't let that be the case. A woman like Kenzie batting for the other team would be a straight up crime against humanity...a blast to watch...but a crime nonetheless.

"*What*? No!"

"Then why won't you go out with me?"

Shit! Me and my fucking mouth! Where the hell was my damn nail gun when I needed it? I needed to go back to bed and start the morning over. Gone was the smooth, flirty Brett who could get whatever woman he wanted. In his place was a mega douche who was still sporting half chub even though the awkward vibes in the room were off the Richter scale.

It was the *FML* moment to beat all *FML* moments.

If a look could melt skin from bone, I had no doubt that the devil eyes Kenzie was shooting at me right then would have turned my flesh into a puddle of goo. As it was, that glare had my balls retreating up into my stomach for their own safety. The good news was that if the discomfort from seconds before wasn't enough to cure the inconvenient case of twitchy dick I'd been suffering from, the look she was currently sporting sure as hell did the trick.

My hard-on deflated like a Thanksgiving Day Parade float that had taken a buckshot.

"Are you really arrogant enough to think that I'd have to be gay in order not to be interested in you?"

I opened my mouth to respond, but quickly clamped my

jaw shut when I realized there was no response to that. I had nothing.

She stood from her chair and sidestepped her table. "I'm glad to know you have such a high opinion of yourself, but the truth is I'm just not interested. Even if I had been before, you just guaranteed that any previous attraction I *might* have felt is dead, buried, and encased in cement and rebar. Now, if you'll excuse me, I have work to do."

With my tail firmly tucked between my legs, I walked over to where my men and Trevor were suddenly very hard at work. And if I had to guess, the assholes were trying their best not to laugh at the epic fail that just took place.

"Here you go, buddy," Trevor said, handing me an empty jar.

"What's this for?"

"Figured you could give it to her to keep your nuts in, 'cause I'm pretty sure she just ripped them off and shoved them in her pocket. That was just pathetic, brother."

"Fuck off and die," I grumbled as I got to work, effectively ignoring the combination of pitying glances and laughs coming from my men, all the while thinking *what in the ever loving hell just happened.*

CHAPTER FOUR

PAST

"I SAW the way you were looking at that man," Lance declared, coming to stand behind me at the stove as I prepared dinner. I struggled to suppress the shiver that was working its way down my spine at his close proximity.

"What?" I asked, looking over my shoulder in confusion. "What man?"

I recognized that face, everything from the ticking in his jaw to the ruddiness of his cheeks. Lance's expression screamed fury and I immediately went on high alert as fear began coursing through my veins.

I should have known.

I never should have allowed myself to fall into the comfortable pattern of the days events, but I'd wanted so badly to believe he was changing, that he'd really and truly meant it the last time when he said he'd never do it again.

It had been such a wonderful day. When the alarm went off hours earlier, I'd shot up to turn it off and go about my morning the way I always did. I was to get up, make Lance breakfast, and then prepare the kids for the day while he ate. Once Cameron and Callie were dressed, I had to make his coffee in a travel mug to his exact specifications—always a splash of milk and one tablespoon of sugar. Any more or less would lead to consequences for not putting forth the effort to take care of my man as he took care of me and our children by working long, hard hours every day so we could live in a nice house and have food on the table—his words. After coffee, I would take the kids and stand in a line by the front door to offer up our goodbyes to him as he headed off for work.

Every morning was the same thing. But that morning when I rolled over to silence the alarm, Lance reached out, wrapping one of his thick, well defined arms around my waist and pulling me back into his body, startling a yelp from me at the unexpected movement.

"Leave it," he whispered as he nuzzled his nose into the crook of my neck. I tried to tell myself that this was wanted attention from him, but the fact was, even though his actions seemed sweet, I still couldn't will my body to loosen up enough to curve into him. I was just waiting for something to set him off, for something to spark that all too familiar anger in him.

"I don't want you to run late, sweetheart," I whispered back, hoping the stiffness of my body against his wasn't something that would cause him to snap. "I need to make breakfast so you have something to eat."

I gasped when Lance shifted quickly, turning me to my back so he could hover over me. The sudden movement and the soft look in his blue eyes as he gazed down at me were completely out of the norm. I couldn't recall him looking at me that way since before the twins were born, and right at that moment, I realized how much I'd come to miss it.

"You take such good care of me, baby," he muttered as he

brushed a piece of hair off my cheek. "How'd I get so lucky?"

Tears welled up in my eyes at his tenderness, and when he leaned in to kiss me, I wanted nothing more than to believe that this was what my life was going to be like from here on out.

"I'm taking the day off," he said with absolute certainty.

"Are you sure?" I couldn't help but ask. Lance had only just made partner at his law firm. It was uncommon for a junior partner to take time off. They usually spent most of their time at the office logging as many billable hours as possible in the hopes of eventually making it to equity partner one day. I knew for a fact that that was Lance's goal, so him declaring he was taking an entire day off in the middle of the week left me stunned.

"I'm positive. I've been so busy concentrating on work that I've neglected my family. I promised you I'd be better and I meant it." His sincerity moved me so much that I found myself lifting my head and pressing my lips against his. This was what our relationship was like in the beginning. That right there was why I was so excited when he asked me to marry him; I didn't even hesitate in giving him a resounding yes, even though, several years and two kids later that marriage still hadn't happened.

"How about you get the kids up and dressed and I'll make breakfast?" he asked. I gave a quick nod, unable to speak past my beaming smile. "And after that, I'm taking my family for a day at the zoo. You think the twins'll like that?"

"I think they'll love it," I said softly as I pressed my palm to his cheek. "And I love you."

"I love you, too, baby. This is just the beginning. I promise. You'll see, from here on out, it's going to be nothing but the best for my girl."

The day had been a dream. The twins laughed and squealed with excitement. Lance and I snuck kisses whenever and wherever we felt like it. We held hands as we trailed after our rambunctious toddlers from one side of the zoo to the other. It was absolutely perfect, and by the time we headed out everyone was thoroughly exhausted. When we got to our car, we noticed one of the tires was flat and as Lance fumbled around trying to get the tire replaced, my anxiety spiked. I started to worry that the difficulty he was having with changing the tire was going to set him off. When a man and his family stopped to offer up help, Lance politely declined and went back to work. I offered a quick thank you to the couple and once Lance got the spare on the car, we were on our way home. Thankfully, he still seemed to be in a good mood.

I was such an idiot.

"Lance, honey," I tried desperately. "I didn't look at any man, I swear. I don't even know who you're talking about."

"Don't lie to me, you stupid bitch! I saw it with my own eyes!" he shouted. "Are you calling me a liar? I take time away from my job, for *you*, and you have the audacity to eye fuck that man in the parking lot while I'm changing the tire? You're a goddamned slut!"

"Please," I plead on a whisper. "The kids will hear you. Please don't yell." That was definitely the wrong thing to say, but damn it, I refused to subject my children to his violent outbursts. So far I'd been able to shield them from it, but he seemed to be getting worse and worse every day.

Unhappy with my response, his face grew even redder as he lifted his hand and slapped me across the face as hard as he could, sending me sprawling to the kitchen floor. Tears burned my eyes and blurred my vision as they streamed down my face.

He crouched down and hissed, "Don't you *ever* tell me what to do. You're nothing but a worthless piece of shit. If it weren't for me, you and those little brats would have nothing. You better learn your fucking place." With that, he stood and aimed a well place kick to my gut, shoving all the air from my lungs.

I lay on the floor, gasping for much needed air as he told me, "You belong to me, do you understand? You will *always* belong to me. If I ever catch you looking at another man, I swear to god, this is nothing compared to what I'll do to you." He calmly strolled from the kitchen but before he cleared the doorway, he turned and glared at me over his shoulder. "Get your ass up and finish dinner. I'm starving so it better be good."

As I tried to push myself onto my hands and knees, my trembling limbs uncooperative in my efforts, I berated myself for being so weak.

I *knew* it wouldn't last. I just *knew* it. But I was so stupid, so beaten down and desperate for things to change, that I believed him when he promised to never lay his hands on me again. Somewhere in the back of my mind, I knew that our day as a family had only been a fluke.

This was my own fault. I'd been so desperate to escape my abusive parents that I ran willingly into the arms of a man so much worse than they'd ever been. Yet, instead of getting out, I let him beat me into submission to the point where I had nothing and no one to help me escape.

I was weak.

And I had no one to blame but myself.

PRESENT

EVER SINCE THAT little scene with Brett in the salon, memories of my life with Lance had shoved their way to the forefront of my mind.

I'd only been seventeen when I met him. A man eight years my senior, and a successful associate at a fancy law firm seemed like a knight in shining armor to a naïve, inexperienced teenager who'd always dreamed of escaping her horrible home life. The fact that he was the only man I'd ever been with was something that pissed me off every time I thought about it. It had only ever been him. From seventeen to twenty-eight, I'd only ever been with one man, and I hated that.

But when Brett asked me out it catapulted me back in time to every single accusation Lance had ever made, to every beating I took when he accused me of looking or flirting with another man. If I were being honest with myself, there was a part of me that was thrilled when Brett asked to take me on a date—well more like told me, but that was semantics, really. My reaction to him had been overly dramatic to say the least, but the head space that situation put me in had been anything but delightful. Over the past few days, I'd tried to talk myself into apologizing to him, but every time my eyes traveled his way, a knot of anxiety twisted up my stomach and I chickened out. It hadn't been Brett's fault, and I felt horrible for my callous reaction, but he couldn't possibly know that.

"You sure you're okay?" Lizzy asked me for maybe the thousandth time that day.

"I'm fine," I insisted.

"I'm sensing an underlying annoyance coming from this general area," she said with a wave her hands in my direction.

"Well, good, because I'm laying it on pretty damn thick," I deadpanned.

"All right, all right. I'll stop asking. Just let me say this one last thing," she rushed, not giving me a chance to interrupt. "You look like you haven't been getting much sleep—"

"So, in other words, I look like shit."

She shrugged noncommittally, not bothering to deny it. "You said it, not me."

"You suck as a person," I grumbled as I went about setting up my station for my next appointment.

"I'm just stating facts, babe. How about this? Why don't I come crash at your place tonight? I'll watch the destructive duo while you go out to movie or quiet dinner or something. I don't care what you do, just take some damn time for yourself."

I looked at her, more than a little leery. "I don't know. I'd hate to come home and find Cameron tied up in a closet because you and Callie ganged up on him for being the weaker sex."

"Nah," she waved a hand casually, "that little dude can hold his own. You can trust me! I'll only let them eat a pound of chocolate and watch *one* scary movie. I was thinking *Friday the 13th* or *Nightmare on Elm Street*. That'll be up to them."

"You know you're the world's worst babysitter, right?"

She smirked and gave me a wink. "Nick Jr. for an hour, max. They'll eat all their veggies. Then it's two readings of *Goodnight Moon* and lights out. I know the drill, honey. Go out tonight and do something for yourself. *Pleeeeeeease*?" she begged, hopping up and down just like Callie did when she wanted something.

It took me a few seconds, but I finally relented. "Fine. But I'm only going out for a few hours."

"Yay! Stay out as long as you want. I'll tell Trevor we're having a little slumber party."

"Great, just what I need. Your husband skulking around my apartment trying to peep through the windows in the hopes of seeing a naked pillow fight."

She chuckled deviously and said, "I might tell him we'll be modeling new lingerie and practicing kissing just to see if I can make his head explode."

We laughed and finalized plans for her to show up at my place around seven. By the time I finished my workday and headed home, I was actually looking forward to the night ahead.

CHAPTER FIVE

KENZIE

THE MOVIE WAS ONLY an hour and a half long. Lizzy had informed me that under no circumstances whatsoever was I allowed back into my house any less than hour hours from the time I left. The evil bitch even had my own kids on her side. I still had two and a half hours to kill before my babysitter from hell would let me through the door of my own damn apartment.

As I drove through downtown—well, as downtown as the small town of Cloverleaf could get—I spotted the neon lights that lit up the parking lot of Colt 45's.

Since there was no going home, my best bet was to stop in for a drink and a bite to eat. Movie theater popcorn wasn't as filling as a person would think, and at that very moment, I was craving a double bacon cheeseburger like nobody's business.

Ooh, and bottle of Saint Arnold's to wash it down with.

That was just one of the many things I'd discovered about myself since I left Lance. I'd spent years sipping martinis, gin and tonics, and expensive red wines at my exes insistence. Turned out, I was a beer girl through and through. I'd gladly take a cold IPA over any of that fancy stuff every day of the week.

Another thing I discovered about myself in the eight months I'd been in Cloverleaf—especially since Brett walked into my life—was that I missed sex. Like really, *really* missed the hell out of sex. Yes, Lance was the only man I had ever been with, and long before that relationship ended, I'd come to despise his touch, but it hadn't always been bad, and my body never forgot what it felt like to be pleasured to the point of exhaustion.

While the idea of another relationship made me cringe, that didn't mean there weren't fantasies about a certain brown-haired, brown-eyed man shoving me up against the wall and turning my body inside out. Honestly, a woman could only go through so many batteries before she started to feel desperate. Since meeting Brett, my rabbit had gotten so much use I was pretty sure I'd chipped a tooth. But those self-induced orgasms were lacking...hollow. I missed the touch of a man's skin against mine as I went over that fine edge. I missed the feel of lips against my bare flesh, the mingled sounds of passion as we both chased after our release. I wanted someone to nip and bite and lick. I wanted to feel a man's fingers squeeze my hips to the point of almost bruising.

Good Lord. I needed to get laid something fierce.

Maneuvering my car into a parking spot, I turned the key and stepped out into the cool night. Fall was an unusual season to experience in Texas, but with the later months, came the lack of humidity and slightly chillier nights. As soon as I walked through the door the smell of good southern cooking and the hoppy aroma of the beer on tap hit my senses, making my mouth water.

I started for the bar, planning to have a seat and enjoy my dinner when the sound of my name being called drew my attention back toward the pool tables.

"Kenzie!" I turned to see Emmy and Savannah waving at me from their table. Smiling back, I made my way over to them, thankful I managed to run into someone I knew. I had already been looking forward to that burger and beer, but knowing I'd get to eat in company made it just a little bit sweeter.

"Hey, girl, what are you doing here by yourself?" Emmy asked from her perch, leaning way back against her chair, legs kicked out in front of her with her hands on her round stomach.

"My house was taken hostage by a crazy redhead. I'm under strict instruction not to return before eleven."

"Can I take your order?" the waitress asked as she stopped at our table.

"Yeah, can I get a bacon cheese burger, extra bacon? And whatever IPA you have on tap."

"A woman after my own heart," a deep voice rumbled from behind me.

Wide eyed, I turned around to see the man who plagued my every naughty, debauched fantasy. Brett stood there, in all his sexy, rugged glory, looking down at me as he leaned on a pool cue, grinning like the cat that ate the canary.

"Hey there, beauty."

The black thermal he wore stretched taut across his broad shoulders and defined chest in such a mouthwatering display of muscular deliciousness that I was rendered momentarily speechless.

"Who won?" Savannah asked as her husband, Jeremy, and Emmy's fiancé, Luke, joined us at the table, each taking a seat next to their significant others.

"You ask that like you don't already know the answer," Brett scoffed as he took the only empty chair left at the table, right next to me. "I whooped their asses. I'm officially a hundred bucks richer."

"Damn it!" Savannah declared, punching Jeremy in the arm. "I said no bets over twenty-five! You know you suck at pool. That's our future kids college fund you're pissing away."

"Asshole cheated," Jeremy grumbled as he took a drink from his beer bottle.

"How did I cheat? You were standing right there!"

"Well, looks like Mini Luke's down fifty bucks for his college fund, baby girl," Luke said casually as he rubbed Emmy's pregnant belly."

"Call him Mini Luke one more time and your P is never getting anywhere near my V again," Emmy replied as she slapped at his hand.

Normally, I'd be laughing as I watched the back and forth banter between everyone, but I was I having trouble concentrating on anything going on around me when the heat from Brett's thigh pressing firmly against mine felt like it was scalding my skin. I'd never in my life felt so in tuned to another person as I was with Brett. My body was insanely aware of every movement the man made.

The waitress blessedly chose that moment to show up with my meal. As soon as the beer was placed in front of me, I snatched it up and took a couple hearty gulps.

"I think you and I started off on the wrong foot."

Brett's warm breath against my ear startled a jolt from me as I spun my head to the side to look at him. He was so close I couldn't concentrate on anything but the hypnotic pull of those rich brown eyes.

"What?"

"The wrong foot," he repeated. "I'd like us to start over."

"And how do you propose we do that?"

Brett leaned back and extended his hand. "Hi, I'm Brett Halstead. It's nice to meet you."

My lips tipped up in a smile at his playful demeanor. "Mackenzie Webster," I responded, placing my hand in his. As soon as our palms touched an electric current shot straight up my arm. "It's nice to meet you, too," I murmured, sinking into his gaze. The rough brush of his slightly calloused finger across the pulse point in my wrist caused my breath to hitch. I was certain he could feel its erratic thrum beneath my skin. I couldn't describe the effect the man was having on me, but the longer I was in his presence, the more difficult it became to resist his pull, and a large part of me—the part deep down in my belly that was heating up—didn't want to.

As the evening wore on, the conversation between everyone kept me entertained as I enjoyed my mouthwatering burger and what had to be the best onion rings I'd ever had the pleasure of eating in my life. Before I knew it, I was on my fourth beer and laughing so hysterically at Emmy and Savannah's antics that my sorely underused stomach muscles ached. My head was fuzzy and I couldn't remember the last time I'd felt so relaxed.

"You have a ride home?" Emmy asked me when the night finally wound down. "If you drove, Luke and I can take you home since you've been drinking."

I opened my mouth, just about to accept her offer, when Brett spoke over me. "No worries, I got her."

I whipped my head around to argue but it was too late. "Perfect," Emmy said with a clap of her hands. It was *not* perfect. I could barely handle sitting next to Brett for a few hours. Being locked in a car with him, no matter how short a time, was bound to make my head explode. To say the sexual tension between the two of us was stifling was an extreme understatement. It was so damn thick I worried I might choke on it.

I was so busy trying to formulate a reasonable excuse as to why I needed to ride with Emmy and Luke that I missed my chance. Everyone at the table said their goodbyes, passing out hugs, cheek kisses, and backslaps while I stood there like an idiot, booze and Brett clouding my brain and taking away all rational thinking.

Chills spread across my skin as he leaned in and spoke softly

—almost seductively—into my ear, "You ready to go or you want to stay for another drink?"

It took an immense amount of willpower to pull my gaze from his soft lips. Staying for another drink with him was a horrible idea. My desire for him was growing with each minute I was in his presence. I craved him to the point of being terrified.

A quick glance at my watch showed I still had an hour before Lizzy would let me through my front door, but sitting outside my apartment seemed safer for me than staying with Brett. "I-I think I should probably head home." I knew...I just *knew,* as I stared into his warm gaze, that any longer with him and I was going to end up doing something I would regret.

"All right, let's get you out of here."

I stood on wobbly legs and slowly made my way to the door. I'd have loved nothing more than to blame my weak knees on the alcohol, but that would have been a lie. It was all Brett. I wanted to run away and jump him all at the same time. When his warm palm landed on the small of my back to guide me from the bar, I had to bite the inside of my cheek to suppress a moan.

Note to self: never drink around Brett again.

Booze plus Brett was a recipe for disaster.

BRETT

SWEET CHRIST, this woman is doing me in.

I'd spent the last hour and a half with a perpetual hard-on that was beginning to ache so badly I could feel it pulsing behind my fly. I wanted to be buried so deep between Kenzie's thighs we wouldn't be able to tell where I started and she began. The sweet smell of her skin, the way those pillowy lips curved into a stunning smile, the way her lush curves pressed into me when I leaned in a little too close to talk to her... she was driving me bat-shit crazy and didn't even know it. There was nothing on this earth more attractive than a sexy-as-hell woman who was unaware of her effect on men. It made her seem so...innocent. But when those hazel eyes met mine, I could see the hunger in their depths. A hunger that matched my own.

I'd watched in fascination all night as her nostrils flared every time I got close. The pulse in her neck pounded notice-ably whenever I brushed my leg against hers. If I had any doubt she wanted me just as badly as I wanted her, it quickly disap-peared the moment I placed my hand on her lower back and guided her from Colt's. Her body instantly stiffened at my touch and I heard the shallow catch in her breath before a quiet, almost silent moan escaped her lips. That was enough to put me over the edge. Images of her soft, silky body writhing under mine as she screamed my name bombarded me. I was making my move. She might have shot me down before, but her body was telling me the truth. I was going to get what I wanted. And I'd keep at her until she finally admitted she wanted me too.

CHAPTER SIX

KENZIE

BRETT LED me to his jeep, never once removing his hand from my back. I kept my eyes trained straight ahead once we made it to the passenger side, waiting for the beep of the doors unlocking, but it never came.

"Beauty," he whispered in my ear after several seconds. A part of me was scared to turn around, knowing what would happen if I looked into his eyes, but with that one whispered word, I lost the fight between my body and brain. My body turned of its own accord, and I was instantly transfixed in his gaze.

"Tell me not to kiss you," he demanded. "If this isn't what you want, you need to say so right now, because once I start I don't think I'll be able to stop."

I opened my mouth to say no, but the word never came. It was only two simple letters, but I just couldn't say them. He stared at me for what felt like an eternity before a knowing smile tipped the corner of his mouth.

"Time's up."

I don't know what I was expecting exactly, maybe for our

first kiss to be a gentle and hesitant, but that wasn't what happened. My lips parted on a gasp of surprise when his mouth crashed down on mine, hungry...dominating. The moment the kiss began, he was in complete control. His tongue darted inside, tangling with my own, commanding a response from me. A moan rumbled from deep in my throat when he pushed my back up against the side of his jeep, pressing every inch of his rock hard body against my own.

Brett wedged his thick thigh between my legs and grabbed hold of my waist as he pressed against me even harder, grinding the most sensitive part of me against the rigid muscles in his leg. His lips moved from my own, down to my neck, nibbling and licking at me as my hips moved against him and my nipples pebbled into hard peaks. I couldn't remember anything ever feeling this good. We were both fully clothed and I was already embarrassingly close to orgasm. I gasped when I felt the bulge of his erection pushing insistently against my stomach and a sense of power washed through me at the thought that I affected him so much.

His tongue traced back up my neck to my ear, where he pulled the lobe between his teeth and bit down lightly.

I was barely able to hear his whispered words over the blood rushing through my ears. "Come home with me."

It wasn't a request, but I couldn't have denied him even if it had been. I *wanted* to go home with him. I wanted more of what he was making me feel. I wanted everything his body was offering.

I nodded vigorously, unable to form words as he assaulted every one of my senses. As quickly as his heat had wrapped around me, it disappeared, leaving me shivering against the cold metal of the car. The locks beeped and he pulled me against him to open the door. I'd barely been able to form a coherent thought when he lifted me up like I weighed nothing and deposited me in the passenger seat. Leaning over me, he buckled my seatbelt, as if he was afraid I'd try to escape if he didn't secure me inside the car. Once he finished, he slammed the door shut and jogged around to his side. In a matter of seconds, the jeep sprung to life and we were peeling out of the parking lot. I counted down the minutes—five in all—before he pulled into a dimly lit driveway. I'd never been happier to live in such a small town. Any longer of a drive and I probably would have had enough time to talk myself out of what I was about to do.

Throwing the car in park and turning the key, he jumped from the driver's side and all but ran to my door, ripping it open and pulling me from my seat. He hoisted me up, forcing me to wrap my legs around his waist as he carried me up a sidewalk and a small set of stairs.

"I can walk, you know," I panted, still breathless from being so close to him as he fumbled with his keys, no doubt trying to get the door unlocked. I almost cried out in relief when I heard to sound of the deadbolt turning.

"Not letting you go, beauty," he muttered, his lips still trailing over my neck. "Won't risk you running away from me." The instant we passed the threshold, he had me pinned against the entryway wall, grinding his hard length between my legs just like he had in my fantasies. I was sure my drenched panties were about to melt away from my body.

"Not going anywhere," I breathed as I writhed against him, desperate for the release he'd been silently promising since we left the bar.

My hand snaked from around his neck, down his chest, across the ripples of his abs until I reached the stiff bulge behind the fly of his jeans.

"Take it out," he growled against my lips as his hips continued to buck, rubbing against me in the most deliciously erotic way. I didn't think it was possible to get any wetter than I already was, but his words proved me wrong.

With his strong body holding my weight against the wall, I was able to free up both hands. They shook as I worked to loosen his belt, causing me to fumble a bit, but when I finally got his cock free of the denim confines several thoughts crossed my mind.

First, how the hell was *that* ever going to fit inside me? I'd never had anything to compare Lance to, but Brett made what Lance was working with look amateurish. Second, was I really doing this? Was I really about to put myself out there to have a one-night stand with a man I hardly knew?

When his head tipped back on a guttural groan as I jacked his thick shaft, and he growled, "God, beauty. You're fucking perfect," the answer to my question was a resounding *yes*. I *was* about to have sex with this man. Hot, sweaty, animalistic—god willing—sex. And my one-track mind couldn't wait.

Taking my cues from how his body locked up and the intoxicating sounds he was making, I tightened my grip around the velvety steel of his cock, and began stroking faster. At that very moment, I wanted nothing more than to throw Brett over the edge. My earlier beers no longer affected me; I was drunk on the power of what I could do to this strong man.

"Stop." One of his hands that had been holding me under my butt grabbed hold of my wrist to halt my actions. "You keep doing that and I'll come before I get inside you."

At his words, my pussy clenched. The thought of feeling him inside me caused a whimper of desire to burst from my throat. Pulling me from the wall, he quickly moved through the house. Never in my life had I undressed as fast as I did the moment my feet hit Brett's bedroom floor. Clothes were whipped off in a flurry, and I was pretty sure my panties were torn to shreds as he ripped them from my body, unwilling to wait for me to pull them down. With one hand behind his head, he tore his shirt off, throwing it over his shoulder without a care. The second we were both naked he lifted me up and tossed me to the center of the bed like a rag doll, and a part of me—a part that would never willingly admit it out loud—loved his alpha-caveman behavior. Had it been Lance, Lord knows I'd have probably been terrified, but something in Brett's eyes called out to me, letting me know he wasn't going to hurt me. I watched in awe as his huge body climbed over mine, every corded muscle, every dip in his tantalizing skin making me even wetter for him.

"Jesus, baby. You have no idea how badly I've wanted this," he mumbled as he leaned over me to reach into his nightstand drawer. The crinkle of the condom wrapper echoed through the room and I stared, transfixed as he ripped it open with his teeth and slide it over his heavy cock. Once he was covered, he used his knees to spread my legs wide and settled his hips between them. With one powerful thrust, he buried himself as deep as he could possibly go.

"Fucking *shit*," he groaned between clenched teeth at the same time I cried out, unprepared for the way he stretched me open.

Brett froze over me, holding himself up on his powerful arms as he looked down. "Christ, beauty. Am I hurting you?"

"Just...just give me a second," I breathed. "It's been a while. And you're...bigger...than my ex."

"I'll stop, Kenzie. If it's too much, I'll stop. Just say the word. I don't want to hurt you."

As he spoke, my walls relaxed and the slight sting subsided, leaving an intense pleasure in its place.

"Don't stop. God, don't stop. I need you to move, Brett. Please move."

"Anything you want, beauty."

With that, he pulled out, only his thick head remaining inside, before shoving back in, forcing a loud moan from deep within my chest. As he pumped into me over and over again, all I could think was that sex had never felt this good. *Never*. Brett had a gift when it came to giving pleasure. Within just a few minutes, I was teetering precariously at the edge of a release so strong I was likely to pass out.

"*Brett*," I whimpered as our sweat-slicked bodies moved together.

"So. Fucking. Perfect," he bit out with each slam of his hips. "Nothing like it, beauty. Nothing fucking like it."

His words sent me over. I yelled out his name repeatedly, mixing it with a few unintelligible words.

"That's it, Kenzie. Come for me, baby. I can feel your pussy squeezing me. I'm so fucking close."

Two more deep thrusts and he drove himself to the hilt, shouting out my name like a curse before burying his face in my neck and biting down on the sensitive flesh. That caused my walls to clamp down around him as another blissful wave crashed over me. Brett's cock twitched as the last of his release filled up the condom. When he finally finished he collapsed on top of me, nuzzling the crook of my neck until we were both able to function again.

Good Lord. That was the best sex I'd ever had, and as I lay there, the euphoria slowly creeping away, reality started to take its place. The realization of what just happened hit me like a ton of bricks. The steel and razor wire reinforced walls I used to protect myself had fallen earlier that evening. But now that my head was no longer clouded and confused, they came shooting back up into place.

I got what I wanted. Now I needed to move on. But something deep in the back of my mind was arguing with me, telling me what I *wanted* was more than just one night with Brett.

That tiny part of my subconscious was why I knew I needed to escape. It was best that I made a hasty retreat as it became all too clear that, if I let it go any further, I could seriously fall for this man.

And that was the most terrifying thought of all.

CHAPTER SEVEN

BRETT

I WAS PRETTY certain I was dead. Had to be. No man on the face of the earth could live through an orgasm like that. When I came, I was sure the back of my head blew right the fuck off. Hell, if my dick hadn't *still* been twitching, I'd have been convinced I died and gone to Heaven. Once I was able to think and function clearly, after having come harder than I ever had before, I realized my weight was probably too much for a petite woman like Kenzie, and quickly rolled to the side.

That was my first mistake.

The minute she was no longer pinned in place, she shot off the bed like her ass was on fire.

"Hey." I reached out to snag her arm, but she was already too far away. "Where do you think you're going?" I smiled as I watched her sexy ass bounce while she darted around the room.

"I need to get home," she answered, never once making eye contact as she picked up her underwear. Seeing they were torn to hell, she threw them down, grabbed her jeans and pulled them on before going for her bra. Usually, the thought of a woman not wearing any panties under her clothes was enough to get me hard as a rock, but what she'd just said, and the tone she said it in, settled heavily on my chest. My smile quickly vanished as I climbed from the bed and pulled my own pants back on, also sans underwear.

"What are you talking about? I'm nowhere near done with you." I walked to her and reached out, pulling her against my chest. Her eyes darted around the floor, no doubt searching for her shirt.

"I have to get back to my kids." She tried to pull away, but I wasn't having any of that. The woman had just blown my mind and not she was trying to run? Like hell. I'd finally gotten a little taste of what I'd been craving for weeks on end. There was no way I was giving that shit up. I was already addicted.

"Beauty," I spoke softly, tucking a strand of hair behind her ear and tipping her chin up so I could see into her beautiful hazel eyes. "It's all right. Just call Lizzy and explain. I'm sure your kids are down for the count. I'll take you back to your car in the morning. Hell, I'll even set the alarm so we get you there before they wake up. They'll never know the difference."

Her eyes widened before a laugh escaped her kiss-swollen lips. "Are you kidding? Brett, I can't just leave my kids with some random person all night. What kind of mother would that make me?" She pulled away from me and snatched her shirt off the floor, jerking it over her head in agitated movements, and covering that made-for-sin body.

"Liz isn't some random person," I told her, my anger rising at the unwanted brushoff. "She's your friend. You can trust her. Your kids love her and she loves them. I'm not seeing the problem here."

She looked at me like I was speaking in tongues before her eyes narrowed into angry slits. "The *problem*, Brett, is that I'm *here* when I should be home with my children."

I took a step back at her venomous tone. "Are you fucking shitting me right now? We just had sex all of one minute ago and you're already fucking bailing. What the hell is that, Kenzie?"

"It's called a one-night stand, Brett. I'm pretty sure you know how those work."

At her biting words, my anger went from a simmer to a rolling boil. "A one-night stand? Are you out of your goddamn head, woman? That..." I said, swinging my finger over to my disheveled bed, "was not a one-night stand!" The more I spoke the louder my voice got, and I quickly saw that was my second mistake as soon as she recoiled away from me. I tried to get myself in check and took a step toward her, but she quickly backed up.

"Please take me back to my car."

Her Ice Queen persona was really beginning to piss me off. What was wrong with her? How could she not see that what just happened in my bed wasn't a fluke? It wasn't a one-time deal. It was proof that the two of us were *more* than perfect together. I was so pissed I didn't think before I spoke.

"I see how it goes. You got off and the sweet, sexy woman I just fucked is gone. The bitch is officially back."

And using that one word was my third and final mistake. I could see it the moment those shutters behind her eyes slammed back into place, effectively closing me out.

"Take me back to my car. Now," she demanded coldly. That was when I knew I'd lost her, but I was too fucking mad to care at that point. She wanted to be gone? Fucking fine by me. I was more than done with her shit for one night.

I laughed caustically, and ripped my shirt over the top of my head. "You got it, babe." I stomped from the room and grabbed my keys, heading through the front door without even looking back to see if she was still behind me.

Not a word was spoken as I drove us the five minutes from my house to the bar parking lot, but from the corner of my eye, I could see her glance in my direction every other minute. When I pulled my Jeep up next to her car, I threw it in park and sat there staring out the windshield as the passenger door opened. She paused briefly and looked back as if she wanted to say something, but thought better of it. When I finally met her gaze, she looked almost regretful.

"Brett..." she started, but then stopped.

It might have been a mistake; I might have let my anger get the best of me, but I needed her to know where I stood.

"Rest assured, beauty, if you're lucky enough to get me back between those luscious thighs, no way in fucking hell will you be running out on me again."

I threw the jeep in gear and took off for home, leaving her slack jawed and shocked in the parking lot of Colt's.

KENZIE

WHAT THE HELL had I been thinking?

But that was just the problem, wasn't it. I *hadn't* been thinking. I'd let my damn hormones take control of the whole situation, and a night that started out wonderfully crashed and burned in a fiery ball of destruction.

Brett's words played on a constant loop in my head the whole next day.

Rest assured, beauty, if you're lucky enough to get me back between those luscious thighs, no way in fucking hell will you be running out on me again.

I had an angel on one shoulder telling me it was for the best, that I didn't need to get tangled up in something messy while I was still trying to get my footing and build a healthy life for

Cameron and Callie. But the horny little devil on my other shoulder was telling me that luck wouldn't even begin to cover it if I were to get Brett back between my thighs, that it would be no less than a freaking miracle.

Damn it. At times like this, I really hated my stupid subconscious. That bitch was making a mess out of my carefully planned out life. A life I was determined would contain *no* men.

By the time Brett had pulled into the parking lot the night before, I was already beating myself up for my overreaction at his house. It seemed I was prone to overreactions where he was involved.

Yes, calling me a bitch was definitely wrong, and I wouldn't excuse that. But part of me knew I'd intentionally led him to that point. I *was* acting like a bitch, and I was doing it on purpose because I couldn't handle what I was feeling. Gut instinct told me to flee and to burn that bridge as soon as I crossed it. I'd opened my mouth to apologize, but his words had struck me mute, and I would have been lying if I didn't admit that they turned me on at the same time.

Good Lord, there was something seriously wrong with me.

"*Mom*! I want pan-a-cakes!" Cameron shouted as he and Callie came barreling into the kitchen.

Luckily, by the time I arrived home it was so late that I was able to feign exhaustion and brush off Lizzy's curious stare before pushing her through the door. I knew that there was no getting away from her third degree when I eventually returned to work—the whisker burn on my cheeks and neck and just-fucked hair were pretty damning signs that something had happened—but thankfully, I had a full day to come up with some sort of plausible story for my unkempt appearance Friday night.

"I want cereal!" Callie shouted, pushing her brother from behind.

"Pan-a-cakes!" Cameron demanded with a shove back. "And you's a butt toot!"

"Hey, no pushing," I scolded, pulling my twins off of each other before bloodshed ensued. "And don't call people butt toots, Cam," I told him sternly.

Butt toots, seriously? Where do kids pick this shit up?

"But sissy's stinky and smells like da stuff that comes outta my booty," he giggled hysterically.

"I do not!" Callie wailed as tears rushed down her cheeks. "*Mooommmy!* Bubby's bein' a meanie!"

My eyelid twitched, and that telltale stabbing pain shot through my skull. That asshole who wrote *What to Expect When You're Expecting* never covered how gross tiny four year olds could be. That would've been a really freaking helpful chapter.

"Enough," I told them both. "Go in the living room and play nice, or so help me, I'll make you both eat asparagus for breakfast."

That threat worked like a charm every time.

I still remembered the first time I put it on their plates for dinner.

"Mommy, deese gween beans taste like crap." Callie told me *as she hesitantly licked the vegetable hanging from her fork. I'd made a special dinner for my and Lance's anniversary, but as usual, he'd been stuck late at the office. He didn't even bother to bring the day up when he called to curtly inform me not to wait up. That was when I knew he'd forgotten.*

"Don't say crap. And they aren't green beans. They're asparagus."

"It tastes like dog poop," Cameron told me with a *scrunched-up face.*

And thus began the stage where my kids viewed everything healthy as tasting like poop.

At the threat of the dreaded asparagus, my kids ran screaming from the kitchen like the boogey man had just jumped out of the pantry. Five seconds later, the sound of the TV coming on echoed into the kitchen, and that damn *Yo Gabba Gabba* song began to play.

That was another thing those stupid parenting books never taught you. Kiddie shows were the worst things to happen to our society since the Kardashians. Those damn songs would get stuck in your head forever. I let out a sigh of defeat and turned back to the stove to make breakfast. I'd decided on a compromise. No pancakes or cereal.

They were getting French toast and they'd better damn well like it.

CHAPTER EIGHT

KENZIE

WHEN I ARRIVED at work the next morning, Brett and his men were already at the salon working on the new rooms Trevor was having built for Lizzy. Our eyes met briefly when I walked through the door, but he turned and continued hammering without so much as acknowledging my existence.

I understood that he was still mad, and part of me was too. We both said some pretty shitty things to each other, but I couldn't stop thinking that I needed to apologize for my part in the whole mess. Just because we had a few hours of naked debauchery before everything had gone south didn't mean we needed to be enemies. We'd made a mistake by hooking up, but I desperately wanted to put it behind us in the hopes of salvaging some sort of friendship. Brett was a nice guy and I was already starting to form relationships with the people in his tightknit circle. It didn't need to be messy between us. I mean, guys did this kind of thing all the time. One-night stands were practically invented by the male species. Just because we had sex didn't mean we couldn't be friends, right?

Right.

I spent hours surreptitiously watching Brett every chance I

got while preparing my speech for when I was finally able to get him alone. My window of opportunity finally opened when I saw him walking down the hall to use the restroom. Deciding that was the perfect time to take a quick break between appointments, I waited a minute then headed to the break room down the same hall to grab a much needed soda from the fridge. I'd timed it perfectly. Just as I was walking back out of the room, Brett was exiting the restroom.

"Hey," I started, trying to sound as casual as possible.

"Hey." His tone was brusque, and it was obvious he had no plans to stick around seeing as he was already turning to head back down the hall. My window was quickly slamming shut.

"Can I talk to you for a second?"

He faced me and leaned one massive shoulder against the wall, effectively blocking my way back into the main part of the salon. His arms crossed over his chest, accentuating his bulging biceps, and flashes of being wrapped up in them a few nights before as he thrust into me flooded my system. I had to shake my head to clear it of the erotic memories so I could concentrate on the here and now.

"I...uh," I began to stutter. Clearing my throat, I started again. "I wanted to apologize for...you know...the other night."

One of his brows quirked up as he asked, "You want to apologize for having sex?"

"What? No! No, not that part..." *Gah*! I was losing my mind. Why couldn't I sound like a smart, confident woman when I was in his presence? I was turning into a bumbling idiot.

I rolled my eyes at him as his lips tipped up in a smirk. "What I'm trying to say is I know I was acting like a bitch the other night, and you weren't *completely* wrong for pointing that out. But let me just add, it's never cool for a guy to actually *call* a woman a bitch. Even if she's being one. Just saying," I rambled nervously. "Anyway...my point is I had no right to treat you that way. I was wrong for how I reacted and I just want you to know that I really am sorry," I ended softly.

Brett's frosty demeanor changed. His face softening as he took a step toward me and tucked a strand of hair behind my ear. "It's okay, beauty," he spoke quietly. "All's forgiven."

A weight lifted off my chest and I let out a relieved sigh as a huge smile spread across my face. "I was so worried this was going to be awkward. I'm glad we can be friends."

"Yeah, we can be...wait. What?" His hand paused mid-stroke on my cheek while his entire body grew rigid. "You want to be friends," he stated dryly.

My smile fell, and unease started to creep through me. The tension in the hallway grew palpable.

"Well...yeah. Or at least I'd hoped that we could. I mean, we hang out with the same people. It'd just make things so much easier if we got along, you know?"

He dropped his hand to his side and took a step back, his anger returning so fiercely it radiated off of him.

"So what happened the other night doesn't matter for shit, then? Are you serious right now, Kenzie?"

"Brett," I sighed. "What happened the other night was a one time thing. We can't get involved."

"Why the fuck not!"

"Because! I have two kids I'm raising all on my own, and a life I'm trying to build for us!" My temper turned up a notch at having to explain myself, and as I continued to shout the words just started pouring out without any thought, revealing things I'd have preferred to stay locked up. "I've made some bad choices in the past. I fucked up a lot, and I'll be damned if I do that again. I'm not putting a man before the welfare of myself or my children ever again, Brett. Why can't you understand that?"

He stood quietly for several seconds before responding, and when he finally did his voice came out so low and filled with concern that it nearly brought tears to my eyes. "What happened to you, beauty?"

He tried to touch my face again, but I wouldn't let him. "That's none of your business," I said bitingly.

"Kenzie, I can't help you if—"

"I'm not asking for your help!" I snapped. "All I was asking for was your friendship, but if you can't give me that, then I guess there's nothing left to discuss."

Without another word, I shoved past Brett and headed for my station to prepare for my next appointment. So much for keeping things from getting messy.

As I walked away from Brett, a knot of sadness formed in my stomach. I kept telling myself I was doing the right thing.

So the question remained, why didn't it feel so shitty?

BRETT

IT'D BEEN a week since my and Kenzie's little blowup outside the restroom of Elegant Nails, and I was still pissed at the stubborn, hardheaded woman. I'd been walking around all week long with a raging case of blue balls and a bad fucking attitude. That was not a good combination. I needed a night out with my friends. I needed to blow off some serious steam.

"Y'all coming to Colt's tonight?" I asked Trevor as we worked on finishing up the rooms he'd contracted me to build out for Lizzy.

He started talking—something about his tattoo shop, but I was too busy staring over at Kenzie's station, and silently stewing, to pay attention.

"So what's going on there?" he asked, dragging my attention

away from the woman who was slowly pulling me in two. A large part of me just wanted to wash my hands of her. She was too much damn trouble, but something just wouldn't let me do that. And damn if that wasn't doing my head in.

"Huh? Oh, nothing," I lied and went back to mudding the joints in the drywall we just installed.

"Doesn't look like nothing. Looks like you have a hard-on for Lizzy's friend."

"Nah." I shrugged, faking casual even though my insides were all tangled up. "Woman's got too much baggage. Two little kids. I'm not looking to play daddy any time soon."

Where the hell had that come from? Christ, I was such an asshole.

"Jesus, man. What the hell?" Trevor barked. It wasn't like me at all to be such a dick, and honestly, I had no clue why I'd just said that. It wasn't like I meant it. I was just so damn mad and letting my anger get the best of me.

I dropped my head on a sigh. "That was harsh."

"Uh, yeah. That's a fucking understatement. What was that all about?"

I turned to look over at Kenzie's table, thanking Christ she wasn't there. For a second, I'd been terrified that she'd overheard me saying something so fucked up.

"I don't want to talk about it. Let's just finish this shit up," I grumbled before grabbing the trowel and slapping down more drywall mud.

I needed to get my shit together before something came out of my mouth I wouldn't be able to take back.

When Trevor headed off to his shop a little while later, I kept working, glancing over at Kenzie's station more than what could be considered healthy. But she'd never come back to her little table.

"Hey," I stopped Lizzy as she walked past me. "Where'd Kenz go?"

The knowing smirk the fiery little redhead gave me almost made me cringe. If I became any more obvious, Lizzy'd be up my ass faster than anything, trying to play matchmaker. I'd already fucked up enough on my own. Last thing I needed was her help.

"Went home sick. Said she was getting a migraine. Poor thing, works herself to the bone then goes home and starts all over again with those two little ones. Don't get me wrong, I adore Cameron and Callie, but they're exhausting."

She'd left?

How had she managed to leave without me noticing?

My brows dipped down as I looked from the front door of the salon back to Liz. "Is she okay?"

She studied my face with curiosity before telling me, "Yeah, she looked okay; just a little down, I guess." With that, she turned and walked off, leaving me with a sense of dread deep in the pit of my stomach.

CHAPTER NINE

KENZIE

WHAT A RAGING HEMORRHOID! I couldn't believe I felt guilty for being rude to such an insensitive prick. Brett Halstead was a douche who didn't deserve the time of day, and I was done worrying about how to keep things from being messy.

Honestly, I was thankful to know what he really thought of me. Hearing that I had too much baggage and he didn't want to play daddy to my kids was a relief. I could finally despise the jerkoff without feeling bad about it.

And *please*! Like I'd ever want that asshole to be a father figure to the twins. Yeah, I didn't think so!

"Mommy, what's a hemrod?"

I looked over at Callie where she and Cameron sat, drawing pictures at the coffee table. "Huh?"

"You was jus talk' to yowself," she told me. "What's a hemrod?"

"Uh..." Since the twins were old enough to start picking things up, I'd worked my ass off to make sure I watched my mouth, but sometimes things just slipped out. "It's an adult word, baby."

"Is asshole an adult word, too?" Cameron asked.

Son of a bitch! Note to self: make sure not to think aloud around impressionable young children who hear every-freaking-thing.

"Yes, honey. Mommy said some bad words that she shouldn't have. I don't want to hear either of you repeating them, got it?"

Luckily, my four-year-olds had the attention span of a flea, so they both simply shrugged and went back to coloring. And with that bullet dodged, I went back to making dinner.

LATER THAT NIGHT, after getting the kids off to bed, I collapsed on the couch, queued up an episode of *So You Think You Can Dance* and got comfortable. I was in the middle of watching one of the boring ballroom numbers when my cell went off.

"Hello?"

"Hey, babe. How's the headache?" Lizzy's cheerful voice rang through the line.

I stretched my legs out and laid my head on one of my throw pillows. "It's better, thanks. Sorry for bailing early on you."

"Don't sweat it. I'm just glad you're feeling better. That headache wouldn't have had anything to do with the fact you came home Friday night looking like you had your brains banged out, then got into it with a certain hottie contractor the other morning, would it?"

A deep sigh escaped my lips. "Really not in the mood to go there right now, Liz."

"Oh, come on! You can't hold out on something juicy like that!"

"There's nothing to tell," I lied. "Nothing is happening or ever *going* to happen between me and Brett."

"Sure as hell looked like something was happening to me."

I felt that annoying twitching in my eyelid again, accompanied by a dull throb behind my eyes. I couldn't stand that stupid little eye tick. I'd had it ever since I was a kid. Whenever I felt extreme stress my eyelid would start twitching uncontrollably. I used to get so much grief about it. First from my father, then from Lance. They loved to make fun of my issue, even though they were the cause of it. Miraculously, after leaving Lance and moving to Cloverleaf, the twitch had diminished, only really occurring when the twins were on a rampage. But ever since I met Brett, the damn thing seemed to have come back with a vengence.

I couldn't hold in my groan as I asked, "Can we please talk about something else?"

I heard a faint giggle through the phone, "Your eye's doing that twitchy thing again, isn't it?"

Damn that woman for already knowing me so well.

"If I say yes, will you drop it?"

"Okay, okay. I'll let it go, but let me just say this; if you're face is getting all ticky just from talking about Brett, how do you think you're going to handle seeing him around town all the time? You can't hide away forever, honey. Not in Cloverleaf."

She was right. And at that moment, I kind of hated her for it.

PAST

WALKING INTO THE HOUSE, I felt that same sense of dread that accompanied me every time I came through the front door. I headed straight for the stairs on quiet feet, prepared to sit in my room for the remainder of the night and do my homework.

That was what I did every night.

Get home from school, close myself in my room, study, read, and then eat my dinner once my father had gone to bed or left to sit at some bar for the remainder of the night. There was one rule in my house I'd learned to abide by at a very early age. I was to never be seen nor heard unless my father demanded it of me. On the rare occasion my parents and I spoke, it was mainly so my father could berate me, or so my mother could blame me for what he had become.

Since I was old enough to comprehend, I'd been told that I was the reason my parents' relationship had gone south. When they'd gotten together, it had been a whirlwind courtship, intensely romantic, the stuff of fairytales to hear my mother describe it. They had been sweet and loving with each other. They had the perfect marriage. That was, until shortly after I was born. The older I got, the more disconnected my father became. He and my mother's relationship stopped being about passion as my father became more and more uninterested. He began drinking, leaving the house and staying gone all night. I'd hear them fighting about his affairs. He'd yell at her that she'd turned into a fat, lazy slob who couldn't keep his interests. According to him, it was all my mother's fault that was no longer attracted to her and strayed from their marriage.

She would spend days crying over his harsh words, then she'd starve herself just to lose a few pounds. At times like that, the only person she would cook for was my dad, so I'd go hungry as well.

All of their marital problems rested solely on my shoulders.

I was told by the both of them that if I'd never been born they'd still be happy and in love.

The older I got, the worse my father became. The verbal and emotional abuse morphed into physical. He loved to take his issues out on my mother and me by using his fists. I used to pray Mom would pack us up and take me away from that awful house. But that never happened. She remained insanely devoted to my dad throughout everything, never once faulting him for his own actions. It was all my fault. *I* was the reason he didn't love her anymore.

"Mackenzie, get your worthless ass down here!"

Already halfway up the stairs, I stopped and turned with a sigh. I dreaded each step that brought me closer to the living room. Closer to a man I hated with an intensity that no fifteen-year-old should even comprehend.

"Yes, Daddy?" I asked once I was standing in front of his recliner. Out of the corner of my eye, I saw my mom perched on the edge of the couch like the good, doting wife. As usual, she was dressed in her very best. Not a hair out of place, the makeup on her face strategically applied to cover up the black eye she was sporting from his vile outburst just two days ago.

"What the hell is this, you little brat?"

He tossed a crumpled sheet of paper in my direction, and I had to scramble to catch it. It was a truancy letter from my school stating that I'd already gone over the allotted number of days I was allowed to miss. It said I would fail tenth grade unless I made up those hours before or after school each day for the remainder of the year.

Of course I missed too many days of school. There was no way my mother would have allowed me to show up with bruises on my face and body for anyone to see. She wouldn't risk people asking questions and finding out my dad liked to beat on his wife and daughter. I wasn't the least bit surprised that Mom hadn't spoken up for me.

"Once again, you've disappointed us, Mackenzie. I can't believe you'd cut class and get into trouble."

"Oh, shut the hell up, Nancy. No one asked for you to open your fat mouth."

Mom bowed her head at my father's insult, offering up a pathetic, "Of course, honey. I'm sorry."

I kept my eyes focused on the pristine carpet under my feet.

"Well, what do you have to say to yourself?" Dad asked.

"I'm sorry," I whispered, knowing that trying to defend myself was pointless. The eye twitch I'd developed a few years ago hit full force as I stood before him.

"Goddamn it. Will you knock off that stupid tick! You look like a retard!" At his words, I squeezed that one eye closed, trying to get it to stop. But no matter how hard I tried, I just couldn't control it. "And you'll make up every one of those fucking hours before and after school. So help me, if you fail this year, I'll make you live to regret it."

With that, he stood from his recliner to go.

"Sweetie, where are you going?" my mother asked, jumping from the couch and following like an obedient dog as my father stormed from the living room.

"I'm going out."

"Please, Gary," Mom pleaded. "Don't leave. I made your favorite. Let's just sit and have dinner together like we used to—"

"Christ, woman! Would you stop your damn whining? It's pathetic."

I was silent as the front door opened and shut on the sounds of my mother's whimpers. Seconds later, his truck rumbled to life and the gravel crunched beneath the tires as he pulled out of the driveway.

My mom stomped back into the room and stood before me, brushing the tears off her cheeks. "This is all your fault," she hissed viciously. "I wish you'd never been born!"

I heard those words so many times growing up, that they no longer affected me. I'd become numb to them. The truth of it was, I wished I'd never been born either.

CHAPTER TEN

BRETT

PRESENT

AS A RULE, all single men hated grocery shopping, it was just a part of our nature. But seeing as I already finished my last pack of Ramen the previous night, and ate my only can of Spaghettios for breakfast that morning, I didn't really have much of a choice but to endure the dreaded super market.

"My mommy says those is full 'a bad stuffs that'll make your tummy hurt," I heard off to my side as I tossed another bad of potato chips into my cart. I looked over, then *way* down to see two little brown-haired, hazel-eyed kids standing next to me, staring up in wide-eyed wonder.

I smiled as I watched the little boy shove half a cookie into his mouth. "Well, hey there. Where'd you two little bits come from?"

"You don't gots no veg-i-tibles," the little girl told me, sounding out the word *vegetables* slowly. It was the most adorable thing I'd ever heard. "You gots ta eat stuff that's good for ya, mister," she scolded before biting off a piece of her own cookie.

"Well, those cookies you're munching on don't look all that good for you either, you know."

"Mommy said we's allowed one cookie if we be good," the little boy said through a full mouth full of cookie, spitting crumbs all over the floor. "Is you a giant, mister?"

This little boy bounced from one topic to another faster than I could keep up. I threw my head back on a laugh. "No, I'm not a giant. I'm just a really big guy, bud."

"Does that mean you ate all your veg-i-tibles like a good boy?" the little girl asked.

"Nah, that's just something parents say to make little kids eat all that nasty shit."

"Ooooh, you said a bad word," the little boy admonished at the same time a woman shouted down the aisle, "Cameron, Callie, there you are! What have I said about running off, huh?"

I spun around to see the woman of my every recent sexual fantasy come storming down the aisle, looking like one pissed off Momma bear. I couldn't help but smile. She was even gorgeous when worry and anger laced through her expression. And at seeing her right then, I momentarily forgot that we were both mad at each other.

"Well, hello there, beauty."

She shot a glare at me before turning her angry gaze to her little rugrats. "What have I told you two? You stay where I can see you at all times."

"Sorry Mommy," the little boy said, having the good grace to look properly chastised. Although a part of me was pretty sure those sad puppy dog eyes were just for show.

I was proven right when the little evil genius turned all of Kenzie's attention back to me by saying, "Mommy, dis man said 'shit' and told us you don't hafta eat veg-i-tibles to grow big and strong like him."

The little monster sold my ass out without so much as blinking.

Kenzie's laser eyes swung back up to me, and I could have sworn I felt the skin on my face start to burn.

"Oh, well that's just great! Want to impart any more wisdom on my kids while you're at it? Why don't you just tell them they don't need to go to school either?"

"Yay!" the little girl cheered excitedly.

"Callie, no. Mommy was just being sarcastic. Don't listen to anything I say for the next two minutes."

"Ah, dang it," the girl pouted.

"If we don't listen, can we hab another cookie?" the boy asked.

I was really starting to dig these kids. They definitely knew how to play to their strengths. I was willing to bet these two would give half the police force a run for their money when it came to interrogations.

Kenzie muttered something under her breath that sounded an awful lot like "Lord, give me strength," as she rubbed at her twitching eyelid.

"You all right?" I asked, pulling her hand away from her face.

She yanked back and scowled. "I'm fine. Kids, let's go. No more cookies." Kenzie started back down the aisle with two moping children following behind her, and I was hit with a sudden feeling of desperation. I couldn't let her to leave just yet.

"Hold on a second and I'll check out with you guys. Help you load your groceries up." She hesitated for a second before turning around and bending to say something to Callie and Cameron. When she did that, I got a peek at her tight ass in those jeans before she made her way back to me.

Don't get hard, Brett. For god's sake, man, don't get hard.

"I don't need your help with anything," she whispered bitingly once she stood in front of me. "And that includes you playing *daddy* to my kids. Consider this your out on having to deal with all my *baggage.*"

Then she was gone, leaving me standing in the chip aisle after just confirming my worst fear. She heard every ugly word I'd said to Trevor.

At that moment, I was so pissed at myself that, had I been flexible enough, I'd have kicked my own ass.

KENZIE

MY BODY FELT like it was running on nothing but fumes. No amount coffee was going to do the trick. But waking up in the middle of the night to toddlers puking like something out of the *Exorcist* would do that to a person. Daycare wasn't an option, at least for the next two days. Luckily, I managed to find a sitter to stay with the twins the first day, but it looked like I'd have to take the second day off. And a day out of the salon was a day without pay that I desperately needed for me and my kids.

The last thing I wanted was to have to deal with a certain construction worker, no matter how good looking he was.

I had just finished with my latest appointment and was sitting at the break room table, trying to rest my eyes before my next one, when a thump on the tabletop startled me awake. I bolted upright to see Brett standing across from me with a hesitant smile on his face.

"Hey, you looked like you could use this." He pushed the Starbucks cup closer and the warm aroma of the espresso nearly made me cry out my gratitude. Right then, I couldn't have cared less if the man who offered it was my enemy.

"Thanks," I muttered, not quite making eye contact as I grabbed the cup and took a huge, unladylike gulp. "Mmm, pumpkin spice."

He reached behind him and scratched the back of his neck uncomfortably.

"Uh, yeah. I heard you telling Lizzy one day that you were excited that that flavor was back."

I sat there in dumbfounded silence for a few seconds. After how we'd been treating each other recently, the kind gesture was a bit of a shock. I didn't want to be moved by the fact that he'd gone out of his way because he saw I was in need of a boost, or that overheard some random conversation weeks ago, and actually remembered it. But I couldn't seem to help myself. My chest started to feel all warm and fuzzy.

"It's seasonal," I muttered idiotically.

"I figured that." One corner of his mouth tipped up on a grin. "Anyway, I thought maybe you could use a pick-me-up or something. You looked tired. Hope it helps."

Despite my best efforts, my heart gave a little squeeze at Brett's thoughtfulness. He turned to leave the break room when my mouth opened and the words spilled out on their own accord.

"Thank you, Brett. Really. This..." I said, indicating the cup in my hands. "You didn't have to do this. I...just...thank you."

He surprised me by turning back around, taking a seat in the chair opposite mine. He looked so serious as he rested his forearms on the table that all I could do was sit quietly as he dove right in to what he had to say.

"Look, what you overheard the other a shitty thing for me to have said."

"It was," I cut in, in complete agreement.

"I was being a dick, and I'm really sorry you had to hear that. I didn't mean it, Kenzie."

I had no idea what to say so I at silently as he continued. "I've acted like a bastard because I couldn't get what I want—"

"What do you want?" I interrupted, my curiosity getting the best of me.

He looked at me in bewilderment, his head tipped to one side. "You, Kenz. I want you. How can you not see that?"

I opened my mouth to reply but couldn't get the words to come out.

"I guess I just wanted you to know that I was sorry, and if you're still willing to be friends, I'd really like that."

"Wow, this is...uh. I have to say, this is a little unexpected."

"Well, what were you thinking would happen? A fight to the death?" he joked.

I let out what felt like my first laugh in days. "With how things have been going between us, something like that."

He flashed me his panty-melting smile and stuck his hand out across the table for me to shake. "So, what do you say? Friends?"

"You sure you can handle being just friends?" I asked tentatively, only then realizing how badly I wanted him to say yes. The fact of the matter was, I really and truly wanted to be friends with this man. I couldn't explain it, but for some reason I desperately wanted to keep him in my life.

"I'll try my best, beauty. I promise. And I also promise to keep my inner asshole locked up tight."

"Now, don't go making promises that are impossible to keep," I teased with a smirk.

"Ouch. Don't leave me hanging here, sweetheart."

Reaching across the table, I took his hand in mine and gave it a firm shake while trying to ignore the electricity that zinged through my body at such a simple touch.

"Friends."

"Good," he said once I'd pulled my hand back and tucked it into my lap, unconsciously rubbing where his work-rough fingers had just been. "Now, friend, want to tell me why you're so exhausted today?"

I let out a sigh as my shoulders slumped. "The twins woke up in the middle of the night with some sort of stomach virus. I kid you not, it was like something out of a horror movie." I watched with humor as he cringed at my description.

"Sorry to hear that. They going to be all right?"

"Yeah, they'll be fine. I just have to keep them out of daycare for a few days. I was able to get a sitter today, but I'll have to take off tomorrow to stay home with them, which sucks because I really can't afford to lose a day's pay."

I didn't know why I was being so forthcoming with Brett, but it felt good to have someone to talk about it with. It was like a weight had been lifted at being able to get that off my chest. However, his response was the very last thing I expected to hear.

"I can watch them for you tomorrow."

I gave a surprised laugh. "What?"

"Seriously, I can watch them. I'm great with kids, and I'm my own boss so missing a day of work is nothing."

"Brett, that's sweet, but I don't think so. I mean, they don't really know you and we only *just* agreed to be friends. Letting you babysit my two sick toddlers will send you screaming toward the hills. Trust me, they're a handful on the best days. When they're sick it's a whole other story."

"It'll be fine, trust me," he told me with a sincere grin. "I know I only met Cameron and Callie for a few minutes the other day, but I have to tell you, you're kids are kind of great, Kenz."

"Thanks," I smiled sweetly, the beautiful compliment melting my heart.

"And Lizzy can totally vouch for me. I'll take great care of them. I promise. And if it makes you feel better, I can stop by your place tonight and really introduce myself. Come on, beauty; it's a win-win."

I sat, uncertain, for several seconds as I studied his expression. Everything in my gut told me he was being completely genuine.

"Okay," I finally relented. "Come by tonight and, if it goes well, you can babysit for me tomorrow."

"It'll be great, beauty, you'll see. I'm awesome with little rugrats."

"You have a lot of experience with kids?"

"Well..." he paused before saying, "not really. But with my sparkling personality, I can win anyone over."

I rolled my eyes and laughed. "Oh, Lord. You're in trouble."

CHAPTER ELEVEN

"HOW YOU FEELING, BABIES?" I asked my little ones after getting home from work and releasing the sitter for the night. Cam and Callie were both lying on the couch watching *Bubble Guppies,* each had their head at opposite ends with their tiny feet tangled together.

"Better," Callie told me. "I didn't frowe up anymore."

"My tummy still hurts, Mommy," Cameron said with a little pout.

I reached up to brush a flop of brown hair off his forehead. "I know, sweetie. I got you some ginger ale to make your tummy feel better." I handed him the cup so he could take a swallow. "Mommy has a friend coming over tonight to meet you guys. He wanted to introduce himself. He's going to stay with you tomorrow while I'm at work."

"Is he nice?" Callie asked seriously.

"He's very nice, honey pot. You'll like him a lot."

Leaving them to watch TV, I headed into the kitchen. Cam and Callie still couldn't really stomach much to eat, so I kept their dinner light and bland, letting them eat on the couch this one time.

As I finished cleaning the kitchen, there was a knock at the door. I wasn't prepared for the way my heart lurched in my chest at just the thought of Brett, so I tried to push it to the back of my mind and went to let him in.

As soon as I opened the front door, my mouth grew dry at the sight of him. His light blue, long-sleeved tee hugged all those delectable muscles, reminding me of how good his body felt against mine. His low-slung jeans did amazing things for his tall, toned legs, and his hair was a shade darker from being damp, like he'd just gotten out of the shower before coming over.

"Hey there, beauty."

My gaze shot back to his face. The way his lips tipped and his eyes crinkled with humor told me I'd just been busted checking him out.

"Uh…" I cleared my throat and tried to get my bearings. "Yeah, hi. Um, come on in."

I heard his quiet chuckle as he walked past me and into my apartment.

I led Brett into the living room and grabbed the remote to put the TV on mute. "Hey, guys, I want you to meet my friend Brett."

"Yous the giant from the food store," Callie said as she stared up at his immense height.

Brett smiled sweetly at the twins and squatted down so he could be eye to eye with them as they lay on the couch. "Yep, that's me. Your mom told me you guys weren't feeling well. I thought maybe these would help to cheer you up."

He lifted up a canvas bag, which in my disgraceful perusal of his body just moments earlier, I'd somehow missed. He reached in and pulled out a stuffed bunny wearing a princess dress and crown, handing it over to Callie before reaching back in and pulling out a superhero action figure for Cameron.

I tried desperately not to melt as my kids' sick little faces lit up at the sight of their new toys, but god, it was hard not to when the man was being so sweet to the two people who mattered most to me in all the world.

"Your mom also told me I could stay here with you tomorrow while she's at work if you guys were cool with that."

"You want to babysit us?" Cameron asked.

"Are you kidding?" Brett responded enthusiastically. "Heck yeah! You're the coolest kids I've ever met! I'd love to get to spend the day with you guys."

Don't melt, don't melt, don't melt.

Christ, the man was killing me!

"Will you bring cookies?"

Brett looked down at Cameron and gave him a little wink. "Let's see how your tummy feels tomorrow, little buddy. If you're feeling better, we'll play it by ear. Sound good?"

Brett held his fist up, and like it was the most natural thing in the world, Cameron bumped it with his own. It was so damn cute that I totally let the whole cookie thing slide.

Brett stuck around for a few more minutes before finally telling the kids to get some rest and he'd see them in the morning. I walked him to the door and stepped out into the breezeway with him, leaving it opened a crack so I could hear just in case one of the kids needed me.

"You didn't have to bring them presents, but thank you. It was sweet and they loved them."

"No problem." His deep, gravelly voice dropped low as he stepped in close to me. "Like I said, I really like your kids. Tomorrow will be fine, you'll see."

"I can't begin to pay you back for this—"

He pressed his finger to my lips to stop me.

"Nothing to pay back, beauty. I'm happy to help. Now, go get some sleep. You've had a long day."

The gentle press of his lips to my forehead made me sigh

and lean into him. But before I could do anything I'd later regret, Brett pulled away, shooting me a wink and that beautiful smile of his before turning and walking away.

BRETT

THERE WAS THE TEENIEST, tiniest, just slightest possibility that I might not have known just what I was getting myself into with my offer to babysit for Kenzie.

When I arrived at her apartment and watched her flitting around like an anxious hummingbird, quickly rattling off a long-ass list of rules, emergency contacts, and the phone number for poison control, I'd ignorantly thought to myself *yeah, I got this* as I took in the two angelic creatures quietly sitting at the kitchen table, eating their breakfast.

I'd pushed Kenzie out the door with a, "You have nothing to worry about," feeling overly confident, and thinking that the twins were always so polite and serene.

Yeah, not so fucking much.

Things had started out so perfectly. We watched some whacked-out movie about talking Legos or some such shit.

Side note, if I had to hear that yellow fucker singing about how everything was awesome one more damn time, I was going to lose my mind. The kids were feeling better by lunchtime so I decided to stray from their premade meal of bland and tasteless that Kenzie left in the fridge and ordered a pizza. Watching their hazel eyes, so much like their mom's, light up like I'd just told them I was Santa was probably one of the best feelings I'd ever had. Of course, the whole pizza thing went down after I had a very long, very thorough talk with them about the importance of the buddy code—which was the term I'd come up with for keeping a secret because I was brilliant like that. Buddy code specifically stated that Cameron and Callie could each get *one* slice of pizza for lunch if they promised it would stay between us. What Kenzie didn't know wouldn't hurt her, and it was just pizza after all. No red-blooded American kid could truly thrive without pizza. That was in a manual somewhere for sure.

About thirty minutes after lunch, Cameron upchucked like he was trying to dispel every ounce of fluid from his body. Seriously, I had never in my life seen anything like it. And if I was being honest, I gave that poison control number some serious thought. Luckily, he seemed to rally pretty damn fast after that nightmare.

Once the puke show was over, it was naptime. And it couldn't have come sooner because I was wiped. I could only host so many tea parties—Callie's idea—or be an evil ninja—Cameron's idea...okay, my idea—and deal with a truckload of puke without needing a breather.

I tucked the kids into their tiny beds and made my way back into the living room, remote in hand, totally prepared to watch something that wouldn't make my balls shrivel up into prune. Princess Elsa was hot and all, but I wanted to strangle the icy wench after the eleventy-billionth "Let it go". *Woman, we get it!*

I flipped through the channels, only to find that there wasn't really anything on that caught my attention. Not one who handles boredom all that well, I started wandering around the tiny apartment, straightening things up as I went. I tried to put the toys back into the plastic bins that lined one of the living room walls, but no manner of stacking would keep the overflow of stuffed animals and action figures from toppling back onto the floor. The twins really needed some place to stash their loot; those bins just weren't cutting it.

Giving up on that project, I wandered aimlessly, inspecting

everything closely, really trying to get a feel for Kenzie. The apartment was homey, but all of the furniture appeared to be second-hand. The kitchen table was scuffed and scratched on more of the surface than not. The mismatched chairs had wobbly legs. The couch, while comfortable, had definitely seen better days; the fabric was so worn and threadbare in some spots, it was just one plop away from tearing open. The one thing that stood out the most as I walked the space was that everything that belonged to the twins appeared to be brand new. They had new toys, boxes of crayons, coloring books, clothes, matchbox cars, and dollhouses. You name it, these kids had it. And no way was any of it second-hand.

That spoke volumes about the woman who'd grabbed my interest and refused to let go. She was a proud woman who busted her ass for what she had, and it was clear that any extra she found herself with she used on her children. I didn't know what happened in her past, but I had no doubt that everything she did, she did with those kids' best interests at heart. Strong didn't even begin to properly describe Mackenzie Webster.

All of a sudden, I was pulled from my musings by a high-pitched scream followed by a splash. I felt like my heart was about to beat right out of my chest as I rushed down the hall. Fear gripped my lungs in a tight hold, refusing to allow any air in or out. As I skidded to a halt in the bathroom doorway, what I saw confirmed one thing.

I was *so* screwed.

CHAPTER TWELVE

BRETT

"WHAT THE HELL do you expect us to do?" Trevor asked in astonishment as Luke and Jeremy stood back with their hands over their mouths, trying their hardest not to laugh.

"I don't know!" I shouted before releasing a string of colorful expletives.

"Uuuuummmm, you said bunches of bad words," Cameron spoke from his place on top of the toilet. Well, to be accurate, it was more like *inside* the toilet.

I leaned in and ruffled his hair. "Hey bud, you remember about the buddy code, right?" He gave me an exuberant nod. "Yeah, why don't we put my bad words under the buddy code, yeah? We won't tell your mommy that I accidentally cussed, and I'll work really hard not to do it anymore. Deal?" I reached my hand out and he grabbed on with his little one to give it an enthusiastic shake.

"Deal."

"Can we gets a cookie for not tellin'?" Callie asked from beside me.

"You bet!"

"Yay!" both kids cheered like nothing was wrong in the world while, internally, I was freaking the ever-loving hell out.

"Hey, ladybug. Can you go look in the fridge and see if your mommy has any butter?"

Callie looked up at me with bright eyes and said, "Mommy says butter's bad for you. We gots mawgin."

That'll work.

"Margarine's perfect, sweetie. Will you go get that for me?" She bolted from the bathroom and took off down the hall as I released a breath and turned back to Cameron. "All right, buddy. Explain to me how you get your foot stuck in the toilet."

"I was tryin' ta flush myself."

I stood there, momentarily speechless with my mouth hanging open, before asking, "Why would you...you know what? Doesn't matter. Let's just try and get you out, okay?"

"Yup." He popped the "p" and stood casually, like he had all the time in the world.

"What are you planning on doing? Greasing him up like a pig?"

I shot a scowl at Jeremy. "What are you even doing here? I don't remember calling you for help."

"You didn't," he grinned. "You called Trevor. Trevor called Luke. Luke called me. No way in hell I was missing this shit."

"That's a bad word," Cameron scolded.

"Yeah, Jeremy. That's a bad word. Watch your damn mouth."

"*Got it!*" Callie screeched about a million decibels higher than necessary as she shot into the bathroom with a tub of Parkay in her hands.

"Thank you, ladybug. Why don't you take Jeremy here and go show him your tea party set? He was just telling me how much he wanted to have a princess tea party."

"Yay! Come on, come on, Jewmy!" He gave me over his

shoulder that promised revenge as Callie pulled him out the door, and I couldn't resist the opportunity to shoot him the finger as I watched him go.

"All right, bud," I said, turning back to Cameron, still hanging out, one foot stuck in the toilet like it was just any other day. "This is what we're going to do. I'll reach in and try to get your foot unstuck while Trevor here gently pulls on your leg." I turned back to Trevor and narrowed my eyes. "You hear that, Trevor? *Gently.*"

"Yeah, I think I got it. Remind me real quick, who was it that got a kid's foot stuck in the toilet while babysitting? Ah! That's right, that'd be you, d-i-c-k-w-a-d."

The bastard actually had the nerve to spell it out.

"Yeah, well, I'm still going to kick your a-s-s when this is over, l-i-m-p-d-i-c-k. Can we just do this, please?"

Popping the top off the margarine, I shoved my hand in and dug out a huge glob before reaching into the toilet bowl and trying as best as I could to coat Cam's ankle so we could finagle him out.

"Okay, Trevor, you pull his leg. Luke, see if you can lift him up. On the count of three. One, two—"

"What's going on?"

Son of a bitch!

KENZIE

WALKING into my apartment after a long day of worrying uncontrollably about both my kids' *and* Brett's welfare, the last thing I expected to see was Jeremy sitting in one of the tiny plastic chairs at Callie's tea party table, wearing a princess crown on his head as he sipped pretend tea out of a purple plastic cup with his pinky poking straight up in the air.

"Uh, hi?"

"Mommy!" Callie shrieked. "Brett and Jewmy played princess tea party with me today!"

"Good deal, honey pot. Where's your brother?"

"Bathroom," Jeremy answered as he dabbed the corners of his mouth with a napkin like he was a member of high society. Who'd have guessed the man would take his tea parties so seriously.

I heard commotion coming from the bathroom as I walked down the hall, and what I saw froze me on site. Brett was crouched down with both hands in the toilet bowl while Trevor had a hold of one of my son's legs and Luke was pulling him from under his arms. And was that...? Why was my butter in the bathroom?

"On the count of three. One, two—"

"What's going on?" At the sound of my voice, three pairs of grownup eyes swung to me, all with different levels of *oh, shit, so busted* reflected back at me.

"Mommy!" Cameron let out a delighted shout. "I tried ta flush myself again!"

I couldn't hold back my laugh at Brett's exclamation of, "*Again?*"

Oh, this was just too damn funny. "Brett, did you try to butter up my son?"

"Technically," Trevor answered, "it's margarine, so there's that..."

"Beauty, this isn't what it looks like," Brett mumbled, all adorable and flustered.

"Really? Because it looks like you got my kid stuck in the toilet, then tried to baste him," I managed to get out between hysterical giggles.

"So it's exactly what it looks like," Luke laughed.

Finally taking pity on the poor guy, I walked over to Cameron. "All right, bub. Turn your foot so your toes are at the front, then point them down." He did as told and his little foot popped right out. When I turned back to the hulking men crowding in my cramped bathroom, Trevor and Luke looked like they were trying their damnedest to keep from laughing while Brett looked like he was about to have an aneurysm.

"Not our first rodeo," I told him with a laugh. "Or our third."

"Mommy, guess what!" Cameron said excitedly as he hopped up and down on the bathroom floor, flushing incident long forgotten.

"What, pumpkin?"

"Brett's the best babysitter ever! He gave us pizza and watched movies with us and we gots a buddy code thats like a secret where we don't tell you when he says bad words by assident! But I can't tell you 'cause its buddy code! *Oh!* And I frowed up... Like a *whoooooole* bunches."

I heard Brett grumble, "Kind of defeating the purpose of buddy code there, little man," before Cameron took off into the living room to go play with his sister.

Luke slapped Brett on the shoulder, telling him, "We're out, man. Don't need to be witness to whatever she's about to do to you." Then he was gone.

Trevor did the sign of the cross on Brett before bailing out, and seconds later I heard the front door open and close.

"Kenz, I'm so damn sorry..." Brett started, but I held my hand up to stop him.

"I'm going to go in order here, so try and keep up. First, no more buddy code, okay? I didn't expect your first foray into babysitting to be a perfect ten, especially with those two, but you can't teach them to keep secrets from me. Not even if it's obvious they can't keep their mouths shut to save their lives." He gave me an ashamed nod. "Second, if something happens like, oh say, my son trying to flush himself down the toilet and getting stuck, all you have to do is call me. Odds are, he's done it before, meaning I'll know how to get him out of whatever he got himself into, so there won't be a need to butter him up like a Thanksgiving turkey. Also, I get you were trying to win cool points, but heads up, any dairy after a stomach virus is a definite no. Same goes with a fever. But I'm pretty sure you learned that lesson the hard way."

"That's the freaking understatement of the century. You must hate me right now," he mumbled with his head hung, but I pushed forward, ignoring his statement.

"And you have to watch your language. I know it's hard, trust me, but they're like little sponges. Those damn kids soak up *everything*."

"That the damn truth."

"And last... Thank you."

His head shot up and he stared back at me with wide brown eyes. "Thank you? For what? I'm the worst babysitter in the history of existence."

I couldn't help myself; he was just so damn cute standing there all disgruntled. I stepped up to him and cupped his cheek. "Thank you for liking my kids so much that you wanted to spoil them with pizza. Thank you for playing princess tea party with my little girl. I promise you, that made her entire week. Thank you for sitting through god knows how many kids movies just because it's what they wanted."

"I think I might just puncture my own ear drums if I have to listen to that fu-freaking *awesome* song again."

I was definitely of the same opinion on that.

"But mostly, thank you for giving my kids such a great day that, even though his foot was lodged in a toilet, my son couldn't stop going on about how much he liked you. There were a few bumps in the road, but you are far from the worst babysitter in history. They've been lacking when it comes to having a man who cares in their lives, so I can't tell you what that means to me."

Brett reached up, placed his palm against my hand that was holding his cheek, and pressed deeper into my touch. "So you'll let me babysit for you again?"

A laugh escaped my throat. "You mean you'd actually *want* to do this again?"

"Are you kidding me? Those kids are awesome! I loved hanging with them today. And now that I know you won't castrate me for any little mishaps, the stress is gone."

The enthusiasm in his voice caused my chest to tighten, and my heart started thumping in a quick rhythm. I had to pull my hand away and take a step back. If I didn't put space between us I was likely to do something that I'd regret. This was friendship, nothing more. That was the only way I could keep this incredible man in my life. Anything else and I'd most definitely end up destroying him.

I smiled to try and cut the tension that suddenly enveloped the room.

"Maybe after a few more practice runs. You know, with me only a few feet away."

CHAPTER THIRTEEN

KENZIE

I DECIDED to take my lunch hour at Virgie May's to try and get some planning done. The twins' fifth birthday was just around the corner and I wanted to do something special for them, but the longer I sat, the more that lead weight in the bottom of my stomach grew as I realized my budget wasn't going to allow me give them the party the deserved.

"Whatcha doing?" Emmy's sing-song voice came from behind me. I glanced over my shoulder to find her and Stacia standing there with smiles on their faces. I'd gotten to know Stacia and the rest of their group pretty well over the past few weeks, mainly because of the drama that had taken place with Trevor and Lizzy almost divorcing not too long ago. I'd stood by and watched as Lizzy crumbled over the loss of the love of her life, and it ripped something apart inside me. Finally, after two weeks of seeing my friend self-destruct, I'd had enough. I had taken it upon myself to step up to the plate and reach out to everyone who cared about her. Seeing as her friends were loving, kind, and all around nosey as hell, we managed to stage an intervention for the slightly insane couple, and helped them see how perfect they were for each other.

I couldn't begin to describe how good it made me feel to witness two people madly in love get the happily ever after they truly deserved. And finding myself being pulled into the fold with these wonderful people was a blessing for me and my kids. It was beginning to feel like I was a part of an actual family.

"Making a list."

"Checking it twice and all that jazz?"

"Something like that," I smiled. "How you doing, preggo?" I reached out to rub her belly.

"Ugh," she groaned as she and Stacia took a seat in the empty chairs around me. "So ready for this to be over. Every time I sneeze and dribble on myself, I pray it's my water breaking." Stacia and I both laughed at her over-share. "How did you do it with two of these things cooking in you?"

"Just be thankful, that's all I can tell you. You don't have much longer."

She rubbed her hands over her belly. "Nah, not much longer at all." Her face became solemn as she looked down and traced a pattern on her tummy with her index finger.

Reaching over, I placed my hand on hers and stopped its movements. "Hey, you okay?"

Her smile didn't quite reach her eyes. "I was pregnant once before," she stated quietly, stunning me speechless. I knew there was some serious history between Emmy and Luke that hadn't all been good, but I didn't know the details, and I never felt it was my place to ask. But hearing that a pregnancy had been involved was shocking. "I was only a few weeks further along than I am now..." Her words trailed off as her voice cracked. When her next words came out, my heart broke for her. "I lost Ella."

"Oh, sweetheart." Stacia and I both stood and wrapped Emmy in our arms, holding her silently for a bit.

When she pulled out of our grip, she was slightly more composed as she smiled and brushed a tear from her cheek.

"I'm okay," she promised. "I'm just..." she huffed out a breath. "I guess I'm just scared. I don't..."

She stopped talking completely and I knew exactly where her mind was going. There was no way I letting her stay there.

"Hey, nothing is going to happen," I told her adamantly. "You hear me? Nothing. Your doctor knows what she's doing. She knows your history and she knows how to prevent it from happening again. You can trust her."

"She's right, babe," Stacia agreed. "You have a high-risk OB and she's already promised that everything is perfectly fine with this little dude. It's all going to be great."

Emmy inhaled deeply, closed her eyes and exhaled. "You're right." The strong chick I had grown to know reappeared before my eyes. "This little spud's going to be terrorizing his mommy before we know it."

We all laughed, and I released a relieved sigh knowing Emmy was all right.

"So, what's your list about? Emmy asked, quick to change the subject as she pulled the pad toward her. "Ooh, fun! A birthday party!"

"Yeah, I'm not really sure how much fun it'll be," I lamented as I pulled my notepad back.

"What are you talking about?" Stacia chimed in. "All parties are fun. Even if they're for five-year-olds."

My discomfort with the conversation was made even worse when Brett, in all his sweaty construction worker glory, came sauntering into the diner.

"Well, if it isn't my lucky day." He shot a devastating grin toward our table before leaning down to plant a kiss on Emmy and Stacia's cheeks. "Ladies, you're looking beautiful as ever."

An unwanted pang of jealousy spiked through me at his

flirty banter with the girls. But before I had a chance to remind myself we'd agreed to be just friends, he stopped at my side and leaned in, whispering for my ears only, "Beauty, you're the most gorgeous of all." The kiss he placed on my cheek lingered a little longer than a friendship warranted, and I felt an instant heat throughout my entire body.

With the new rooms at the salon being finished, I'd begun to really miss seeing Brett every day. Each morning I walked into work and didn't see his smiling face was like a punch to my chest. I hadn't realized just how much seeing him all the time brightened my day. Despite the fact we both said we could be nothing more, my traitorous feelings for him refused to go away. Trying to maintain a healthy friendship with him while replaying our one night together in my head was proving to be exceedingly difficult. Especially when he flirted so easily, or said things to me that made my body quiver.

"So, what's going on?" he asked casually as he took the empty chair right next to me.

"We're just talking about the twins' birthday party," Emmy replied before I could come up with a believable lie and switch the subject to something else.

Brett's bright eyes met mine as he asked, "Cool, so what's the plan then, Momma?"

I tried not to sound upset as I told them, "I'll probably just take them to Chuck E. Cheese."

"Oh, no! You have to have a party," Emmy told me. "They're turning five. We need to have a big blow out."

My shoulders slumped. That was exactly what I was hoping to give them but the money just wasn't adding up. "A big blow out isn't something I can afford right now," I spoke in a hushed voice, embarrassed to admit I couldn't throw the kind of party that turning five warranted.

"Well what the hell do you think you have us for?" Emmy

asked. "Sorry, babe, but when you stepped up for Liz, you officially became part of the family. That means we all chip in to throw those precious little hellions a kickass birthday."

"I can't ask you to do that—"

"You didn't ask," she interrupted. "That's the beauty of this little gang right here. We horn in and take over before you even get to ask for the help. We're awesome like that."

"And I throw *amazing* parties," Stacia chirped excitedly. I could practically see the ideas floating around in her head.

"But where will we have it, huh? I live in a two-bedroom apartment, guys. On the second level. A bunch of kids running around like crazy is just screaming, 'hey, evict me! Evict me!'"

"We'll have it at my place." Brett's gravelly voice jerked my attention his way.

"What?"

"That's perfect!" Emmy cried. "Brett has the best backyard *ever*! It's huge and backs up right to the woods behind his house. Great idea, Brett."

"You guys, I can't—"

Brett leaned in so close I could smell the strong sent of laundry detergent and fresh air that came off him. "Yes you can, beauty," his tone soft yet commanding. It was a tone that garnered instant attention.

"We're offering because we *want* to. That's all. I want to help give Callie and Cam a great party any way I can. Just let us help, babe. Those kids mean something to us. They mean something to *me*."

There was no way I could stare into those rich brown eyes after hearing him say such wonderful things about my children and not allow him to help me.

"Okay, fine." Stacia and Emmy let out squeals of delight. "But let's not go overboard, okay? I know it's a big birthday, but they're still just five. No need to get crazy."

I got the distinct impression that the girls chose to stop listening as soon as I agreed. They leaned in together and scribbled frantically in my notepad, saying words like "petting zoo" and "pony", and the scariest of all "Elmo performers."

When I looked away from them, Brett's eyes were still on me, and that smile that made my insides melt was at full wattage.

There was no fighting my smile in return.

CHAPTER FOURTEEN

KENZIE

BRETT: *Where are you?*

I'd exchanged numbers with everyone so we could all stay in contact while planning the kids' birthday party, and for the past week I'd been getting at least one text from Brett a day. Some were sweet, wishing me a good day, some were teasing, some asked about the kids, and some were flirty and playful. Those were my favorite.

Me: *At the park with the Tiresome Twosome.*

When we woke up, the sun had been shining brightly in the sky. The temperature was just perfect, humidity low, with a nice fall breeze; it was the perfect day to get the twins out for their daily dose of vitamin D.

Brett: *Awesome. On my way.*

I couldn't help the ridiculous smile that spread across my face.

Me: *I don't recall inviting you.*

Brett: *Didn't have to. I can read your mind. You want me there. Admit it, beauty.*

The urge to tease him was just too enticing to ignore.

Me: *You're an ass. Also, don't you ever work?*

The bubbles showing he was typing popped up instantly.

Brett: *I could ask you the same thing.*

Me: *Ha! Day off, asshole.*

Brett: *See you in 5. Try to hold your enthusiasm in.*

"Mommy, watch!" Callie called out as I laughed off Brett's last text and dropped my phone back into my purse. I spent the next few minutes watching Callie and Cam take turns going down the slide. So far, the trip to the park had been successful with only one wrestling match breaking out between the two over who got to slide first.

Then God laughed.

"Cameron Michael. Don't pull your sister's hair!" I called out when things started to quickly deteriorate.

"But she's bein' a poop face!"

"No name calling or I'm taking away your Spiderman toy when we get home."

Good Lord, where did kids come up with these insults?

"Have to give the kid an A for creativity. Don't think I've ever heard the name 'poop face' before."

I let out a started yelp and spun around at the deep rumble of Brett's voice in my ear. Only an inch or two separated his body from mine, and the close proximity was doing crazy things to my head.

"Don't sneak up on me like that," I grumbled, trying my best to ignore my body's desire to lean in closer to him. "You scared the crap out of me."

His gravelly laugh was like music to my ears. "Sorry, beauty. Didn't mean to startle you."

He reached up and brushed a strand of hair from my face and it took everything in me to suppress the shiver his touch caused.

I tried my hardest not to notice how sexy he looked in just a plain white t-shirt and jeans, the perfect amount of scruff that covered his cheeks and chin, or those gorgeous brown eyes of his hidden beneath the brim of a tattered ball cap, but I just couldn't do it. His clothes did wonders for his body. And even if I didn't know the perfection that lay beneath, I'd still have found his strength and size mouthwatering. Self-consciousness hit me like a freight train as I glanced down at my frumpy get-up. A day off for me meant yoga pants and ratty tee, my hair up in a sloppy bun, and no makeup whatsoever. Why, oh, why couldn't I have been bothered to put in just a *little* effort when I woke up this morning?

"Brett!" the kids shouted boisterously as they came barreling toward us.

I took a quick step back, immediately missing the heat from his body as they plowed into his strong legs, not budging him a muscle.

"Did you come to play with us?" Callie asked with a bright smile.

"Of course I did. I missed my little buddies." He swooped down and grabbed Callie by the waist and tossed her in the air, delighting in her shrill laughter before putting her safely on the ground and doing the same to Cameron.

"Come slide with us!" Cameron shouted before he and Callie took off in that direction.

Brett followed after, shooting a wink at me over his shoulder. Damn that sexy wink! Being friends with this man was killing me. If him being hot as sin wasn't bad enough, watching him climb up that stupid slide and go down with both kids in his lap just about did me in. That was it. I needed at least an hour alone with my vibrator if I was going to make it through this *friendship.*

It wasn't lost on me that every other mom in the park was

keeping a close eye on Brett's every movement. I couldn't blame them. There was nothing more attractive to a mother than a sexy man getting down in the dirt, not the slightest bit embarrassed to sit in a sandbox if that's what made the kids happy. But that didn't stop my nagging jealousy from rearing its ugly head every time one of them dared to get a little too close. Thankfully, he simply smiling politely as he brushed them off and went back to playing with the twins.

I watched as he made my children laugh and squeal in delight while he followed them from play set to play set, never once losing his patience like Lance had been so prone to doing.

About an hour later Callie and Cam came running back over to me, out of breath and smiling a mile wide, with Brett trailing closely behind.

"Mommy, did you see how high I swinged?"

I scooped my little girl up in my lap and gave her a nuzzle. "I did! I was afraid you were going to swing all the way to the moon."

"Silly Mommy," she giggled, kissing me on my cheek.

"I'd have missed you *soooo* much if you went all the way to the moon."

I felt a shift on the bench as Brett took a seat next to me and pulled Cameron onto his lap, pulling his ball cap off and plopping it on my son's head.

"Hey, Mommy. Brett said I can wear his hat *all day!*"

"That's really awesome, bub. It's a great hat." I smiled. "Did you tell him thank you?"

"Yu huh. He said it haves magical powers. It'll make me strong like Spiderman!"

"That's right, bud." Brett gave the brim a little flick. "My granddad gave it to me so I could grow up strong, and look at me now."

Cameron stared up at Brett in wonder, awed that the magic

hat could possibly make him so big. "Wow. Cool," he breathed out.

"Yeah, my granddad was a pretty cool man."

Cameron turned back to me and asked, "Is my granddad as cool as Brett's, Mommy?"

I felt my smile falter at that question. I'd been dreading questions like that for the longest time, knowing I'd have to lie.

"Yeah," I croaked out, trying to maintain a cheerful face as I spoke past the lump that had formed in my throat.

"How come we never seen our granddad?" Callie asked. My eyes went wide as I stuttered, trying to come up with an appropriate answer.

Thankfully, Brett seemed to be in tune with my sudden mood shift and quickly jumped on a subject change.

"Hey, guys, I'm starving. How about we go get ourselves something to eat, huh? I know Emmy's dying to see y'all. We can head over to the diner for lunch."

"*Yay!*" they cheered, hopping off our laps and jumping up and down.

We grabbed our stuff and left the park. As we walked, I looked over to catch Brett's eye, mouthing a silent *thank you* to him. He smiled politely, but what I saw in his eyes told me he was just as curious for an answer to my kids' questions as they were. That was a conversation I had no intention of ever having with him

---

ALL THOUGHTS and talk of their grandfather was completely forgotten by the time we walked through the door of Virgie May's. After eating a delicious lunch and visiting with Emmy, where she plied my kids with pie (whoever said sugar doesn't affect a child's energy level was a complete jackass.

Science got that one seriously wrong), we spent the rest of the day running around, enjoying the beautiful weather.

By the time the sun started to set, Callie and Cameron were dead to the world and I was thankful to have Brett there to help me carry them up the stairs and into the apartment. He put Cameron on his bed as I laid Callie down on hers and stepped out so I could get them in their jammies and tucked in properly. Neither of them flinched as I got them set.

Stepping to the doorway, I flicked the switch off and turned to look at my two tiny angels sleeping peacefully in their beds before pulling the door to and heading back into the living room.

"Thank you." I reached for the beer Brett offered and plopped down on the couch, sucking back a generous gulp before dropping my head and closing my eyes. The couch dipped with Brett's weight as he took a seat next to me, both of us sitting in companionable silence for a few minutes.

"I appreciate you coming with us today," I spoke, breaking the peaceful quiet. I felt him shift next to me and my eyes popped open at the sensation of his fingers brushing along my cheek.

"I had fun. I always have fun when I'm with those two."

The grin on his face as he tipped his head in the direction of the hall caused butterflies to take off in my belly. He was always so genuine when he talked about my kids.

"They really like you," I whispered, emotion clogging my throat as I thought back to how he was with Cameron and Callie earlier that day. I'd never seen a man connect so well with them before. Lance was always too busy or too tired to be bothered with them, but Brett had the patience of a saint. It pulled at something inside of me that I was trying so desperately to ignore.

"I really like them, too."

WORTH THE WAIT   105

I studied his face, trying to find something that indicated what he said was a lie, but I came up empty.

"You really mean that, don't you?"

His eyes narrowed as he studied me intently, like he was trying to see all of my secrets. It was such a disconcerting feeling that I found myself leaning away from him.

"Why is that so hard to believe?" he asked softly. "You're a fantastic woman who, in turn, is raising two fantastic kids."

I turned away and took another sip of my beer with a mumbled, "Thanks," not knowing what else to say.

Obviously having had enough of me evading his gaze, Brett took my chin between his fingers and tilted my face toward his.

"What happened to you, beauty? You can tell me."

"There's nothing to tell," I lied, standing from the couch and taking a step away. All of a sudden, I needed space from him and his questioning eyes. I hated how he was looking at me. The pity and the concern cut through me like a white hot blade.

He stood as well and reached out for my hand, but I quickly pulled it away. "Kenz, I saw how you reacted when Callie asked about her grandfather. There's something there, something you're keeping locked up. You don't have to do that, baby. You can trust me. I would never judge you."

What a joke. If there was one thing I'd learned growing up, it was that you could never trust anyone but yourself. Trusting people—especially men—had never caused me anything but pain. Emotional *and* physical.

"It's late and I'm tired," I muttered, choosing to ignore his declaration like the coward I was. "I think you should probably go. I'll give you a call tomorrow." I walked over to the front door and pulled it open, giving him no choice but to leave.

Brett calmly placed his half-full beer on the coffee table and made his way over, stopping just in front of me.

"You ever plan on trusting me, beauty?"

Lifting my chin in the air, I looked him directly in the eyes, working hard to make sure my voice didn't waver as I answered, "I don't trust anyone, Brett. I learned that lesson a long time ago."

Something flashed across his face that looked a lot like disappointment. The thought of him being disappointed in me sent a spike of pain through my chest.

"That really makes for a sad, lonely existence, Kenzie."

He didn't say anything else as he walked away, not once turning back to see just how badly his parting shot had gutted me.

CHAPTER FIFTEEN

KENZIE

I DIDN'T CALL Brett the next day like I said I would, or the day after, for that matter. And before I knew it, six days had passed without any communication. My stomach was in knots as the twins and I drove to his house to help set up for their birthday party that was set to start in only a few hours.

My emotions were completely off kilter. I was nervous about seeing him for the first time since kicking him out of my apartment a week ago. I feared he'd give me the cold shoulder for how I'd been acting. But what worried me the most was how much I had missed him.

By the time we pulled up, the driveway was full of cars. I got the kids out of their boosters, hauled the cake from the back seat, and started carrying it up the front walk.

"Brett! Brett!" the kids shouted excitedly as they barged through the door without so much as knocking.

"Callie, Cameron! You don't just run into someone's house," I scolded as I followed after them, trying to catch up and not drop the cake at the same time.

"Hey, birthday buds!" Brett replied just as excited as they were. He bent down and scooped them both up, one in each arm, and looked over at me with that signature grin of his. The nerves in my belly began to uncoil. The relief I felt that he didn't appear mad was almost overwhelming.

"Is that the cake?" Emmy and Savannah came rushing up to me, pulling my attention off of Brett as they peeked through the clear plastic lid to the birthday cake I'd spent *way* too many hours making last night.

"Oh my god, that's so pretty!" The rest of the girls ran over to inspect my work, oohing and awing over the two tiered, pirate-themed cake. The bottom tier was black, with white skulls and crossbones for Cameron, while the top tier was pink with black pirate accents. The twins loved it and I was ecstatic that I only had to make *one* cake.

"How did you do that?" Mickey asked me.

"It was my first foray into fondant, and I'll tell you this now, I'm *never* doing that again. There's no freaking reason it should take me four hours just to decorate the damn thing!"

Brett set Cameron and Callie back on the floor and looked at the cake over my shoulder. As it did every time he was close, my body reacted to him, flushing with an attraction I couldn't beat down.

"You did good, beauty. Why don't you go put it in the kitchen? I have something I want to show you."

"Hey, you two, why don't you come with me?" Emmy waddled over to the twins and took their hands. "The guys are in the backyard. We have some surprises for you."

I watched with a smile on my face as Cam and Callie jumped up and down as they let Emmy lead them out.

Grabbing my hand, Brett led me away from the back door. "Come on. I want you to see this."

I blindly followed him down the hall, reveling in the feel of his palm against mine as memories of our one and only night together flashed back through my head. Arousal flowed over me the closer we got to his bedroom door. I couldn't help but remember exactly how he'd manipulated my body in the very best ways in that room.

Pausing outside a door one room down from his own, Brett turned to look at me. I could tell the moment he realized what I was thinking about. His lids lowered half-mast as he took me in, his gaze trailing down my neck and chest before returning to my own.

"You're remembering it, too, aren't you, beauty?" he asked in a low, velvety voice as he stepped in closer to me, crowding me against the doorframe. He leaned in and ran his nose along the bend of my neck to my ear. "I can't stop thinking about that night, Kenzie. It's burned into my fucking brain."

"Brett," I panted.

"You still feel it, don't you?"

I reached up and placed my palms on his hard chest to push him back, but he only moved just enough to look at me.

"Please, Brett. Don't do this. Especially right now."

A growl rumbled deep in his chest before he dropped his forehead to mine and let out a deep breath.

"I'm sorry," he said, taking a step back. "It's just so goddamn hard not to touch you, Kenz."

Trying to push down the feeling of just how badly I missed his warmth or how deeply his words penetrated my heart, I attempted a smile and cleared my throat. "It's okay. What did you want to show me?"

At my question, his face lit up, making him look like a little boy and endearing me to him that much more.

I followed him into the room and stopped while he walked over to whatever it was he wanted to show me, and whipped the sheet covering it off. My breath stalled and tears instantly filled my eyes as I took in the sight of the most beautiful toy chest I'd ever seen. It was made of solid wood with a hinged lid. The craftsmanship was like nothing I'd ever seen before. The wood was stained a beautiful cherry with hand carved toys, everything from trains to teddy bears. On the lid, in carved scrolling letters, were my children's names. If not for that detail, I would have taken the toy chest for an expensive antique. It was absolutely stunning.

"Oh, Brett," I cried before I covered my mouth with both hands, tears breaking free and running down my cheeks.

His brow furrowed with worry as he took in my tear-stained face. "Ah, Christ, beauty. Don't cry." He rushed to me and scooped me into a tight hug. "I won't give it to them if it upsets you. It was a stupid idea. I shouldn't have built it without talking to you first."

I pulled back, stunned. "You made this?"

"Well, yeah." He let me go and reached back to rub his neck at the same time an adorable blush crept into his cheeks. "I saw the small bins you were using when I watched the kids that day. I just figured you could really use something to keep their toys in so they weren't spilling out all over the place. I didn't think—"

"Brett," I interrupted, placing my palms on his cheeks so he'd look at me. "I love it."

"Yeah?"

"Yeah. This is, by far, the most thoughtful gift anyone has ever given my kids." I let him go and walked over to the chest, running my finger along the intricate carvings. "It's so beautiful. I can't believe you made this. It's almost too much."

He stuffed his hands in his pockets and rocked back on his heels. It was charming how embarrassed he seemed at my compliments of his work.

"I just wanted them to have something special. You think I should have gone with a Toy's R Us gift card instead? What if they don't like it?"

Oh my god, I thought, taking in the uncertainty on his face.

It didn't hit me until that very moment just how much he cared for my babies. He was genuinely worried they wouldn't like his gift. I wanted nothing more than to erase all the concern that marred his expression, but just as I opened my mouth to speak, Cameron and Callie came rushing into the room.

"Mommy! Mommy! Brett got us a bouncy castle!"

"*What*?" My head shot back in Brett's direction, my eyes the size of salad plates. "Now, *that's* too much."

He shrugged casually and shot me a wink that made my belly flutter. "What can I say, I love spoiling them."

Gah! Could he just stop being so wonderful for one damn moment so I could get my head straight?

"What's that?" Callie asked, running over to the toy chest with Cameron right on her heels.

"Wow," they gasped as they ran their little hands over all the different toys carved into the wood.

"Do you like it?" I asked, already knowing the answer.

"This is so cool!" Cameron shouted.

I walked over and pointed to their names on the lid. "Look here. This says Cameron and this says Callie." I traced each letter for them. "Brett made this for you all by himself so you can keep your toys in it."

They jumped up off the floor and ran straight for Brett, wrapping their arms around his legs as they told him thank you over and over. He squatted down to their level and hugged them both tightly. My heart squeezed violently when Callie took his face in her itty-bitty hands and planted a kiss on his lips.

"Love you."

"Me too, me too!" Cameron cried, not to be outdone. And with that, the twin tornados were back out the door and, no doubt, heading straight for the bouncy castle while Brett stayed hunched down, looking like his world had just been rocked. I knew the feeling.

"I think it's safe to say they love their present," I whispered, my voice coming out scratchy as I tried to get a hold of myself. I'd never in my life seen my kids take to another person the way they'd taken to Brett. It moved me in a way I couldn't possibly describe.

Before Brett could stand to his full height, I took the opportunity to step past him and start out of the room. I needed to try and get my head straight, and I couldn't do that when I was near him. But his next words stopped me in my tracks.

"I love them, too, you know."

The only movement I could make was to look over my shoulder as my eyes stung with tears and my jaw dropped.

"I really do, Kenz. I love those two kids something fierce."

He walked past me and down the hall while I remained frozen in place, attempting to process what he just said. As I played his words on repeat, there was no denying it.

I absolutely believed him

CHAPTER SIXTEEN

BRETT

I WASN'T MUCH of an expert on parties, but this one seemed to be going off without a hitch as far as I was concerned. The girls had all the food and decorations set up. The guys and I had set out the tables and chairs, the guests—little demon spawns from the twins' daycare class—were running around like a bunch of rabid hyenas hyped up on speed, and best of all, the bounce house was still in working order, no little devil child had popped it yet.

I'd say that was a success. Cameron and Callie were having the time of their lives so even if the skies opened up and flooded the shit out of everything, as long as those two kids were smiling, I was happy.

"I still don't get it," Trevor stated from where he was standing in a group next to me, Savannah, Jeremy, and Luke. "Why can't *I* have a turn in the bouncy castle?"

"Because you're a grown man!" My eyes rolled skyward, thoroughly fed up with having to explain it to him for the third time. He was worse than the damn five-year-olds.

The son of a bitch actually had the nerve to pout. "That's not a very good excuse."

"Oh my god!" Savannah exclaimed. "I'm not having this conversation *again*."

"What's happening?" Lizzy asked as she walked up to us.

"Your husband's throwing a damn hissy is what," Savannah answered.

"Ah, damn, baby. What did you do now?"

Trevor threw his hands up in the air. "I just don't see why I can't get in the damn bouncy castle!"

"Shit, honey, do we really need to have this conversation again?"

"For the love of..." I started. "Can y'all please watch your language?" I griped. How hard was it for a group of adults to remember to watch what they said around little kids?

Luke looked over at me with a shit-eating grin on his face. "Looks like someone's turning into a big boy."

I opened my mouth to spell out what I thought when I felt a tug on my pant leg. Cam was standing next to me doing a funny little dance, hopping around from one foot to the other.

"What's up, little man?"

Grabbing hold of my shirttail, he pulled me down until he could whisper in my ear. "I gots ta go potty."

I looked up and scanned the backyard for Kenzie but didn't see her anywhere. "Where's your momma, bub?"

"In the kitchen makin' dip. I really gots ta go, Brett," he answered, speeding up his little dance. "And there's a line for the potty."

"That's okay, you can just go out by the trees."

His eyes grew wide as his jaw opened slightly. "You mean tee-tee outside?"

Oh, this poor little guy. Being raised by a single mom, he'd lost out on all of the cool shit us boys got to do. "Yup, just one of the things that makes being a guy awesome. Come on, little man. Let's go."

I took him toward the back of the yard by one of the trees so he'd have a little more privacy.

"Here you go, dude. Have at it." I turned around and crossed my arms over my chest, standing sentry for my little guy while watching all the kids running amuck around my backyard.

"Uh...Brett?"

I turned to look at Cam over my shoulder, his little back to me and the rest of the backyard.

"Yeah, bub?"

"I can't go."

"Huh?"

"I can't potty. People's watchin' me."

"No one's watching you, little guy," I encouraged, but apparently he wasn't buying it because he asked, "Can you do it with me?"

"Uh, not really sure if that's kosher, dude."

He peeked over his shoulder with his big ole' hazel puppy dog eyes. "Pleeeeeease?"

Letting out a sigh, I finally relented, "All right, all right. You stay there and I'll go over here." I moved further into the privacy of the trees so no one could see, and prepared to take a leak.

"Uh...what are you doing?"

I spun around, zipping up so fast I almost caught my junk in the fly. That would have been a disaster of epic proportions.

"Mommy! Brett's teachin' me to tee-tee outside 'cause we's cool guys!"

Kenzie glowered at me before turning back to Cameron. "Yeah, bub, let's go ahead and shut this down. Zip up, you got a party to get back to."

Cam quickly finished up his business and ran off toward the piñata, leaving me to deal with his mom's wrath, all on my own.

"Seriously, Brett? During a *party*? Is it so hard to use a damn bathroom?"

I held my hands up in surrender. "In my defense it's a rite of passage for boys to pee outside. It was only a matter of time."

"I swear to god, Brett, if I get a phone call from the daycare saying he dropped his pants to piss on the playground, I'll kick your ass."

"Look, beauty, this is the kind of stuff you'll just have to deal with. It's every penis-carrying member of society's god given right to whiz outdoors. Don't be jealous."

She smiled brightly, and I could have sworn I hadn't seen those jade eyes light up like that since I met her. It hit me right then and there that I'd do anything to put that smile on her face as often as possible. A woman that beautiful should always smile that happily.

"This is an amazing party, Brett. I can't even begin to thank you and your friends enough for helping me pull this off."

I couldn't keep myself from touching her right in that moment. Reaching up, I brushed a strand of hair from her cheek. "They're your friends too, Kenz, and we'll always be here to help you and those kids, any way you're willing to allow us to."

She studied me closely, her smile fading until a frown marred her beautiful face. I missed her smile immensely the moment it disappeared.

"I'm not good for you, Brett. I need you to know that."

The moment she said that a massive knot coiled in my gut. How could she not see how wrong she was? The more time we spent together, the clearer it was becoming that she was perfect for me.

"Kenzie—"

"No, please," she interrupted. "Hear me out." Closing her

eyes, she took a deep breath before concentrating on me once again.

"You're an amazing guy, Brett. I know that, and I also know that the twins and I are beyond lucky to have you in our lives. But *I'm* not good for *you*. If I let this go any further than friendship things would eventually go bad, and you'd end up resenting me. It's happened before. I'm too damaged, and I'd hate myself if I let a wonderful man like you get pulled down into the mud all because of me. You deserve so much better than what I have to offer."

I could see the determination in her posture, the sincerity that shined through her eyes, and I knew that arguing with her at that moment would be a lost cause. She was too strong in her convictions to believe anything I would say. But I'd be damned if I was giving up on her.

"I'll let you have this win right now, baby, because I can see how much you believe what you're saying."

"It's the truth," she insisted, but I just pushed on, taking a step closer to her so she could see the sincerity in my eyes.

"But I know what you really are. I know how amazing you are as a person, and how wonderful you are as a mother. And I'm not giving up on you. I don't know what bullshit you've been dealt in your life, but I'm not like any of those people from your past who let you down. You *will* trust me one day, beauty, and until that day comes, I'll be here waiting."

Taking full advantage of her stunned silence, I leaned forward and planted a chaste kiss on her gorgeous lips.

"Now, let's get back to the party. We've got two five-year-olds in serious need of cake."

KENZIE

WE'VE GOT two five-year-olds in serious need of cake.

Not *you...We.*

That one little word was like a wrecking ball to the walls I had surrounding my heart. This man loved my kids. And despite my warnings, he still insisted in believing in me, no matter what.

I didn't see how it was going to be possible to keep that man at arm's length for much longer.

The truth was, I was falling hard for Brett. One more hit to those well-constructed walls and they were going to come crumbling down around me.

For good.

CHAPTER SEVENTEEN

KENZIE

PAST

THE DAY I met Lance I thought my life had changed for the better. I'd been waiting tables at a local restaurant when a handsome, older man came in and sat at one of the tables in my section. I could recall thinking that I'd never seen such a good-looking man in all my life. His dark, hard and chiseled features, his icy blue eyes framed by long dark lashes were all beautiful enough to draw my immediate attention. But it was that perfectly straight, white smile that had me enamored.

"H-hi," I stammered as I stepped up to the table. "Uh...Can I help y-you?"

I kept my eyes trained on the floor, feeling awkward and frumpy in my waitress uniform standing next to him in his fancy three-piece suit.

"You know what would really make my day?" he asked, his voice sending a shiver through me. "If you'd let me see those pretty eyes of yours."

There was no stopping the huge grin that spread across my face. I slowly lifted my head to find him grinning back.

"There they are. So beautiful. What's your name, sweetheart?"

"Mackenzie," I replied shyly.

"Well, Mackenzie, I'm Lance. Nice to meet you."

For the rest of his meal, he made a point to start a conversation with me any time I'd stop at his table for a refill, or to drop off his plate. He asked for my suggestion on what to order. He asked how I liked waitressing. He seemed thoroughly interested in everything about me. I told him about wanting to be a nail technician and owning my own spa. By the time he'd finished eating, I was completely smitten with him. So when he asked me how old I was, my heart sank because I knew I'd never see him again when he found out I was only a teenager. He was a lawyer. He was well aware of the trouble he'd get in for dating a minor.

"Hey, why the sad face? What happened to my beautiful smile?" Lance asked me when he saw my frown.

"I-I'm only seventeen." I answered softly, too nervous to meet his clear blue gaze.

"How much longer until you turn eighteen?"

I quickly looked up, surprised by his response. I was so certain he'd brush me off when he found out how young I was, even though my life had already made me feel decades older.

"Three months," I answered, my voice full of hope.

"Well then, it looks like we're just going to have to spend the next three months as friends. You see, I know a good thing when I see it. And, Mackenzie, something tells me you and I were meant to meet each other." His smile was so charming I felt my heart squeeze. "I feel a strong connection to you, Mackenzie. Don't you feel it?"

"I do," I breathed, stunned that he felt the exact thing I was feeling.

"Good. Until then, I'd love to get to know you, sweetheart. What do you say?"

I nodded, grinning like a little schoolgirl. I felt it down to my bones. Lance was the man who was going to make my life better.

THE NEXT THREE months were heaven. Lance came into the restaurant as often as he could, just to see me. He even bought me a cell phone so we could talk at night after my parents had gone to bed. I'd talk to him about how miserable I was and how I just wanted to escape, and he'd tell stories of all the wonderful things he planned to show me when he got me out of that godforsaken hellhole. He was going to take me on trips, show me the world. He talked about putting me through school and buying me my very own salon. He said he wanted nothing more than to spoil me every chance he got, and how, when we were married, he was going to make my life so happy I'd never leave him.

I was in love. Lance was my knight in shining armor. He was going to save me, give me a good life. He was so patient, so kind and loving as he waited out the days for my eighteenth birthday. With my future before me, and Lance waiting in the wings, I was able to get through those three months knowing what was waiting for me on the other side.

On the morning of my eighteenth birthday, I woke with a sense of happiness I'd never experienced before. It was finally the day my life would start.

I went to school that morning, my senior year coming to a close in less than a month. Lance showed up at the front of my high school as I was walking out, holding a dozen long-stemmed red roses. When I worked my shift at the restaurant that afternoon, he was there with the most beautiful heart-shaped pendant necklace. After clasping it around my neck, he gave me my first kiss. The sweetest, most romantic kiss ever. It was truly the stuff of fairy tales.

Later that night, he drove me home and accompanied me inside. It was the last time I'd ever step foot inside that house again. As I packed up what little belongings I had, my father ranted and raved that I would never be allowed in his house again if I left with Lance. That was fine with me; I had no intentions of ever seeing either of my parents again for as long as I lived.

"Gary, just let her go," my mother pleaded. I could hear the excitement in her voice as she spoke. "With her gone, things can go back to how they used to be. We can be happy again. She's the reason we've been so miserable!"

"Shut your fucking mouth, Nancy!" my father hollered. "You're both fucking poison. I should have left you both years ago." He stepped up to Lance as we headed for the front door. "I should be thanking you. You're taking this worthless piece of shit off my hands."

Lance took my hand in his and led me away without so much as a word to my father. He dropped my bag in the trunk of his car and walked over to open my door for me before going around and climbing into the driver's seat. As we pulled away, I looked back one last time. My father was rushing out the door toward his truck, my mother close on his heels, crying and begging him not to leave. He shoved her to the ground and climbed in, peeling off to whatever bar or whatever mistress he was in the mood for. Something deep in my gut told me he wouldn't be going back, that he was leaving my mother for good. And as we pulled around the corner, away from that horrible house, I couldn't find it in myself to feel sad for her.

THE ABUSE BEGAN SO SUBTLY, so methodically, that it took me looking back on that time to realize exactly when it had started. Lance managed to alienate me from everyone in my life, but he did it in a way that made me believe it was my idea.

He'd talk about the time I spent with friends and co-workers. He'd lay on the guilt, making me feel as though I'd neglected him until I pulled away from anyone who could have taken my time away from Lance.

I became so obsessed with making him happy that I hadn't even realized I made him the only person in my world. Everything I did was to please him. My sole reason for existing was Lance. Unfortunately, by the time I realized what was happening, I was in too deep. I had nowhere to go, no one to turn to for help.

I'd mistakenly thought I could rectify the situation simply by talking to him. One night I voiced my concerns about not having a social life outside of our relationship, so sure he'd understand my dilemma and support me in building a life outside of *us*.

The problem was, I'd unknowingly tied myself to the worse kind of abuser. As the years passed, it became evident that Lance was even worse than my father. His abuse started out mental and emotional long before the physical violence.

It had been three years into our relationship before he'd even taken his hands to me. But the night I brought up wanting to spend more time with friends was the night everything changed. My face was so bruised I had to take an entire week off work before the swelling and discoloration went away enough for me to cover them with makeup. He'd come home the day after with an engagement ring. He got down on his knees, crying and begging, swearing over and over it would never happen again. And like a fool, I believed him. I accepted his proposal, naively thinking that nothing like that would ever happen again.

I was so very wrong.

The beatings grew so frequent that I was let go from my job at the salon for missing too much work. I had no money, no friends, and no family. I was, once again, well and truly alone.

I was trapped.

Every time he hit or kicked me, it was my fault. My fault for burning dinner, my fault for knowing how to push his buttons, my fault for not understanding the stress he was under at his frim. He thrived on letting me know that I was the reason for his anger and violence. He was the second man in my life who I'd turned into a monster.

I was cursed.

The only time he didn't hit me was when I was carrying the twins, but that didn't mean all forms of abuse stopped.

Oh no, I was told daily how fat I was getting, or how undesirable I'd become. When I didn't have the energy to clean the house, I was a disgusting, lazy slob. When my back hurt to the point of tears, I was being dramatic. I was to blame for Lance's cheating because I'd let myself go and he couldn't stand to look at my body.

Once the twins were born, I'd worked tirelessly to get my pre-pregnancy body back. But there were just some things that carrying two babies did to a woman's figure that couldn't be undone, no matter how many hours were spent in a gym.

It was during one of those grueling workout sessions with the personal trainer that Lance hired that I realized something that rocked me to my core.

I had turned into my mother.

CHAPTER EIGHTEEN

BRETT

PRESENT

"YOU TRACKED Kenzie's every move at the party last week. I don't think you took your eyes off her for more than a minute. Might as well admit it, dude. You've got a serious hard-on for that woman." Trevor had been at it since we sat down at Colt's. So far, beers with the guys consisted of them giving me shit about Kenzie. And as usual, Trevor was the worst.

"You won't hear me denying that, brother."

"You want to wife that chick and you know it."

I looked over at Trevor with a look that screamed *you're one to talk.* "This coming from the man who got Lizzy loaded just to get her down the aisle?" I scoffed.

"Eh, if it works, it works. At least I'm getting it on the regular now."

"I said I had a hard-on for her. Not that I wanted to marry her."

"We all saw you at that party, man," Luke chimed in. "You're more whipped than poor Ben over here."

Ben's offended gaze shot towards Luke. "What the hell? I'm not whipped."

Trevor let out a snort before saying, "I work with that woman. I know the set of balls she's got on her. Any man dating her doesn't have a choice but to be whipped. It's your cross to bear, Benny boy, just accept it. Only reason we don't give you more shit about it is because she's hot as hell."

Ben's eyes narrowed on Trevor. "You know Lizzy's keeping me on retainer, right? Just in case you fuck up and she needs a good defense for murdering you."

Just as everyone burst into laughter, Luke's phone went off.

"Ah, hell," he muttered, looking down at the screen before sliding it back into his pocket. "I have to go."

Something about his demeanor got my hackles up. "I thought you weren't on call tonight," I stated.

"I'm not, but I want to be on scene." Concern spread over is features as he said, "I think you need to come with me."

Icy dread filled my chest at the look on Luke's face.

"What's going on?"

"String of break-ins. Someone's been shot." He shook his head sullenly before adding, "It's Kenzie's apartment complex, man."

He barely had enough time to complete the sentence before I was out of my chair, heading for the door at a run, my heart firmly lodged in my throat.

KENZIE

BANG!

I was jolted from a dead sleep by what sounded like a

gunshot. Disoriented and shaking, I thought for a moment that it had just been a dream. That was, until the twins came running into my bedroom, their eyes bugged out in fright.

"*Mommy*," Callie shrieked as she and Cameron dove onto my bed, scrambling toward me and climbing under the covers.

"It's okay. It's okay," I soothed, wrapping the both of them in my arms at the same time I tried to steady my own heart rate.

The sound of sirens, accompanied by blue and red lights, came through my bedroom window. I had no idea what was going on, but whatever it was, it wasn't good. My mind immediately went to that dark place. *What if he's out there? What if Lance found us?*

The commotion from outside grew louder and louder, causing my fear to grow along with it, until it was squeezing my chest like an ice cold fist.

"Mommy, what's happenin'?" Cameron whimpered from beneath my arm.

"I don't know, baby. But it's all going to be okay. It's going to be okay," I repeated on a whisper, trying to remind myself that Lance had no clue where we were.

A loud pounding on the front door startled screams from all three of us.

"Kenzie! Open the door!"

Oh god. He's here. He found us. No! No no no no.

"Beauty, it's me. I need you to open the door, baby."

Beauty. Lance never called me *beauty*. It was Brett. Jumping from the bed, I ran down the hallway as fast as I could. My hands shook uncontrollably, my fingers fumbled with the deadbolt and chain lock. As soon as I got the door open, Brett barged through and wrapped me in his tight embrace. The moment I was in his arms, all of the fear disappeared. I was safe. My kids were safe. I was overwhelmed by how much I trusted Brett at that very moment. I knew...I just *knew* that if he was there, my children and I had nothing to fear.

"Brett! Brett! Brett!"

The twins came barreling down the hall, not stopping until they'd latched onto both our legs, forming a big group hug in the middle of the doorway.

"Let's move this all the way inside, yeah?" Brett asked softly, finally pulling from our little huddle and guiding us into the living room before shutting and locking the door behind him.

"W-what's going on out there?" I asked, wringing my hands nervously in front of me.

"A bunch of apartments were broken into tonight. One of the men drew a gun on the intruder and fired. Luckily, no one was seriously hurt. Stupid fu—I mean...uh, the police arrested three teenage boys for the break-ins. Apparently they thought it'd be funny to take a dare from some of their buddies at school. Now two are in the back of squad cars and the other is on the way to the hospital to have bullet removed from his leg."

"Oh god," I gasped, covering my mouth with my hands as Brett stood from the couch.

"I need to you pack a bag for you and the kids. Just enough to get you through tonight and tomorrow. I'll bring you back for the rest of it later."

Um...what?

My brain must have still been rattled from my Wild West wakeup call because he wasn't making a damn bit of sense.

"Why do we need to pack?"

The *well, duh* expression he wore kind of made me want to punch him a little bit. "Y'all aren't staying here, Kenzie. Four apartments were broken into and someone was shot two doors down from you. You're moving in with me."

I choked on a laugh at the same time the twins started jumping up and down screaming "*Yay*! Sleepover!" at the top of their lungs. They took off to their room, no doubt to pack their own bags, before I could get a word out.

"Are you kidding," I hissed out once the kids were out of earshot. "We aren't staying with you!"

His chin lifted and put his hands on his trim hips. "No use arguing, beauty. I'm not leaving here without you and those kids. It's not safe."

"Oh my god! It was *one* incident. It's not like this place is the epicenter of an underground crime ring. This isn't *Breaking Bad*, Brett. It's a perfectly safe complex."

"A perfectly safe complex with a few additional bullet holes," he countered. "Now, pack your shit."

"No," I answered defiantly as I crossed my arms under my chest, immediately realizing my mistake when Brett's full attention zeroed in on my unrestrained boobs. "Hey! Stop looking at them!" I shouted, smacking him in the arm as hard as I could.

"Feel free not to pack a bra, babe. Won't get any complaints from me."

"We. Are. Not. Moving. In. With. You." I sounded out every syllable, convinced he must have been a little slow.

"All packed!" Cameron yelled as he and Callie ran back into the living room, their cartoon character rolling suitcases dragging behind them.

"See," Brett said with a smile as he pointed at the twins. "At least *they* know what's good for them. You know, I expected more cooperation from the *adult* of the household. It's a sad, sad day when five-year-olds listen better."

My eyes rolled dramatically at his pathetic lecture. "I can guarantee those suitcases are full of nothing but toys."

Brett looked over at Cameron for confirmation that his bulging bag was full of stuffed animals and action figures, getting a proud, "Yep!" from my son.

"Told you," I gloated.

Brett's eyes narrowed as he stepped close to me, his joking demeanor from moments ago gone. I could see the seriousness radiating through his gaze. "I'm not playing a game here, baby. I really don't like the idea of you and the rugrats staying here one second longer than you already have. And by *really don't like it*," he whispered for my ears only, "I mean I can't fucking stand it. The only way I'm getting a halfway decent night's sleep is if I know for certain y'all are safe. And the only way I'll know that is if you're under my roof. Now, please, for the love of all that's fucking holy, will you *please* stop arguing and just go pack a damn bag?"

Well, when he put it like that how was I supposed to argue? I couldn't.

"Fine." I threw my hands up in a defeated huff. "I'll go pack, but I'm packing every bra I own a-s-s-h-o-l-e."

I stomped away to the sound of Brett's laughter, making sure he didn't see my smile as I headed to the bedroom while he tried to wrangle Cam and Callie into packing something a little more useful.

CHAPTER NINETEEN

BRETT

IT WAS easy for Kenzie to put on a brave front around me when there was a way for her to keep me at a distance, but having lived in my house for the past week, there were certain things she couldn't hide. Things that made me want to find the fuckers who had hurt her in the past and pound the ever-loving shit out of them. What was worse, I was beginning to see things in the twins' actions that made me downright murderous.

The evening after they moved in, Callie was drinking a glass of juice and accidentally spilled some of it on the floor. She immediately dropped her head and closed herself off. I couldn't get her to talk to me for the rest of the night, no matter how hard I tried.

When I'd get home from work, dinner would already be done, the table set, drinks poured. It was a full on *Leave it to Beaver* family spread. After the third night, I'd informed Kenzie that she didn't have to make me dinner every single night, but she was insistent. When I told her the least I could do was clean the kitchen after she cooked, she simply shrugged and told me she was just doing her part. If it wasn't the cooking, it was the laundry, or the cleaning, or the yard work. If she could find something that needed to be done around the house, she was determined to do it.

But the moment that finally did me in was when Cam was playing in the living room and accidentally knocked a picture frame off one of the shelves, breaking the glass. I rushed over to make sure he hadn't cut himself, but he'd cowered away from my touch before finally taking off into the bedroom he and Callie were sharing. Enough was enough. I'd had it with the fucking walking-on-eggshells routine.

Storming into the kitchen, I'd found Kenzie exactly where I knew she'd be, perched in front of the stove, watching over dinner like a hawk. It was as if she was terrified to let anything burn. Flipping off the burners, I ignored her protests and grabbed her by the wrist, dragging her through the back door and into the yard.

"What the hell, Brett! I'm in the middle of making dinner. It's going to burn if I don't get back in there."

"Then let it burn, Kenzie! That's what happens sometimes. Dinners burn. Drinks spill, glass breaks, *accidents happen*. It's not the end of the world." I saw those shutters of hers start to slide into place, and I knew I couldn't let that happen.

"Beauty, you and those kids don't have to be perfect, not here. You don't need to do all of this. You don't have to work all day, then come home just to start all over again. I moved y'all in here because I wanted you safe, not because I wanted a maid service."

Her head dipped down in an attempt to hide the tears that were forming in her jade eyes. Jesus Christ, the woman was killing me.

Taking her chin between my fingers, I forced her to meet my gaze, trying to make her see how sincere I was. "I can't stand that you, Cameron and Callie feel the need to walk on eggshells when I'm around. I want y'all to be comfortable. Twice this week one of the kids has done something by accident, and the result has been them running off to their room and hiding from me. That guts me, Kenz. I *hate* it when they won't talk to me."

"I'm sorry," she whispered, those tears breaking free and making tracks down her cheeks.

Seeing her pain was tearing me apart. "Don't apologize, beauty. *Talk* to me. Please. You can trust me, baby. I can help you if you'd just let me," I pleaded, needing her trust more than anything.

"I do trust you."

I couldn't explain why, but those four words made me feel invincible. Reaching up, I brushed her tears away with my thumb. "Then trust me to be able to help you. Talk to me, Kenz."

We stood in silence for a minute before she finally spoke. "Okay." Her voice was so soft I barely heard it. "After the kids go to bed. I don't want to talk about this when they can hear."

I nodded. I could give her that.

KENZIE

KNOWING what I had to do and being prepared to do it were two different things entirely.

I'd left Brett standing outside and gone back into the kitchen to finish dinner. The conversation around the table was stilted, and no matter how hard Brett tried, he just couldn't get the kids to interact. I had every intention of talking to them, letting them know that Brett wasn't upset about the broken picture frame, but I wanted to do it with just the three of us. Apparently, Brett had other ideas.

He stood from the table without a word and headed into the kitchen. The sound of cabinet doors opening and closing echoed into the dining area until he came walking back in with a small stack of plates and glasses. Sitting the dishes on the table between Cameron and Callie, he picked up one of the glasses, took a few steps back, and dropped it right on the floor, sending shards of glass flying everywhere.

The three of us sat in shocked silence as he picked up a small salad plate and did the same thing, breaking it into a million pieces before turning his full attention to my kids.

"Things break. Accidents happen. I'm not going to get mad at y'all for breaking something as minor as a picture frame. I can replace a picture frame. I can buy new dishes." He crouched down so he was eye level with them. "I don't need those things. What I *need* is for y'all to be happy here, to be comfortable with living in this house and with me. You two are more important to me than a stupid picture frame. Understand?"

Callie and Cameron nodded silently, their jaws hanging open as they stared at Brett with curious little faces.

"Good, now..." He stood up handed each of them a plate. "Your turn."

They sat there frozen for several seconds. Finally, Callie dropped her plate on the floor, letting out a peel of innocent laughter. Cameron quickly followed suit. The three of them dropped dish after dish, until only one glass was left.

"Mommy, your turn," Callie told me, sliding the glass my way with a wide smile. Her enthusiasm was contagious. Unable to deny her when she was just so damn happy, I picked up the glass and tossed it down where all the shards of broken dishes lay, letting out my own laugh as the glass broke.

It might not have seemed like much to Brett, but what he'd just done for my children was *everything*. A few broken dishes had given them a confidence I'd never seen in them before. He'd done that. And in doing so, Brett had given me a gift that meant more than anything money could ever buy. He'd given me and my children safety and security. I'd never be able to repay him for that.

After we finished our little Greek wedding celebration, I took the kids to give them their baths and get them ready for bed while Brett swept up the mess we'd made.

"Mommy, Brett's the coolest guy ever!" Cameron said, his voice chock full of excitement as he styled his hair into a shampoo mohawk.

"Yeah! Can we stay here forever?"

I dipped a cup into the water and dumped it over Cam's head to rinse the soap out.

"I don't know, babies. But we're here now, so let's just enjoy it."

After finishing their baths, I got them in their jammies, read *Goodnight Moon*, and was getting ready to tuck them in.

"Mommy," Cameron asked as I leaned in to kiss his forehead. "Can Brett make me a burrito tonight?"

My chest warmed as a smile tipped the corner of my lips. "Sure, bubs."

Brett looked at me with such adorable confusion when I told him what the twins requested, but after explaining how to wrap them in tightly like a burrito, Brett went into their room and proceeded to tuck the covers around their tiny bodies.

"Night night kiss," Callie told him when he stood to walk away.

Brett stood there for a moment, seeming surprised by her request before leaning down and placing a sweet kiss on her forehead. He walked over to Cameron and did the same.

"Love you, Brett," Callie whispered as her eyes grew heavy.

"Yeah, Brett. Love you."

He paused briefly, and what I saw on his face made my

heart start beating frantically in my chest. He looked down at my angels, his face full of more pride and love than I ever thought possible. "I love y'all, too," he said, his voice gravelly with emotion. That was the last hit the walls around my heart could take. They were done for, destroyed and crumbled down to dust.

The problem with that realization was that I now had to tell Brett about my past. Every sordid, ugly little detail. And I could only hope he'd still look at me the same way he did just then by the time I was done.

AS I ROUNDED the corner into the kitchen, Brett stood from pulling two beers out of the fridge. Popping the cap off both, he handed me one before taking a pull from his own.

He pointed at my bottle with his own, "Figured you might need that."

Putting the chilled glass to my lips, I sucked down half of my beer in just a few gulps. "You figured right," I told him. "Just a heads up, I might need a few more before this conversation's over."

A smirk tipped up one corner of his lips, "That's what tequila's for, beauty."

"Ah, yes. Because hugging the toilet and sleeping on the bathroom floor would be the perfect capper for this night." I tried for light and joking but knew I'd fallen short.

"Why don't we go outside? It's a beautiful night."

I blindly followed after him as he stepped through the back door onto his deck. I pulled my sweater tightly around me as I took a seat on one of the patio chairs, telling myself that the chill running through me was caused by the nip in the night air, not because of my trepidation at telling Brett the truth. But I wasn't fooling anyone, least of all myself.

Brett sat on the chair next to mine, resting his elbows on his knees as he studied me. "You know, you can tell me as much or as little as you want, Kenzie. I'm not here to push you. I just need to know what I'm up against here."

My brow furrowed in confusion as I asked, "What do you mean?"

Leaning back with a sigh, he reached around and rubbed at the back of his neck. "I'm going to be honest here, so just hear me out. I know I said I was fine with just being your friend, but that's not working for me anymore. I know you've felt this insane connection we have. It's been there since we met, and now I've gotten to know you better, know your kids better...well, it's changed things. You need to know that, from here on out, I'm pulling out all the stops."

My heart pounded so strongly I was sure he could hear it. His brutal honesty sent my emotions into a spiral that I wasn't sure how to deal with.

"I want to be with you," he continued. "And I want to be a part of those kids' lives. And I'll do everything in my damn power to get what I want. I just need you to know that. Might as well start preparing now, because you aren't going to know what hit you."

I couldn't understand why he felt so certain, especially without knowing my story. Sucking in a fortifying breath, I prepared to tell him the truth. A truth that would, no doubt, send him running in the other direction.

CHAPTER TWENTY

KENZIE

"I'M CURSED," I started, and then waited to see his reaction. He sat there quietly for several seconds before finally opening his mouth.

"Um... Okay?"

"Well, not like, an *actual* curse or anything like that," I stumbled over my words. "I just mean...well...I—"

"Breathe, beauty," he soothed.

Trying to rein in my emotions, I closed my eyes and inhaled a deep, cleansing breath. Then deciding to just rip the Band Aid off once and for all, I dove in.

I told him *everything*.

I started by explaining what my parents' marriage had been like before I entered the picture. I told him all about their abuse, my father's affairs, how they blamed me for everything that was wrong. I told him how my father said I was the reason he was so unhappy, that if I'd never been born, he and my mom would still be happily married. I didn't leave anything out, giving him all the gory details so he could see exactly how bad it was and why I was so desperate to escape by the time Lance came into my life.

I told him everything about my relationship with Lance. How he waited until I was eighteen to pursue me, how he would talk about taking me away from everything bad and giving me the life I deserved. I explained how I fell hard and fast for the man I *thought* Lance was. I didn't hide anything. I didn't hold a single detail back about how Lance went from a man I thought would save me into someone so much worse than my father could have ever been.

The entire time I spoke, Brett sat rigid in his chair, his knuckles white from how tightly he was gripping the arms of his seat. He didn't say a single word until I finished, but I didn't miss that ticking in his jaw, or the way his whole body tightened when I detailed some of the worst of the abuse. He was wound so tightly, he looked like he might shatter at any moment.

But I'd done it. I'd gotten through the entire ugly story. It took what felt like years to tell and three additional beers for courage, but I managed to spit all that nastiness out without shedding a single tear. I was proud of myself for that alone.

Neither of us spoke for several minutes after I finished, and my discomfort grew to the point where I couldn't bring myself to look at him, scared to see the disgust in his eyes.

"What made you leave?" Brett asked, finally breaking through our thick silence.

I kept my eyes trained on the beer bottle in my hand, tearing at the label as I answered. "I'd been planning a way out for a while. I'd been stashing cash away, small amounts he wouldn't notice, you know? I wanted to make sure I could support my kids when I finally left. I needed to make sure they would be safe and secure."

"But something happened." It wasn't a question. Brett's statement told me, loud and clear, that he knew there was something ugly there.

"But something happened," I whispered back, still peeling at the label until the shredded ribbons lay in my lap.

"What was it, beauty?" I heard the legs of his chair scrape across the wooden deck before he took my chin between his fingers and forced my head up. What I saw in those deep brown eyes wasn't disgust. Not even close. It was anger, not at me, but at my situation. It was sorrow and pain. From just one glance at his face, I could see how much he hated what I'd gone through. But there was something else there as well, something I couldn't quite place.

"He came home from work one night and I'd burned dinner. It was an accident. I didn't mean to. But he was so *angry*. I tried so hard to keep the kids away when he got like that. I made sure they were never around to see him hit me. I tried to protect them from all of that. But that night, Cameron came into the living room when Lance was hitting me. He ran up to him and started punching him in his legs, yelling at him to let his mommy go—" My voice cut off on a sob at the memory of my little boy running in to try and rescue me. My self-hatred returned in full force at the thought of what I'd made them live with for four years. Remembering that, the tears ran down my cheeks, unchecked.

"That set Lance off. He spun around and raised his hand at Cameron, but I grabbed a hold of his arm. I'd tolerated Lance hitting me for almost ten years, but there wasn't a chance in hell I was letting him put his hands on my babies. He'd never touched them. Hell, he hardly ever treated them with anything more than indifference, but after that, I couldn't do it anymore. I was finished. When he left for work the next morning, I packed our shit and got the hell out of there."

"And he hasn't come after y'all?"

I lifted one shoulder slightly and gave Brett a wobbly smile. "He doesn't know where we are. My dad grew up in Cloverleaf until he left for college in Ohio. He only came back once when his mother died. I was just a little girl. I never talked about this place with Lance. I knew he'd never find us here. Besides, it wouldn't matter if he could find us anyway. He's not looking."

Brett's dark brows dropped over his eyes in a deep frown. "What makes you think that?"

Sitting back, I took a sip of my now warm beer. "I have stuff on him. Before I left, I hacked his email accounts and found out some things that he'll *never* want leaked. I used that against him. Told him if he came after us, I'd send it to the lead partner at his firm. It would destroy him."

"Christ," he sighed, flopping back in his chair. "I'm afraid to even ask."

"Then don't," I answered simply. "This isn't your fight, Brett."

"Bullshit it's not my fight," he ground out between clenched teeth. "Didn't you hear a damn word I said to you earlier?"

My eyes bulged out as I stuttered, "But...what about...I just...Brett, you can't be serious. What about everything I just told you?"

"What about it?" he asked, infuriating me by how casually he was acting.

"I'm cursed, Brett! I've had *two* men in my life and both of them have turned into monsters. I'm the only common denominator here! I can't let that happen to you, too. Don't you see that?"

He instantly shot forward in his chair, grabbing my hands in his. "You aren't cursed," he demanded earnestly. "You were dealt a fucked-up hand in life. That's not your fault. And I'm not like your dad or that piece-of-shit ex. I'd *never* lay my hands on a woman, and I'd rather lose my goddamn arm before I hurt those rugrats. So you have nothing to worry about there."

"Brett—" I pleaded, but he cut me off.

"You know what I see when I look at you? I see a woman tougher than any person I've ever met. I see a mother who'd go to the ends of the earth for her children. I see a person who'd do anything for those she cares about. *That* right there proves you're a good person. You aren't cursed, Kenzie. Don't ever let anyone make you feel less than you are."

My head dropped as tears burned my eyes again. "I'm not a good mother, Brett. Look at what I put them through. For *years*! All because I was too weak."

"News flash, beauty. You aren't fucking perfect."

At that, my head shot up and my eyes narrowed in a glare.

"None of us are. You made mistakes; I'll give you that. But you came out on the other side of all that shit. And can you honestly tell me that you don't spend every single day thinking of different ways to make those two kids even happier than they were the day before?"

I couldn't argue that point.

"They love you something fierce, baby. I've never seen a better mom. When you're with them, they're faces are lit up like a goddamn Christmas tree the whole time. That's all you, beauty. That's what you give to them."

"I...you...*Gah*! Stop being so sweet! I can't argue with you when you're being sweet!"

His rumbling chuckle did unimaginable things to my belly. "Hey, I told you to prepare, baby. Not my fault you didn't listen."

"So, what, this is part of you pulling out all the stops?" I asked, using finger quotes as I rolled my eyes.

"Like I'm giving away all my secrets right out of the gate," he teased with a sexy wink that pulled a laugh from my throat. "Now, come here and give me a kiss."

"*What?*"

He stood from his chair and moved toward me, his eyes narrowing like he was about to pounce on his prey.

"You've been craving it just as much as I have. But that doesn't matter. Right now, after everything you just shared with me, I need something good to burn away the images I have floating around in my head. I need to feel you and know you're here, that you're really with me, and that you're safe. I need you to give me that, beauty, because I'm hanging by a very thin fucking thread."

He was undoing me, unraveling me completely with every word. Unable to speak past the lump in my throat, I nodded.

In the blink of an eye, he was right in front of me, pulling me up, and taking hold of my chin gently between his thumb and forefinger.

"Once I start, this isn't stopping. I need you to get that, baby."

A huge, goofy smile spread across my lips. "I trust you," I told him truthfully. I'd opened myself up to Brett completely. I'd exposed everything to him, made myself vulnerable.

Because I trusted him.

I trusted him in a way I'd never trusted anyone before, not even Lance. This wasn't the young, naïve faith I'd put in Lance. It was pure, honest, heartfelt trust. I told him the worst of my past, and he was still standing there. He hadn't run. He hadn't looked at me with disgust. He still wanted me, just as much as he did before he knew the truth.

I was no longer *falling* for him. I'd already fallen, hard as hell.

"I'm not planning on stopping you this time."

His smirk widened until his smile matched mine. Then he went in, his lips crashing against mine in a fierce kiss. It was as if he was marking me with his lips.

And I loved every second of it.

His tongue pushed in to tangle with my own, and a deep moan tore from my throat as his taste exploded in my mouth.

"God," he groaned, his voice thick and gravelly as he trailed his tongue down my neck, nipping as he went. "I've been going crazy for another taste of you, beauty."

A flood of arousal pooled at my core. I clenched my thighs together tightly, desperate for some sort of relief. His words were enough to make my panties unbelievably wet, but I needed more. I needed his touch.

"*Brett,*" I whimpered wantonly against his mouth. "Please."

"What do you want, baby?"

"Touch me. God, *please* touch me."

Brett pulled his lips from mine and I cried out at the loss. "You mine, Kenzie?"

"What?" I asked in confusion, my head a cloud of lust and need.

"Are you mine? You want me to touch you, baby, I need to know you're mine."

"I am," I replied desperately. "I am, please just touch me."

"You done making me chase you?" The small, stinging bite he gave my lower lip pulled a groan from deep inside my chest.

"For fuck's sake! I'm yours, Brett! No more chasing, now touch me, damn it!"

I felt him smile against my lips as his hand squeezed my breast roughly, sending shots of pleasure straight between my thighs. "There's my tough girl," he muttered before hoisting me up.

Wrapping my legs around his waist for leverage, I let out a startled yelp. "Where are we going?"

"To bed. I want to spend the night devouring every goddamned inch of you. I'll be damned if I'm doing that on the back deck."

CHAPTER TWENTY-ONE

KENZIE

I GROUND myself against the thickness of his hard-on and dropped my head back. "Oh god, *yes*," I hissed.

He walked through the house and down the hall with me wrapped around him like a second skin the entire time. The laugh I let out as he dropped me onto the bed turned into a sharp gasp as he reached down to rub at the bulge in his jeans. Watching him squeeze himself sent shockwaves through me. Christ, I wanted his cock. I was going crazy for it.

Brett stepped away from the bed and shut the bedroom door, clicking the lock into place before he reached behind his neck and pulled his shirt over his head.

"Just a warning, beauty. You try to bail on me this time, I'll tie you to this bed and fuck you until you can't walk for a week."

Propping myself up on my elbows, I shot him a wicked smile before saying, "You realize that's only incentive to bail again, right?"

His lips twitched with humor, "You're right. Maybe I won't let you come tonight. How's that for incentive?"

My bottom lip poked out on a pout. "That's just mean."

He popped the button on his jeans and pulled the zipper

down. My mouth watered as Brett pulled his rock-hard length from his jeans and began to stroke.

"You want my cock, beauty?"

My own hand trailed down my stomach and between my legs as I moaned, "Yes. Brett, please."

"No bailing?"

"I swear," I panted as I rubbed myself through the denim. "No bailing. I'm not going anywhere."

He let out a feral growl before stalking to the bed. When the mattress dipped under his weight, I almost threw my hands in the air in victory.

His mouth came down on mine as his hands worked the button and zipper of my pants. Scraping my nails down his back lightly, I shoved at his waistband, trying to get his jeans completely off.

"I can't go slow right now. I want you too much," Brett panted as he slid his fingers inside my panties, finding me already drenched and needy for him.

"That's okay. I don't want you to."

At the feel of him plunging one finger deep inside me, I let out a loud cry that he silenced with his mouth. "If I'm too rough, tell me. I swear I'll stop, beauty. I don't want to hurt you."

I snaked my hand between our bodies and grabbed hold of his cock, pumping up and down until I forced a low grown from him.

"It's fine. I'm fine, Brett. Please, just fuck me already," I begged. I was close to losing my mind if I didn't get him inside me soon.

"Yes, ma'am," he said with a smile against my lips before nipping at my mouth. He stood from the bed and kicked the rest of his clothes off, then reached for me and whipped my jeans down my legs, underwear and all, tossing them over his shoulder recklessly as I pulled my shirt over my head and unhooked my bra.

His weight was on me instantly, and he drove his cock into me with one powerful thrust. The moment our bodies connected, I cried out in relief.

"Yes! Oh, fuck, yes, baby," I called as he thrust into me over and over again, like a mad man.

"Have to be quiet, beauty," he warned, but I was too far gone.

My hips met his, stroke for stroke, until I thought my body might explode.

"So fucking tight," Brett grunted. "Fucking perfect, Kenzie. Christ, you're perfect for me."

His hips circled with each slide into my body, grinding against my clit in the most delectable way, pushing me closer and closer to the edge of sanity until I thought my body couldn't possibly take any more pleasure.

"Baby, you have to keep quiet," Brett grunted as he fucked me, my moans and sighs growing louder and louder the closer I came to climax.

"I can't. Oh, shit, *Brett!*"

His hand covered my mouth to keep me from screaming out as my release washed over me, almost painful in its intensity. Lost in a haze of exquisite ecstasy, I bit down on his hand and raked my nails across his back so hard I was sure I'd drawn blood.

"*Fuuuuuck!*" Brett grunted, his eyes rolling back in his head. "Fucking *shit!*" Then he buried his face in the pillow beside my head as he roared out his own release, his hand still over my mouth as he emptied himself inside me, every twitch of his thick shaft sending shockwaves through my pussy.

Bliss.

That was what I experienced with Brett. Sheer, unadulterated, body draining bliss.

"Shit," he sighed, still out of breath. He lifted his head and pushed up onto his forearms to look me at me. "Baby, I forgot a condom."

I gazed into those worried eyes and couldn't help it—maybe it was because my brain had been turned into post-orgasmic mush, or maybe it was because he just looked so adorable, all concerned, but a laugh bubbled up from my throat.

His brows dipped down further as he said, "Well, I'm glad you find this funny."

"It's okay, honey," I giggled as I reached up to rub his cheek. "I have an IUD. It's all good."

"I'm clean, beauty, I swear. I just had a physical a month ago."

"I trust you," I told him with a sincere smile. "I trust you, and I'm clean, too."

He let out a huffed, "Thank Christ," and dropped his full weight back down on top of me, sending the air from my lungs in a loud wheeze.

"Can't. Breathe," I grunted as his body shook with laughter. "You weigh a ton!"

Lifting back up with a chuckle, Brett looked down at me with smiling eyes as he brushed a strand of hair off my forehead.

"Hey," he spoke softly.

"Hi."

"You still with me?"

"Not bailing," I promised. "I'm right here."

"Good, beauty. I like you right here."

In that moment, wrapped in Brett's warm embrace with him staring at me with so much adoration, I kind of liked being there myself.

It was perfect.

Everything about being with him in that moment was just so wonderful. I opened my mouth to say so when our little bubble popped with an unexpected, "Mommy? I'm thirsty," being called from the kids' bedroom.

Brett rolled off me, and I moved to get up when he grabbed my wrist. "You stay here. I got it."

I watched with a perma-grin, admiring his ass as my man climbed from the bed and shrugged on a pair of sweats before heading to the bedroom door. That was when it hit me.

My man.

Brett insisted I give all of myself to him, but at the very same time, he'd given me all of him in return. He truly was *my man*. I laid back and basked in that knowledge as I heard Brett talking from the hallway.

"Hey, little guy. You want some water?"

"Yeah. Is Mommy sleeping?"

"She sure is, bud, but I'm always here to help you out."

And I knew he spoke the truth.

"Will you make me into a burrito again?" Cameron asked, their voices growing quieter as the made their way into the kitchen.

"Any time, bud. All you ever have to do is ask."

The last thought I had before sleep claimed me was, god, that man. He made it impossible not to love him.

CHAPTER TWENTY-TWO

WHAT THE HELL happened to my sweet, angelic little rugrats that I'd come to know and love over the past few months? Gone were the toddlers who looked up at me with loving smiles and bright hazel eyes. In their place were demented soldiers of Satan's army, hell bent on annihilating all of humanity.

And no, I didn't feel I was being dramatic in the slightest.

"I don't wanna go to daycare!" Callie shouted, flinging herself onto the floor in a tantrum that would have given that little bitch from *Willy Wonka* a run for her money.

"Ladybug," I coaxed. "You have to go to daycare. Mommy and I will be at work all day. There isn't anyone here to stay with you." I didn't know why I tried reasoning with her. I was ill equipped to say the least. I needed a goddamned hostage negotiator.

"I'll stay by myself," she pouted from the floor, arms crossed over her tiny chest as she stared up at the ceiling.

"What if I stop and buy donuts on the way to school, huh? If you get dressed, I promise to get you and bub a donut."

"For the love of god," Kenzie grumbled as she rushed into

the kitchen, pouring a bowl of cereal with one hand and trying to button the last few buttons on her blouse with the other.

"Cameron Michael!" she shouted. "If you don't get your little behind out of that bed this minute, I'm cancelling the Fall Festival! You have to the count of three. One! Two!"

Before she got to three, Cameron came running down the hall and skidded to a halt in the kitchen. His hair stuck up in every direction, eyes still heavy with sleep as he plopped his butt at the table and started in on the cereal Kenzie set in front of him.

She spun around and gave her daughter, still sprawled out on the floor, the stink eye. Hell, even I had to cringe at Kenzie's glare.

"Callie Anne. Get your butt off that floor and finish your breakfast. You're two seconds away from losing the Fall Festival *and* Halloween. Don't test me, little girl."

Bottom lip still poking out, Callie climbed from the floor, parked her rear end in the chair, and finished breakfast as I watched on in wonder at how Kenzie took seconds to get a handle on a situation I'd been drowning in for the past half hour.

"You can't bargain, sweetie," she said, planting a kiss on my parted lips as I stood in awe of her. "They'll eat you alive if they sense the slightest weakness."

Kenzie puttered around the kitchen, pouring herself a cup of coffee and adding half a bottle of creamer to it as I kept my eyes firmly planted on the twins, just waiting for one of their heads to start spinning around on their shoulders. The house had gone from chaotic to peaceful in sixty seconds. I didn't trust it.

"I have to tell you, beauty," I whispered to her. "I'm a little scared right now."

Kenzie reached up and patted my cheek sympathetically. "Never let them smell your fear, honey. They'll tear you apart."

She turned casually to the kids and started barking out orders like a drill sergeant. "Clothes, shoes, teeth and hair brushed. You have ten minutes. Go, go, go!"

"What just happened?" I asked as Cameron and Callie scampered from the kitchen to get dressed. "You've been living here for two weeks and they've never acted like this."

"Welcome to parenthood," Kenzie replied casually as she took a sip of her coffee. "I tried warning you that it wasn't always sunshine and roses. You sure you want to deal with this? These mornings will be pretty frequent now. You wanted them to be comfortable here and with you. Well, this is them when they're comfortable."

Reaching over, I snagged her coffee cup and sat it on the counter before wrapping her arms around my waist and pulling her body firmly against mine.

"Hell yeah, I still want to deal with this. I'm in it for the long haul; I've told you that. And if this morning's behavior means they trust me enough to let their real selves show, then I'm all fucking for that. I just need an instruction manual or something to deal with times like this."

Standing on her tiptoes, she gave me a little peck and smiled against my lips. "You're kind of amazing. You know that?"

"I've been told a time or a thousand," I answered with a sarcastic grin.

Kenzie let out a laugh, "And so humble."

"What can I say, I'm a catch."

"Ready!" Cameron hollered as he and Callie came darting back into the kitchen.

"All right, rugrats, let's hit the road."

Shoving my wallet and phone into my pants pockets, I stole one more kiss from Kenzie before heading out. Right before we got to the door, Callie asked—very loudly, "Brett, can we still gets donuts? You promised."

I looked over my shoulder at Kenzie just in time to see her throw me a wink. "I'll see about ordering that manual from Amazon."

My girl. Always looking out for me.

"AFTERNOON, LORI. LOOKING BEAUTIFUL AS EVER," I told the daycare worker as I walked up to the front desk. The older woman had been in Cloverleaf since before I was born. Her daycare was the one I'd gone to when I was a child myself.

"Well, if it's not Brett Halstead. What can I do for you today, darlin'?"

"I'm here to pick up Callie and Cameron Webster. Their mom should have put me on the pickup list this morning."

She typed away on the keyboard in front of her before stating, "Ah, yeah. Looks like she did. I'll just need to see your license and you'll be all set."

After handing my license over, Lori made a photocopy of it and slid it back to me before directing me to the twins' classroom.

"You know," she called out as I started to walk away. "Those kids and their momma are something else."

I shot her a smile over my shoulder. "Don't I know it."

"Any man who lands them is one lucky son of a gun, if you ask me."

"Preaching to the choir, Lori." I gave her a wink, and then made my way down the hall to their room. The minute I pushed it open, I was overthrown by two mini tornados.

"Brett! Brett!" the twins shouted as they latched onto my legs.

"Hey there, rugrats. You ready to go home?"

As they ran to their cubbies for their jackets, a pretty teenage girl with a shy smile approached me. "Hi there, I'm Megan, the twins' teacher."

"I'm Brett, nice to meet you," I said, extending my hand for her to shake. The moment her palm touched mine her eyes cast down and her entire face flushed bright red as a girly giggle rose from her chest.

Great, a teenage girl with a crush. Yeah, I wasn't touching that with a ten-foot pole. Time to go.

"Hey guys, you ready?"

Seeming to snap out of it, Megan declared, "Oh! Don't forget their art folders." She ran over, grabbed two folders and brought them back to me. "Today's project was for them to draw their family."

I took the folders in my hand and raised them in a wave. "Thanks. Have a great evening."

We made our way out of the daycare and over to my Jeep where I loaded the twins in the booster seats I'd bought to keep in my car. As I buckled them in, I couldn't help but remember just how appreciative Kenzie had been when I informed her I bought my own seats so we didn't have to keep switching. She showed her gratitude with her mouth...and her hands...and pretty much every one of my favorite parts of her rockin' body for hours.

Just like Lori had said. I was a lucky, *lucky* man.

KENZIE

WALKING into Brett's house after work, I was beyond surprised to see dinner was almost finished and the twins were sitting at the dinner table coloring. In all the years I had been with Lance, he never once cooked dinner for me. That had always been my job, or, in Lance's words, the *woman's* job.

"Hi, Mommy!" Callie called when she saw me. I dropped my purse by the door and walked over to the table.

"Hey, honey pot." I leaned down to place a kiss on her head before walking over to do the same to Cam. "You and bubs have a good day?"

"Yeah," she answered, Cameron still silently engrossed in coloring a picture of Spiderman.

I walked over to the stove where Brett stood, stirring a pot of something that smelled delicious.

"Hey, beauty," he said, planting a kiss on my lips.

"Hi," I smiled. "You're making dinner?"

"Mmm hmm. Fried pork chops, mashed potatoes, green bean casserole, and homemade gravy."

I leaned over the stove, inhaling deeply before whispering, "Dear Lord, I'm so hot for you right now."

Brett chuckled and pulled me flush against his strong, hard body, saying, "That so? Well then, maybe you'll be willing to show your gratitude tonight."

"Mommy," Cameron called. "We got to go to Viwgie May's after school. We gots to see Emmy, and Brett bought a whole bunches of yummy food for dinner!"

I pulled away from Brett with a glare and walked over to the trashcan. Sure enough, a bag from Emmy's diner and a bunch of to-go containers filled the can.

"It's the thought that counts," he informed me casually. "You're lucky I went this route. Can't cook for shit."

My head fell back on a laugh. Whether he cooked or not didn't matter to me. The fact that he even thought to handle dinner before I got home was what really counted. He was so getting lucky.

"Mommy, look it." Callie came running up to where Brett and I stood. "We drew pictuws of our family at school today."

I took the picture from her hand and studied the stick figures she'd drawn on the page. Brett's chest pushed against my back as he leaned over my shoulder to take a look.

"That's me, and bubs, and you, and Brett. See? He's wearing a toow belt." She pointed to a yellow scribble around one of the stick figure's waists. The breath whooshed from my lungs as she spoke. My little girl drew a picture of her family, and there Brett stood, right there in the middle of stick figure Callie and stick figure Cameron.

Brett's body went stiff as a board behind me and I could have sworn he'd stopped breathing.

"Do you like it, Brett?" Callie asked, staring up at him with wide, innocent eyes.

Brett's chest rumbled as he cleared his throat, his voice thick with emotion as he answered, "I love it, ladybug. Best picture I've ever seen."

She jumped up and down excitedly, clapping her little hands. "Can we put it on the frig-a-rader?"

"Heck yeah." He stepped from behind me, took the picture from me, and stuck it front and center on the refrigerator door.

"*Yay!*" Callie yelled as she bounded up to Brett. "Now everybody will see our family." She hugged his legs tightly, muttering a quick, "Love you, Brett," before going back to the table to finish her coloring.

When I turned to catch Brett's eyes, the love I saw shining in their warm brown depths made my heart squeeze.

"Christ, I love that little girl," he mumbled in a thick, hoarse voice.

Walking up to him, I put my arms around his waist and

squeezed tightly, burying my face in his chest and inhaling his clean scent. "Thank you," I whispered against the ball in my throat as tears pricked the backs of my eyes, threatening to spill over.

He reached up and tucked a stray strand of hair behind my ear. "For what, beauty?"

I pulled back and stared up at him, hoping he could see the sincerity in my eyes. "For being so wonderful. How'd I ever get lucky enough to have you?"

The kiss he placed on my lips was feather light, but full of emotion. "I'm the lucky one, baby."

God, this man undid me in every way. I had no walls left. He'd shattered through ever defense I had. I could finally admit it to myself.

I was crazy in love with Brett Halstead.

CHAPTER TWENTY-THREE

KENZIE

"OH GOD. HARDER, BRETT. FASTER," I begged helplessly, writhing beneath him as he thrust into me with slow, torturous strokes.

"Eyes on me, baby," Brett panted as he continued to drag his cock in and out, driving me out of my mind.

Using all my strength, I peeled my heavy eyelids open and stared up at the man doing insanely erotic things to my body, manipulating it in ways no one ever had before.

"Fuck me, your pussy's so perfect," he ground out, making my walls clench around him. I was never much for dirty talk, but there was just something about when Brett did it that set my blood on fire. Just his words were usually enough to send me careening into a blinding climax, but this time was different. It was as if each thrust was calculated to drive me closer and closer, but not enough to send me over. He was intentionally denying me my release.

"Baby, please," I whimpered, on the brink of tears.

Slow thrust in. Slow drag out.

"Say it, beauty."

Thrust in, drag out.

My brows dipped in confusion. "Say what?"

Thrust in, drag out.

His deep brown gaze bore into mine. It was as if he was seeing every single thing I felt. "Say it, beauty. I know you feel it. I want to hear you say it."

Thrust in, drag out.

Oh shit. He knew. He *knew* how I felt about him. My breath stalled completely. "Brett," I whispered on an exhale.

Thrust in, drag out.

"Say it, Kenzie. Tell me what I want to hear and I'll let you come."

Thrust in, drag out.

My head shook frantically, my eyes wide as fear took over.

Thrust in, drag out.

"Yes, baby. I know you do. Just say it."

Thrust in, drag out.

Yes, I knew I loved him. But knowing it and saying it were two different things. Somewhere in the back of my mind, I was still terrified that admitting it out loud would change everything... That it would change Brett.

Thrust in, drag out.

"I'm not going anywhere, beauty," Brett murmured as he dragged his nose against the side of mine. Sweat coated our bodies and I could feel him tensing up. He was as close as I was but refused to let go. "I swear to you, Kenzie, I'm not going anywhere and I'll never change on you," he said, reading my mind. "This is me. This is *us.*"

My hips moved up against his as I fought him, trying to grab at my climax. "*Brett.*"

Thrust in, drag out.

"I love you, baby. I love you. Just say it. *Please,* just say it."

Thrust in, drag out.

Oh god. He loved me. Brett loved me. I could see the

honesty reflecting back at me in his eyes. I knew they weren't just words to him. He meant them. He truly did, and that thought alone cracked my heart wide open.

Thrust in, drag out.

Lifting my head to bury it in the crook of his neck, I moaned, "I love you. God, I love you so much."

That was all it took. With my admission, Brett's control snapped. He pulled almost all the way out and drove back into me with a fierce snap of his hips, causing me to cry out as that sweet combination of pleasure and pain began to take hold.

"Again," he growled as he pounded into me, fucking me like a man possessed.

"I love you."

"*Fuck*, beauty," he groaned. "Love. You. Too." Each word was punctuated with a violent drive of his cock. "Want you to come, baby. Want you to scream it as you come all over my cock."

That was all it took. I spiraled down into a release so strong I thought I might drown, yelling out *I love you* as it pulled me under.

"That's it, Kenzie. Give it to me, baby. Fuck, you're so beautiful when you come." His erotic words only fueled my orgasm, causing tears to slide from the corner of my eyes as I came long and hard.

"So close, baby. So fucking close. Christ, I love you." I felt him swell even thicker moments before he buried himself to the hilt and dropped his head into my neck, groaning out my name as poured into me.

"Fucking perfect. So fucking perfect," he mumbled minutes later once we'd both managed to catch our breaths.

When he pushed up on his forearms and looked down at me, I couldn't help but smile at what I saw staring back at me.

"Love you, honey," I whispered, pushing a hunk of hair from his forehead.

Lowering his head to nuzzle his face against mine, I felt his own smile against my cheek as he told me, "Love you more, beauty. Always."

Only moments later, exhaustion pulled me under into a peaceful sleep. My life had never felt more wonderful.

I WOKE hours later to the whispered sound of Brett's voice. "Hey, ladybug? What're you doing up at this hour?"

At Callie's whimpered confession of, "I had a bad dream," I quickly sat up and swung my legs over the side of the bed, prepared to take care of my daughter in her time of need. But apparently, the job was already being done.

The hall light cast a glow through the crack in our bedroom door, and I saw Brett's strong form crouched down in front of my baby girl as he asked, "Well we can't have that, now can we? My beautiful girl needs her sleep. What'd you dream about, sweetheart?"

"A monster was under my bed. Yous big and strong. Will you beat the monster up for me?"

I heard the determination in Brett's voice as he answered, "I'll kick any and every monster's butt who bother's my girl. Let's go. I'll show him who's boss."

Second's later I heard the twins' bedroom door creak open, and Brett's muffled threats of a beat down. And knowing my precious baby was safe and taken care of, I laid back down with a brilliant smile on my face. It only took a few minutes for me to drift back off to sleep, and when I did, the smile remained firmly in place.

I HONEST to god believed that the Cloverleaf Fall Festival was created in order to kill me. That wasn't an exaggeration.

Brett, unable to deny the twins' manipulative innocence, had already gotten them cotton candy, funnel cake, and hot chocolate topped with three inches of marshmallows to wash it all down with.

I had to put my foot down on the caramel apples. Callie and Cameron were running around, screaming at the top of their lungs like—well, like two five-year-olds hopped up on sugar. But it wasn't just the twins who had my head pounding so bad it felt like my eyeballs were about to pop out.

Oh, no.

The *real* problem was those two combined with Trevor. *That* was a combination created by the devil himself.

"*Mommy*! I wanna ride that Ferris wheel again!" Cameron yelled at the top of his lungs—because a kid on a sugar high can't possibly speak at a regular decibel.

"*Yeah*! The Ferris wheel!" Trevor shouted. "Let's ride it again!"

"We're doing the pumpkin patch," I answered. "You can ride the Ferris wheel again later."

"Ahhhh," all three—yes, *three*—of them whined.

Throwing my hands up in defeat, I turned and looked at Brett who was trying his hardest not to laugh his ass off.

"This is all your fault," I hissed out.

"What'd I do?"

"You fed the kids a pound of sugar each and let Trevor off his leash!"

"Hey! In my defense, Lizzy's the one in control of Trevor's leash. If you're gonna blame anyone for him, blame her!" he shouted, pointing his finger in Lizzy's face.

She just looked at me with an *eh, what are you going to do* expression and shrugged. "I gave up trying to rein all that crazy in. It's best to just let him run the energy out of his system until he exhausts himself. Kind of like a puppy."

Letting out an exasperated breath, I turned around to find Emmy, Luke, Savannah and Jeremy laughing so hard they were hunched over with tears in their eyes. At my murderous glare, Stacia and Gavin slowly backed away, stating, "Uh, we're just... going to go look around. We'll meet y'all over at the pumpkin patch." Then they took off, smart enough not to stick around.

"Hey, guys, check it out!" Ben called as he and Mickey came walking up to our group. "They have deep fried Oreo's." He took a huge bite and let out a groan. "Best. Thing. Ever."

"I WANNA DEEP FWIED OREO! I WANNA DEEP FWIED OREO!" Callie shrieked, jumping up and down.

"No more sugar," I said a little too loudly, drawing the attention of the families all around us.

"All right, rugrats," Brett spoke up in order to diffuse the situation. "Time to hit up the pumpkin patch. Let's go find the biggest pumpkin they have." He scooped up a squealing Cameron and plopped him on his shoulders then took Callie's hand and led the way.

"Come on, Momma," Emmy said, throwing her arm over my shoulders. "Let's go get our pumpkin picking on." We all trailed after Brett and the kids, laughing and joking around as we walked through the pumpkin patch. Eventually, Gavin and Stacia made their way back to us once the threat of my head exploding had passed.

I lost track of how long we'd been wandering around in search of the perfect damn pumpkin. All I knew was that I wanted to cry out in thanks when I heard Cameron shout, "Brett! Look at this one. It's *huge!*" We all looked over in time to see him try to pick up a pumpkin almost as big as he was.

"Whoa, little man," Brett called over as he rushed to where Cameron was huffing and puffing away. Was it possible for a five-year-old to get a hernia? "That thing's huge, bud. You sure that's the one you want?"

Cameron's head bobbed up and down animatedly. With a laugh, Brett stood and went to collect one of the red wagons the pumpkin patch provided for the pumpkins that weighed too much to carry. Then the girls and I stood back, watching and laughing as Brett and the rest of the guys struggled to get the ginormous pumpkin into the wagon.

"Luke! Don't you dare throw your back out!" Emmy yelled. "This baby's coming soon. I won't be taking care of it all on my own 'cause your old butt was trying to show off and slipped a disc!"

"Thanks for the vote of confidence, baby girl," he hollered back, his face so red I was a little scared he was close to rupturing a testical.

I felt a tug on the hem of my jacket and looked down to see Callie standing there, holding a tiny pumpkin the size of her fist. "Mommy, can I have this one?"

"Sure thing, honey pot," I told her, squatting down to her level. "But are you sure you don't want to get one a little bigger?"

"Nah, bubby can get the big one. I jus want this baby punkin."

I placed a kiss on my little girl's head and smiled brightly. "Well, if that's the one you want, that's the one you're getting."

She whooped with enthusiasm before asking, "Can I have another funnel cake?"

I opened my mouth to shoot her down just as Trevor made his way over to our little group. "Ready."

We all turned our eyes his way to see him standing there with a pumpkin twice the size of his head.

"What the hell do you need that for?" Lizzy asked, exasperated.

"Uh...to carve," Trevor answered, his *well, duh* face causing laughter to bubble up in my throat.

"Trevor, you're a grown man with no kids. Why do you need to carve a pumpkin? Especially one that size."

"It's not just to carve, *cher*. You're also going to make me a pumpkin pie. Now, chop chop. Callie said something about funnel cake and I want one."

The ladies and I had a bet going on whether or not Lizzy was going to let Trevor live to see Christmas. I had my money on dead by Thanksgiving. And after what I'd witnessed, I felt pretty confident I was about to be two hundred bucks richer.

CHAPTER TWENTY-FOUR

THE KIDS WERE at daycare and Brett was at work, so I had the house to myself all day long. I was looking forward to complete silence. I had a ton of books on my Kindle just begging to be read. I also had a backed-up DVR with hours of shows to watch. If I wanted a bubble bath, I could sit in there all day long. I could even put on a facial mask and give myself a mani-pedi. The options were endless.

I'd just finished applying my mud mask and sat on the couch. *Criminal Minds* was queued up to play and I held a bottle of OPI My Paprika is Hotter than Yours, ready to paint my nails. The orangey color was perfect for Halloween just days away.

I was one coat down on my toes when the front door burst open, startling a screech from me. Lizzy, Emmy, Savannah, Mickey, and Stacia came sauntering in and planted their butts on the living room furniture like they lived there.

"Uh...hi?"

"What up, babe?" Emmy asked as she plopped her pregnant self down on the couch next to me. "Ooh, mani-pedi time. Fun."

"Honey," Lizzy said, taking the bottle of polish from my

hand and propping my foot on her lap so she could take over painting. "You could have come by the salon. I'd have done you for free."

Savannah let out a giggle. "Kinky. I like it. But if you don't record that for Trevor, he might die of disappointment."

Laughing off Savannah's comment, I turned back to Liz. "No offense, sweetie. But the salon's the last place I want to be on my day off."

"Understandable." She moved my foot off her lap, grabbed hold of the other and got to work on it.

"Sooooo," I dragged out, looking around at the women filling the living room. "To what do I owe the surprise visit? In the middle of the day. On a Wednesday." Didn't these people work?

"Ah, yes," Lizzy said with a laugh. "You've never experienced this particular benefit of being part of our gang."

"And what benefit is that?"

"The benefit of having a key to everyone's house," Stacia said with a laugh.

Oh yeah, I recalled Savannah and Emmy telling me it was something I'd get used to the night we staged Trevor and Lizzy's intervention.

"So you decided to stage a B&E to, what, raid his fridge?"

"Actually," Mickey leaned in close, her face a mask of seriousness. "We have something we really need to talk to you about." I had no idea what they needed to talk about, but by their somber expressions, I was a little concerned. What if they didn't think I was good enough for Brett? What if they came here to tell me to leave their friend alone? Could I walk away from him if that's what they all wanted me to do? I knew the answer to that. No way in hell. I'd just have to prove to them I was deserving of his love.

"What do you need to talk about?" I asked them quietly, cautiously.

Savannah leaned close, resting her elbows on her knees. "We need to know, how big is he?"

Huh?

"What?"

"Brett," she said simply. "How big is he?"

My eyes bounced from one woman to another. "Sorry, guys, I'm not following."

Stacia spoke up. "Look, each one of us has been with one of the guys in our group. So we're able to report back to each other what each dude is packing. For instance, Gavin's a good eight inches and curves a little to the left."

"Ben's turns kind of purple when he's close," Mickey said. "I'm talking, it actually looks a little angry when he needs to come."

"And Jeremy's has a tendency to hook up in this perfect way that hits just the right spot to—"

"Enough!" I shouted to stop Savannah before I heard something that I would never be able to un-hear.

"Luke's seriously blessed in the girth department," Emmy told me.

"And when I first saw Trevor, I freaked the hell out. I'm talking Hulk dick here. I was like, there's no way in hell that'll fit!" Lizzy shared.

"Okay, first of all...Son of a *bitch*! I never needed to know any of this about any of the guys. Seriously, I'm going to giggle and blush like a damn schoolgirl every time I see any of them. I'll have to work to keep my eyes off their crotches. So thanks a lot for that," I deadpanned.

Stacia continued like I hadn't said anything, "The only one none of us has seen naked is Brett. That's where you come in, Kenzie."

"So let me get this straight. You all left work early and let yourself into Brett's house because you're dying to know about his dick size?"

Each woman nodded, eyes wide as they waited for my answer.

I shrugged and replied, "I can get down with that."

"Score!" Mickey fist-bumped Emmy before turning back to me, each of them giving me their full attention.

"Okay, so, I only really have one other person to compare him to, but when I saw Brett the first thing I thought was that he made Lance look like an amateur."

"I knew it!" Savannah cried out, smacking Stacia in the shoulder. "I told you! Didn't I tell you? I *knew* he was working with something good."

"But it's not his size that's the most impressive," I continued, stunning them all silent. "It's how he uses it."

Emmy's elbows rested on her stomach, her chin propped in her hands as she looked at me in wonder. "How do you mean?"

"Well, he's able to hold off from coming for like, ever." I got a collective gasp from the room. "And he uses it against me."

"Shit. That's hot," Lizzy whispered in awe.

"Yeah. Just the other night, he did this thing where he went super slow, like *agonizingly* slow. He kept me right on the edge the whole time, but wouldn't let me come until I told him I loved him."

"No way!" Savannah squealed.

Emmy clapped like a little girl, saying, "I knew that man was a freak. So hot!"

"And the man has a gift for dirty talk," I told them excitedly. "I mean, I could get off from just his words alone!"

All of a sudden, Mickey stood from her seat and started for the door.

"Where are you going?"

She turned back to me as she shrugged her jacket on. "I

suddenly need a little afternoon delight. I'm going to surprise Ben at work."

"Ew!" Savannah shouted. "Not in his office! I go in there. I don't need to walk into work every day and try to figure out what all surfaces your naked ass has been on!"

"Then I'll just have to bend over it instead." Mickey shot Savannah a saucy wink, causing her to gag. "See you bitches later."

After about another hour of sharing naughty stories, the rest of the girls took off to either go back to work or go find their man and work out some suddenly very pent up frustration.

I spent the rest of the day doing exactly what I'd wanted to do. With Lizzy having finished my toes, I worked on my fingernails, washed my mask off, watched a few episodes of *Criminal Minds* and read smut while soaking in a bubble bath.

I'd put a pork roast in the slow cooker earlier that morning, so by the time I got back from picking the twins up from daycare, it was ready to be served. I'd just finished setting the table when Brett came walking through the door.

Nothing bad had happened in our relationship since saying those three little words to each other. If anything, it had become even better. Every evening he walked through the door from work, I melted at the sight of him. No matter what he was wearing, no matter if he was sweaty from work or not, I always wanted him. He showered my kids and me with so much love that it was impossible not to fall for him over and over again.

The first thing he did every evening was scoop Callie and Cameron up in big bear hugs, squeezing them until they squealed with delight. Then he'd make his way to wherever I was and plant a kiss on my lips so tender and heartfelt that my brain would fry on the spot. He made sure to ask all of us how our day had been as we sat down to eat. And it had officially become Brett's job to handle burrito duty at bedtime. I'd read the twins *Goodnight Moon* and give them their kisses, then Brett would wrap them up tightly before turning off the light and pulling the door to. Hardly a night passed where we weren't all over each other like two horny teenagers sneaking around behind our parents' backs. Unfortunately, some nights were harder than others with two kids under the same roof. But on the nights where there were no interruptions, Brett made certain to show me as well as tell me just how much I meant to him.

And I made sure I showed him the same. *I love you* was something that was said in his house multiple times every single day. I was living a life I was so unaccustomed to, that I sometimes had to pinch myself just to make sure it was real. Each night, I went to sleep wrapped in the arms of the man I loved, and each morning I woke up clinging to him like a second skin, so afraid I'd wake up to discover he was just a dream. I was desperate to keep him, to keep this perfect life we seemed to be building together. But in the back of my mind, I always had that niggling doubt that it would all be taken away from me in the blink of an eye, disappearing like a puff of smoke if I didn't protect it with everything I had.

Pulling me from my musings, Brett walked over to the stove and planted a mind-numbing kiss on my lips.

"Hey, beauty. You have a good day?"

I smiled against his lips and twined my arms around his neck, basking in the feel of him pressed against me.

"I did. Had a little pampering time and the girls stopped by for a visit. It was a pretty great day. How was yours?"

"Good. A little weird, but good."

"What made it weird?"

"Well, I stopped by Virgie May's for lunch. Savannah was there with Emmy. They were just acting strange."

Biting my lip to keep from laughing, I had to ask, "Yeah? How so?"

"Well, they turned bright red when I walked through the door and kept giggling like idiots. And I swear to god, I kept catching Emmy staring at my junk. What's up with that?" I had to fight to suppress my own giggle as I looked at his confused face. "I think Savannah even called me a super freak at one point. I swear, Jeremy and Luke have their hands full with those two."

My laughter couldn't be contained any longer. My head fell back on a deep belly laugh that made Brett look even more bewildered.

"I'm guessing you know something about Crazy and Crazier's issues today?"

I gave him a wink and a smirk, saying, "Maybe, but I'm not telling you. You know, *buddy* code and all."

"Uh, huh," he mumbled, one side of his lips tipping up in a grin.

"But just know this, you should be very, very proud."

With a laugh of his own, he leaned in to give me another kiss. "Yeah, you fit in just perfectly with those whackos."

Being held in his arms and having spent a great day relaxing and hanging with friends, I took that as a compliment. I couldn't think of any other group of people I'd want to fit in with more.

CHAPTER TWENTY-FIVE

KENZIE

PAST

"WHAT THE FUCK IS THIS?" Lance shouted, holding up a piece of paper in his hands. Unsure of what it was, I remained silent, knowing whatever I said would only make matters worse.

"Sixty dollars at Party fucking City? What the hell did you buy, Mackenzie?"

"Th-the kids' Halloween costumes," I stuttered, my eyes glued to the ground, too terrified to meet his hate-filled gaze. "I asked you if I could go buy them," I whispered, knowing that the reminder wasn't going to help any. "You said I could."

Charging me, he gripped my chin in a brutal hold that I knew would leave bruises come the next day. He roared in my face, "I didn't say you could spend sixty dollars, you stupid cow!" His yell was followed by a strong backhand across my cheek that sent me flying into the kitchen island, the corner of the counter jabbing hard into my side.

"Take those stupid fucking costumes back," Lance hissed at

me. His bright blue eyes sparked with so much hatred I thought his look alone would cut through my skin.

"Lance," I pleaded, even though I knew it was pointless. But the thought of disappointing my children hurt more than anything he could ever do to me. "They've already seen them. They're so excited. Please, don't make me take them back."

He grabbed a chunk of my hair and jerked my head to an awkward angle, pulling some of the strands from my scalp and making me cry out in pain. "Take. Them. Back. Or so help me, I'll make you wish you were dead. Do you understand me, you stupid bitch?"

"Yes," I whimpered as tears streamed down my face.

Without another word, Lance hauled my head back by my hair and slammed my face into my counter. Through my scream of pain I heard the startling sound of bone crunching, knowing good and well he'd just broken my nose.

"I'M SO SORRY, BABIES." I tried my hardest not to cry as I dressed my kids in costumes I'd managed to make using clothes I found in my closet. The thick concealer I wore to hide the fading bruises on my face would run, but more than that, I didn't want my babies to see me cry, not when they were putting on their own brave faces.

"I's okay, Mommy," Callie told me, but my poor little girl couldn't even muster up a smile. They'd been so excited when I brought home their costumes. Callie was going to be a princess, Cameron a ninja. But now I had to find a way to make something out of nothing. I'd wrapped Callie in one of my white button down shirt, tying a belt around her waist to make it look like a dress. I still had my apron from when I waitressed. Pairing that over the shirt and tying her hair up in a high ponytail, her costume was complete.

I'd managed to scrounge up a few bucks and made a trip to the dollar store where I found a clip-on bowtie and toddler suit jacket only a size too big for Cameron. I put him in a pair of his black dress pants that were for special occasions and his black tennis shoes, slicked his hair to the side in a neat part and told him he was a fancy man in a tuxedo.

I hated it. I hated that my angels grew up in a home where, at such a young age they had already learned to put on a brave face and not to throw fits over what they couldn't have. That was when I made my decision. I was done with it. I couldn't live like that anymore. And I couldn't put my children through it any longer. I was going to give my children a better life. It was time to start planning.

He'd taken my kids' Halloween. I wouldn't let him take anything else from them. Starting right then, I'd put the wheels into motion.

BRETT

PRESENT

"NUH UH, no fucking way in hell, beauty. I love y'all, but I have to draw the line at this."

The pouty expression on her face was almost enough to do me in. But when I glanced back at the costume that lay across the bed, my balls shriveled up and I practically felt myself growing a vagina.

"That's all right," Kenzie spoke softly as she picked up the costume from the bed and shoved it into the back of the closet. She called it a Prince Charming costume. I called it a straight man's nightmare with tights, sparkles, and puffy fucking sleeves. "If you don't want to go trick-or-treating with us, it's no big deal. I'll take the twins and you can hand out candy here."

Son of a bitch. I got the distinct impression that I was being manipulated. But damn if I wasn't letting myself fall for it, hook, line, and sinker.

"Now hold on just a damn minute. I didn't say I didn't want to go trick-or-treating. I'd love to go. I just don't want to have to dress up like a fruit loop to do it!"

"Prince Charming isn't a fruit loop! He's the ultimate ladies' man," Kenzie argued. "He's the one who basically started the whole swoony male thing. I mean, without Prince Charming, all those fairytale chicks would have grown into old spinsters. Honestly, if you really think about it, the guy basically laid the foundation for men everywhere. Prince Charming *created* the woman's ultimate fantasy guy."

Damn the woman and her valid argument. Still didn't mean I was cool with dressing up like an old-school douche. I'd never live it down. "I don't know," I whined. Yes, me, a grown-ass man was whining about wearing a freaking Halloween costume.

"Baby," Kenzie said, walking over and placing a hand on my cheek. "I don't want you to do anything you don't want to do. If you aren't comfortable dressing up like Prince Charming to go with Callie's princess costume, that's okay. I love you anyway."

She looked so damn sincere as she said it that I couldn't help but cave. "All right, beauty. If it'll make you and ladybug happy, I'll wear the costume."

Kenzie let out a squeal as she jumped at me, wrapping her

arms and legs around me like a monkey. "I knew you'd do it, honey," she said as she planted kisses all over my face. "You're such a good guy."

A deep laugh rumbled up from my chest as soon as I realized what had just happened. "You totally played me, didn't you?"

"Maybe." She was just too fucking cute when she giggled that I couldn't help but to forgive her.

"Christ, I'm such a sucker for my ladies."

"DUDE!" Luke shouted. "What the fuck are you wearing?"

"Watch your mouth!" I yelled back, hitting him upside the head with my plastic sword.

"Luke said a bad word. Luke said a bad word," Callie and Cameron sing-songed as I hit him one more time.

"Why'd you have to invite everyone over?" I turned back to Kenzie, pouting like a giant pussy.

"The girls wanted to see the twins in their costumes," she smiled innocently.

Emmy shot me a cheeky grin and said, "And we may or may not have found out what you were dressing up as and wanted to get photographic evidence to blackmail you with."

Callie and Cameron had run from the living room to get their candy buckets so I was safe for a few choice words. "This is bullshit!" I whisper-yelled. Turning, I pointed my finger right at Kenzie. "Why do you get to be the pink Power Ranger and I'm stuck looking like an asshole?"

She propped her hands on her hips and narrowed my eyes at me. "Because Cameron wanted me to be a Power Ranger with him and Callie wanted you to be her Prince Charming. That a good enough reason for you?"

I let out a huff and several quiet choice words while all of our friends stood around laughing.

"You owe me," I warned loud enough for only her to hear, my arms crossed over my chest. "I'm talking handing out blowjobs like lollypops. I look stupid." My bottom lip may or may not have been poking out just a little bit as I spoke.

"Aww," she cooed as she slid her hands up my chest and around my neck. I couldn't lie; she was kind of rocking that pink Ranger outfit. I saw some role-playing in our future, for sure. "Poor baby. You're so adorable when you're all pouty and grumpy."

"I'm not being pouty and grumpy," I argued. "I'm being broody and aloof. Like a man."

"Yeah, keep telling yourself that, baby," she said with a roll of her eyes. "Now, suck it up and let's get our trick-or-treat on."

After kicking everyone out of my house, and Kenzie, the twins, and I took to the streets. I had to admit, I was having a hell of a time. Turned out, it wasn't all that uncommon for parents to dress up with their kids. I even got a few nods and chin lifts from dads dressed just as douchey as I was. It was a weird kind of bonding moment for us men.

After about an hour or so, Cam and Callie seemed to be dragging so I shuffled them back to the house. The poor kids were so tired they didn't even eat any candy before passing out. Kenzie and I had to peel their limp bodies out of their costumes and tuck them in. They remained comatose the entire time.

After getting changed and throwing that damned Prince Charming costume in a pile to burn the following day, we headed into the living room to cuddle up on the couch. That was when Kenzie introduced me to one of the perks for parents when it came to Halloween. The candy tax. It was our responsibility to go through all the candy to make sure it was safe. Then we got to take our cut.

Another good thing I learned about Halloween was Kenzie had a thing for melting down those mini Three Musketeers bars and licking them off my body.

Oh, yeah, I could totally get into the whole trick-or-treating thing.

CHAPTER TWENTY-SIX

KENZIE

"THIS SHIT IS NOT SUPPOSED to be for men. I don't understand why I need to be there."

For the fifth time that morning, I had to explain to Brett why he was being dragged to Emmy's baby shower.

"Because," I said *again* as I applied one final coat of mascara, "Emmy and Luke are two of your best friends in the world and they want you there. They wanted to do a coed shower, so all the men are required to go. Quit your belly aching."

From my vantage point in front of the bathroom mirror, I could see Brett throw his head back and stare up at the ceiling. "Why, God? Why have you forsaken me?" he cried out dramatically. It really was pathetic to watch.

"Honey," I giggled. "It's three hours of your life, not the end of the world."

"It's three hours I'll never get back, and I run the risk of losing my man card afterwards. I'm telling you right now, I'm not eating any of that fucking slimy shit babies have to eat, or letting you try and pin a diaper on me, or whatever the hell you women do to torture us men at things like this. I've heard stories. I'm watching you."

Damn, there went my plan for the baby food guessing game. I'd been looking forward to seeing Brett's expression when I made him eat a jar of turkey and green beans. That would have been classic.

"You're no fun."

"And you women are evil. The only reason y'all want us there is to degrade us."

I had no response for that. He was absolutely right.

We'd left the kids with a sitter and took Brett's Jeep to the shower at Emmy and Luke's house, with Brett sulking the entire way.

The second we walked through the door, it became clear that the coed themed shower wasn't Luke's idea at all. He stood in the corner, flanked by Trevor, Jeremy, Gavin, and Ben, all wearing matching expressions of misery.

Oh, this was going to be fun.

"Go play with your friends," I said sarcastically with a pat to Brett's cheek. He immediately took off in their direction, taking the beer that Trevor held up for him. A baby shower with booze. Thank god for that. I wasn't going to admit it to him, but I felt the same way about these parties as Brett did. I mean honestly, who in their right mind actually *liked* sitting around for over an hour watching a woman unwrap gifts and coo over the eleventy-billion onesie she got for the kid she was cooking. I was a mom and I hated these damn showers.

"Kenzie! Over here." I turned to find Savannah, Mickey, Lizzy, Stacia and Emmy standing around the kitchen island with a few other women I hadn't met. The house was packed with people. It was as if the entire town had come out to cele-brate with Emmy and Luke.

I made my way over to the girls, my heart swelling at just

how welcomed they made me feel. I was quickly introduced to the other women standing in the kitchen. Savannah's mom, Victoria, and her mother-in-law, Kathy, were there. I also met Lizzy's mom, Diana, and her Nana, as well. And I had to admit, after only five minutes of conversation with the old woman, I was pretty damn sure I wanted to be Nana when I grew up. The woman was something else.

The last woman I was introduced to was Luke's mother, Ilene. She was a sweet, quiet woman who had the same bright green eyes as Luke's. Just by looking at her, I could tell she was ecstatic to be meeting her grandson soon. She doted on Emmy and kept rubbing on her belly every so often. Emmy just stood there, a bright smile on her face, and let her. Obviously she had a wonderful relationship with Luke's mom.

Standing around so much family, I couldn't stop the pang of sadness that shot through my heart. That was what I'd always wanted...a family to stand around the kitchen with me, laughing at the most inane things. A mother who would rub on my swelling belly, beyond excited for her grandchild to come into the world. It had been over a decade since I'd spoken to my own mom. I was certain she didn't even know she had two grandbabies.

"You want something to drink, Kenz?" Lizzy asked, pulling me from my depressing thoughts.

"Uh, yeah." I cleared my throat, trying to rid it of the ball of emotion that had formed. "I'd love a beer."

"Coming right up."

The mothers and Nana took their leave to give Luke a hard time, leaving just the girls and me in the kitchen. As I tipped my beer bottle up and took my first sip, Emmy asked, "So Kenzie, what was your baby shower like? I bet you got a shit-ton of gifts since you were cooking up two."

I ended up choking as my drink went down the wrong way,

sending me into a coughing fit so bad that Savannah and Lizzy both had to pound on my back.

"You okay?" Mickey asked once I was finally able to breathe again.

"Yeah, sorry. Went down the wrong pipe." I tried to make light of it by plastering a fake smile on my face, but I knew they saw through it.

"I, um… I didn't have a baby shower for the twins." I kept my concentration centered on the countertop, not wanting to see the pity I was sure was in each of their eyes. "I didn't really have many friends, and…well, I haven't spoken to my parents in years."

"Looks like you lucked out, if you ask me," Emmy harrumphed. "This is *booooring*." My eyes finally darted up to see the rest of the women staring at her with the same *what the hell* expressions on their faces.

"What?" she asked defensively. "Oh, come on, like y'all aren't thinking the same damn thing. It's a party centered around a baby who's not even here yet. The games are all lame as hell. All of the presents are for the alien currently taking over my body, not for me. And my giant ass can't even drink!" she finished, then stated, "Oh, don't you give me that look, Savvy. Your bitch ass is just as bored as the rest of us."

A sly smile pulled at Savannah's lips. "Okay, you're right. I'd take a game of Flip Cup over Pin the freaking Diaper on the Baby any day."

"Thank you!" Emmy harrumphed. "This shit's for the birds."

"Then why'd you insist on a coed shower?" I asked.

"Because if I have to suffer through having every damn person in this house rub my belly like a freaking magic lamp, I'm going to make damn sure Luke's just as miserable as I am."

Lizzy leaned in to tell me, "We get our kicks from making the men in our lives suffer. It makes us all smiley."

"Cheers to that!" Savannah yelled, and the rest of us raised our drinks in a toast. I smiled and laughed when I was supposed to, and I couldn't put into words how much I appreciated Emmy jumping in to divert the conversation away from me. But I couldn't push away that part of me that wished I'd had exactly what Emmy had. I'd have given anything to have a house full of people rubbing my belly and wishing me luck. Emmy was an amazing person, and because of that, the whole town had turned up to celebrate the family she and Luke were creating together. I was just glad she was the kind of person who could appreciate all of the love she had.

"Hey, beauty," Brett's deep voice rumbled in my ear as his arms snaked around my waist. The warm comfort of his arms around me instantly pulled me out of my slump.

"Hey, honey," I grinned as I leaned back into him and turned my face up so he could give me a kiss.

"You looked a little sad for a second there. Everything okay?"

My sweet man.

I was constantly asking myself how I'd gotten so lucky to have such a wonderful guy in my life. Even from across the room, he sensed my mood and came over just to check on me, unknowingly decimating all my negative thoughts with one loving embrace.

"I'm perfect."

"You sure?" he asked against my lips.

Squeezing his arms tighter around me, I answered, "Yep." And I was. Just being in his presence was a calming breath of air for me. As long as he was around I was always going to be okay.

"All right, good." He leaned in closer and whispered in my

ear, "Now can you tell me why the girls are staring at me funny?"

I turned my gaze from Brett to see the girls all huddled together, snickering and whispering, every now and then their eyes wandering down just below the belt. Yeah, I knew why they were looking at him funny. But I wasn't about to rat anyone out.

"Our friends are weird," I simply state.

"That they are, beauty," Brett chuckled. "That they are."

After several more torturous hours of games which consisted of melting candy bars in diapers and guessing baby names, it was finally time to go. *Thank god*. At one point, Emmy broke down crying when we played the game where everyone used toilet paper to guess how big around she was. Luke had unknowingly set off the waterworks when his guess was double the size of her belly. There were several choice words thrown around and accusations that he thought she was fat. All of which he vehemently denied. But the damage was done. Men needed to learn, when it came to a pregnant woman's hormonal rages, they were *always* in the wrong...even if they weren't.

I seriously thought Luke was going to have an aneurysm when it became obvious he wasn't going to be able to console his hysterical fiancée.

While Emmy raged and Luke begged forgiveness, the rest of us were trying our hardest not to burst out in laughter.

"So..." Brett dragged out, breaking the peaceful silence of the car ride back to his house. I turned from the passenger window to look at him and noticed him tapping a quick rhythm on the steering wheel.

"So...?"

"Uh...well..." He cleared his throat, seeming almost nervous. "I was just wondering...um..."

"Wondering what?" I coaxed, trying to get him spit it out.

"Wondering if you ever planned on having any more kids."

Well, that wasn't what I had been expecting. I was silent for several seconds, trying to wrap my head around an answer. Did I ever plan on having any more children? When I was with Lance, that answer was a definitive *no*. And after I left, my sole focus was Callie and Cameron. Having more kids wasn't something I'd really given much thought to, but now that Brett had asked, there were so many different scenarios bouncing around in my head.

Our relationship was still so new, but there was a part of me that felt excited about the thought of having children with Brett. Unfortunately, for all the excitement, there was still that niggling doubt that things might not work out. My fears that Brett would pull the same Jekyll and Hyde routine that Lance and my father had wasn't really something I worried about anymore. I *knew*, soul deep, that Brett was a good man. He could never be the kind of monster they were. But what if he grew tired of my hang-ups? What if he decided a ready-made family wasn't for him? That he wanted to start fresh, have a clean slate with a woman who didn't carry more baggage than a 747?

"I haven't really thought about it. It wasn't something I ever considered after the twins were born," I answered, turning to stare out the windshield. I didn't want to see his face if my answer disappointed him.

"That's cool." He answered so calmly that my eyes shot back to his, wide in shock.

"Really? Do you not want kids?"

He looked thoughtful for several seconds before answering. "To be honest, I do want kids. It's just always something I've seen happening in my life, you know? Get married, start a family. That's always been the direction I knew my life would take eventually."

I wasn't sure I was following him. Was he trying to tell me our relationship was over if I didn't want more children?

"But then I met you and the twins, and in the blink of an eye, I had everything I could ever want."

My head quickly turned on a surprised gasp. "But what about kids of your own?"

He looked over at me for a second, his expression fierce before turning back to the road. "Those kids might not be mine by blood, Kenz, but as far as I'm concerned, they're *mine*. I love them like they're my own. I'd do anything for them. From everything you've told me, that ex of yours is a piece of shit. He never did right by them and, if I have to, I'll spend the rest of my life trying to give them all the happiness that he never did. The three of you are my world, baby. Don't you get that by now? I don't have a life if y'all aren't in it. You and those kids are all I'll ever need to be happy. You're my family."

Oh god, it felt like my heart couldn't physically contain everything I was feeling at that very moment. Tears rushed down my cheeks as I stared at the man who'd shown me the true meaning of happiness.

"I love you." My voice came out raspy as I continued to cry.

"I love you, too, beauty. More than fucking life itself. And I know you still have your doubts, but I'm just giving you a heads up. One day, I'm going to ask you to marry me. You're going to say yes, and we'll spend the rest of our lives being happy. Now, that doesn't mean I'm not going to piss you off on the regular, because I'm a guy and that's just the shit we do, but for every time I piss you off, I'll bust my ass to make it up to you ten-fold. You have my word on that."

"Do you have any idea how happy you make me?"

"If it's anywhere close to how happy you make me, then you are a lucky, lucky woman, baby," he joked, pulling a heartfelt laugh from my chest.

"I'm not opposed to having more kids," I whispered happily. "You know, just giving you a heads up on that."

His face broke out into a bright smile as he kept his focus on the road ahead.

"Good to know, beauty."

CHAPTER TWENTY-SEVEN

BRETT: *Need you to go in the closet and find your hottest dress and heels. I have plans for you tonight, beauty.*

Me: *I'm not wearing heels and a dress to make you dinner. I don't give a shit if it is a fantasy of yours. Not. Happening.*

Brett: *You're not making dinner tonight, baby. We're having a date night.*

Date night: a concept single mothers worldwide were unfamiliar with. I looked up at the clock to see if I had enough time to find a sitter when my phone pinged again.

Brett: *And wear some sexy as fuck underwear, too. You got a thong? You should totally wear a thong!*

Me: *It's 3:00! I don't have time to find a sitter. Have you forgotten those 2 little people who live under the same roof as us? The ones who can't feed or wash themselves?*

Brett: *Already have that taken care of. Lizzy and Trevor are on kid duty tonight. Be sure to pack them an overnight bag.*

"Lizzy!" I yelled from my station. "You volunteered to keep Cameron and Callie overnight? Have you lost your damn mind?

You already have Trevor at home. You really want to add to that headache?"

Lizzy's laughter rang out through the salon as she walked over to me. "He promised to behave if I ordered pizza for dinner. Hope you don't mind the rugrats eating junk tonight."

If it meant that Brett and I got an entire night to ourselves she could feed them whatever the hell she wanted...you know, as long as it wasn't poisonous.

"That's all you had to bribe him with?" I asked skeptically. That just sounded too easy. I'd gotten to know Trevor pretty well, and I was fairly certain that pizza wasn't a sufficient enough bribe for that man.

"Well...pizza and I might have promised to act out one of his role play fantasies."

"Ooh, that could be fun."

She narrowed her eyes and gave me a *you've lost your damn mind* look. "Yeah, then *you* dress up like Maggie from *The Walking Dead* and tell me how much fun it is."

I couldn't control the hysterical laughter that escaped me as I pictured Lizzy in torn up, dirty clothes and a brown wig. I was talking full-on, snort inducing laughter.

"Seriously, Kenz! Who in their right damn mind gets turned on pretending to fight in a freaking zombie? He even wrote a script. A *script!*"

"So he's going to dress up as Glenn?" I giggled.

"No," she sulked. "He's Merle. That asshole's had a sick obsession with that man since we made the mistake of introducing him to the show. He even found that stupid metal thingy to put on his hand so it looks like it's missing."

"Stop...stop," I choked, tears running down my face. "I can't breathe."

"Yeah, you're welcome, bitch," she grumbled before going back to work. I tried desperately to control myself, but every time I pictured them in full TWD regalia, another fit of laughter started up.

Me: *Trevor tell you what he conned Lizzy into doing to agree to babysitting?*

Brett: *Yes. And don't remind me. I just got that fucking visual out of my head.*

Me: *What's wrong with your friend?*

Brett: *So damn much. Don't forget the thong!*

Woohoo! I couldn't wait for date night!

BRETT

FOR THE LOVE OF CHRIST. This date night was the worst date night in the history of the world! I needed a motherfucking redo like nobody's business. I'd spent countless hours putting the damn night together, and it'd been one epic screw up after another right out of the freaking gate.

I had stopped at the florist's to buy the most expensive bouquet of flowers I could find, thinking, surely *every* woman loved flowers.

Yeah, not so much.

When I walked through the door, flowers held behind my back, I was stunned speechless and semi-erect the moment I laid eyes on my girl. The little black dress she was wearing hugged her curves so well my mouth watered. From head to toe, she looked like perfection.

"Sweet Lord, baby. You look fantastic."

"Thanks," she smiled then proceeded to have a little sneezing fit.

"You okay?"

"Yeah. I'm good. I'm good." She stepped up to give me a kiss, but as soon as she was in front of me she sneezed in my mouth. "Shit! I'm so sorry. God, that was so gross. I'm so sorry, honey."

"It's okay," I soothed, wiping the back of my hand across my face. "Here, I got you these." I pulled the flowers from behind my back with a shit-eating grin, so damn sure they were going to get me laid. To say her reaction was a bad one would have been an understatement.

Covering her nose and mouth with both hands, I heard a mumbled, "Oh god," as she took two giant steps away from me. "Are those stargazer lilies?"

I looked down at the bundle in my hand and shrugged. "I don't know. What the hell is a stargazer lily?"

"Shit." *Sneeze.* "I can't be..." *sneeze...* "around stargazer..." *sneeze...* "lilies. They make my..." *sneeze...* "allergies act up..." *sneeze.*

Son of a bitch. "Beauty, I'm so sorry. I didn't know."

Her eyes began to water, making black shit run down her face. "It's okay..." *sneeze.* "Can you just..." *sneeze...* "take them..." *sneeze...* "out of here?" *sneeze.*

"Shit. Yeah," I rushed out, heading for the backdoor. I threw it open and hurled the bouquet into the backyard like a football without a second thought. What a waste. I'd spent two hundred bucks on fucking flowers that almost made my girlfriend sneeze herself to death.

"I'b jus gonna..." she started, beginning to sound like she had toilet paper shoved up her nose. "...take an antihistamine and fix my makeub."

Fuck me sideways. The night was already going down the toilet and the date hadn't even officially started yet.

The evening only got worse from there. I'd made reservations at a fancy restaurant about thirty minutes outside of town. It was the most expensive Italian place I could find within a fifty-mile radius of Cloverleaf, and everyone on *Yelp* said it was the shit. I was certain the place was a winner.

"You sure you don't want to just go home?" It was the third time I'd asked her that since leaving the house. We'd just been seated at our table. The lighting in the restaurant was dim, the glow of the candles on the tables made everything seem more romantic. But I was still able to make out her red nose and puffy, watery eyes perfectly. She looked miserable.

"I told you. I'b fine," she mumbled, trying her best to give me a sincere smile, which couldn't have been easy considering she had to breathe through her mouth. "Let's just order and enjoy ourselbes. This place is so nice. Look," she said, pointing to the menu excitedly. "Eberything's in Italian."

I loved seeing her face light up like that, even if it was still slightly swollen.

The waiter came over with our drinks and took our order. We spent the time waiting on our meals talking quietly about where we saw our relationship heading. It was amazing. If someone had asked me to draw up the perfect woman for myself, I never would have come close to all that was Kenzie. It was as if she had been born just for me.

Our food arrived and we both immediately dug in. The next minute or so was filled with nothing but moans over how fantastic everything tasted.

Yeah, *Yelp* knew its shit. The restaurant was phenomenal.

"Oh, baby," I groaned as I took another bite. "You have to taste this. It's so damn good." Spearing a piece with my fork, I lifted it to her mouth for her to try.

"Mmm, that is good," she said around the bite. "What is that?" she asked once she finished chewing, having savored the bite for as long as she could before swallowing.

"Lobster ravioli. Excellent, right?"

I was already chewing another bite when I noticed her face had turned an unhealthy pale color and a weird wheezing sound was emitting from her chest.

"Lobster?" she croaked. She started trying to suck in deep breaths, but seemed to be having trouble.

"What's happening? What's going on?" I rushed out when she grabbed her purse and began to dig around frantically.

"Allergic to shellfish," she wheezed.

The white of her face quickly morphed into an angry purple-ish color. This was not good. *Not good!*

"EpiPen," she choked out, still digging in her purse.

"Shit! *Fuck!*" I jumped from my chair so quickly it went flying into the table behind me, but I didn't give a damn. I was by her side in a flash, jerking the purse from her grasp and upending it onto the table, sending the contents scattering.

"Found it!" I shouted triumphantly, holding the pen up in the air like a goddamned trophy.

"In…" *wheeze…* "my…" *wheeze…* "thigh."

"Shit, right!"

Popping the top off, I quickly stabbed the needle in Kenzie thigh and depressed the button, praying that she'd soon start to breathe normally again. That blue-ish color her face was turning couldn't have been a good sign.

After a few seconds, she relaxed back in her chair and sucked in a deep breath.

Thank baby Jesus.

The waiter came scurrying over in a panic. "Is everything all right?"

"Check, please," I grumbled dryly.

I was officially calling it. I'd unknowingly almost killed my girlfriend twice in one night. It was safe to say that date night was a bust.

CHAPTER TWENTY-EIGHT

KENZIE

POOR BRETT. He'd tried so hard to put together a romantic evening for the two of us, but it had just ended in disaster. After my near run-in with anaphylaxis, he'd insisted that I go to the emergency room. I tried convincing him that there was no need. The EpiPen had done the trick; I didn't need emergency care, but he wasn't hearing it.

We spent the remainder of the night at the ER, waiting to be seen by a doctor, just to be told four hours later that everything was fine. I just needed to rest and stay away from anything that could cause another allergic reaction.

Basically, the good old doc confirmed everything I'd already told Brett.

He gave me some strong meds to ward off the breathing issues the flowers had caused, so by the time we were in the Jeep on the way home, I was finally able to breathe through my nose again. Looking back on the night, I wanted to laugh. I mean, come on! It was funny if you really thought about it. But judging by the white-knuckle grip Brett had on the steering wheel and the ticking in his jaw, I knew laughing would have been a huge mistake. I'd just wait a day or two for him to finally see the humor in the situation.

But there was no doubt that I was filling the girls in on our epic date night as soon as freaking possible. I was positive they'd get a major kick out of it.

"I'm so sorry," Brett mumbled for the gazillionth time. "Shit, beauty. I'm so fucking sorry."

"Honey," I laughed. "It's okay. Really. Years from now, we'll look back on this night and laugh our asses off. This is the kind of story we'll be able to tell our kids when they're grown up. Mommy and Daddy's very first date led to near-death and a trip to the emergency room."

He didn't say anything for a solid two minutes.

"Our kids?" he finally asked, his tone soft and filled with awe.

"Well...yeah. I mean, you already *told* me you were going to propose one day, and that I'd be saying yes," I joked. "And I already told you I'm cool with more kids."

"You love me, beauty?" he asked in a ragged voice.

My own voice came out in a whisper. "You know I do, honey. I love you more than I ever thought possible."

Finally, after all the drama of the night, I *finally* saw his lips quirk up in a grin. "Even though I tried to kill you...twice?"

There was my guy.

"Yes, even though you tried to kill me," I giggled.

"You're my other half, beauty. Without you, I'm not whole."

"You make me whole, too, Brett," I replied past the lump of tears that had quickly formed in my throat. "I wake up every day thanking God that he put you in my life."

Reaching over the console, Brett took my hand and pulled it to his lips, placing a gentle kiss on each knuckle. "Love you, beauty."

"Love you, too, honey."

The rest of the car ride was spent in silence, our fingers twisted together. There wasn't a need for more words. We'd already said everything that needed to be said.

BRETT

I WAS HAVING the best dream. Kenzie was on her knees in front of me, giving a gold medal worthy performance of her oral skills. Jesus Christ, there was nothing sexier than when my beauty looked up at me with her gorgeous jade eyes as her plump lips stretched around my aching cock.

I was pulled from my slumber by the sound of a guttural moan, the vibrations shooting straight up my dick.

"Fuck me," I groaned once the fog of sleep had lifted completely and I was able to see and feel what was *really* happening.

Kenzie pulled away from me, releasing my cock from her mouth with a loud pop. "In just a minute, honey. I want to taste you first.

My head fell back on a gasp as she swallowed as much of my hard length as possible. "Baby," I managed to grind out between clenched teeth. "You gotta stop. The doc said you needed to rest."

"I've rested enough. I want you."

Not one to deny my woman's wishes, I lay back, propping my hands beneath my head, the glow of the moon through the blinds giving me just enough light to make out the erotic sight of Kenzie's head bobbing up and down between my legs. With each upward stroke, she hollowed out her cheeks, sucking me so hard the telltale tingles erupted at the base of my spine. It was by far the best blowjob I'd ever had. But I didn't want to come in her mouth. When I came, I wanted to be buried inside her, feeling her pussy squeezing me as she screamed my name.

"Beauty, stop," I panted. "I'm about to come."

She wasn't deterred. At my words, she moved faster, her hand around the base of my cock moving up and down to meet her lips. Her wicked tongue flicked the underside of the head until I thought I was going to lose my mind.

Fuck me, I was so close.

"Don't want to come in your mouth, beauty. I want you to ride me."

That seemed to get her attention. Finally releasing me, I watched in wonder as she slowly crawled up my body until she was straddling my erection. The heat from between her legs as her slick pussy rubbed against me made me tremble.

"Ah, *fuck*, baby. I need to be inside you."

Reaching between her thighs, she grabbed hold of my shaft and lined it up with her entrance. Before I could even process what was happening, she slammed down quickly, taking every inch of me in to her body with a deep moan. It was heaven. The only words to describe what being connected to Kenzie like this felt like were pure heaven.

"God, Brett," she whimpered as her hips moved back and forth, up and down. The rhythm in which she fucked me was absolutely mind blowing. I was never going to get tired of this.

"That's right, beauty. Fuck me. I want you to make yourself come all over my dick.

"Oh, yeah. Keep talking, honey."

My girl, always so turned on by my dirty talk.

"You love my cock, don't you, Kenzie?" I asked, knowing every word was sending her closer and closer to the edge.

"God, yes."

"Your pussy's so goddamned tight, baby. Never felt anything like you. So fucking hot and wet."

"I'm close," she gasped, grinding down on me. I wanted to give her what she needed, but I couldn't lay there helpless any longer. I needed to fuck her. I needed to pound into her until she felt me *everywhere*.

Grabbing hold of her hips, I sat up, still buried inside her and shifted so she was on her back. She cried out at the movement as I pushed deeper into her.

"Oh god," she whimpered as I slammed my hips into hers at a relentless pace.

"Need you to come for me, beauty," I panted as the tingle in my spine grew to an almost painful level. My balls drew up tightly and I knew I wasn't going to last much longer. I had zero self-control when it came to Kenzie. The desire I felt to mark every inch of her body was undeniable.

Lowering my head, I sucked one of her pretty pink nipples into my mouth, biting down just hard enough to make her entire body quiver.

"So close. God, Brett, I'm so close."

My hand snaked between our bodies to where we were connected in the most intimate way, finding that tiny bundle of nerves. Knowing just what she needed to go flying over the edge, I pinched her clit between my index and middle finger as I fucked her hard and fast. Seconds later her walls clamped around me like a vice as she yelled out her release, chanting my name like a prayer over and over. The grip her pussy had on me was too much; I couldn't hold back my own orgasm any longer.

"*Kenzie*," I shouted out loudly as I came so hard I thought the neighbors would be able to hear me. Three more thrusts was all it took to empty myself in her. For the love of everything holy, making love to Kenzie was no doubt going to be the death of me one day.

Once we caught our breaths, I rolled onto my back, making sure to keep us connected as I lay with her soft body on top of mine, basking in the afterglow of world class sex. My life couldn't have been more perfect than it was at that very moment, Kenzie's soft curves pressed against me, still buried deep inside Heaven.

Pure perfection.

Her breathing had slowed to the point that I thought she'd fallen asleep. That was, until she spoke, her words muffled as she nuzzled her face into my chest.

"I'm going to marry you one day," she whispered dreamily.

"I know, beauty."

"One day soon."

"Yeah," I answered softly as my chest expanded at her words, causing me to tighten my grip on her. I never wanted to let her go.

"You make me whole, honey," she told me on a yawn. "Love you."

"I love you, too, Kenzie." Then I followed her into a deep sleep with a smile on my lips and my girl wrapped in my arms.

CHAPTER TWENTY-NINE

KENZIE

PAST

"LANCE," I gasped, trying my hardest to sit up in the bed. I tried doing those breathing exercises I'd seen on TV to work past the pain, but it was pointless. Lance said Lamaze classes were a waste of time and money. He claimed that he wasn't going to throw away billable hours at the office to attend some stupid class that only reminded you to breathe.

Well, as another contraction shot through me, I'd have given anything to have taken those damn classes. I needed relief.

"Lance." Reaching over, I tried to shake him awake. We needed to get to the hospital. I wasn't scheduled to have a C-section for another nine days, but my water had just broke. My little babies decided they were tired of waiting and wanted to make an early appearance. The contractions came on fast and strong, getting closer and closer together as the minutes passed.

"Lance, honey. Wake up."

"For fuck's sake, Mackenzie, will you please shut the hell up? I'm trying to sleep!"

"I'm in labor. We need to get to the hospital. Now."

With an angry grumble, he finally pushed off the bed and started tugging his pants on. "Well, that's just fucking perfect. It's the middle of the goddamned night, and I have a deposition in the morning. How the fuck am I supposed to get through that with no sleep, huh?"

I couldn't concentrate on his rant, and honestly, at that very moment, I really couldn't have cared less about his stupid deposition. I was in too much pain.

"Well, you going to just fucking sit there or get your lazy ass up? Come on!"

Lazy? I was in fucking *labor,* for Christ's sake!

Knowing that arguing with him would only cause an even bigger fight and delay me getting to the hospital in time, I clenched my teeth and moved off the bed, trying to breathe through the contractions.

"ALL RIGHT, Ms. Webster, it's time to move you into surgery. Are you ready to meet your little ones?"

Nerves coursed through my body as they prepared to wheel me into the room to begin my C-section. I was terrified and excited all at the same time. "Lance, honey, you ready?" I turned my head to look over at where he was sitting with his laptop perched on his lap as he typed away.

"I've got a lot of work I need to get through," he answered, only looking up from the screen to address the doctor. "You can come and get me once she gets into recovery. I'm sure everything will be just fine. You don't need me there."

"Lance," I gasped, tears burning the backs of my eyes before they broke free and slid down my temple onto the bed I was laying on. "We're about to have our babies. I'm scared. I want you there with me."

He let out a frustrated huff and finally deemed me worthy of a look. "Tomorrow's a big day for me, Mackenzie. I need to get this finished. I'll see you when you come out of surgery."

"Sir," the doctor cut in, "your wife could really use your support in the operating room—"

"She's not my wife," he answered, his tone full of disinterest. He'd already gone back to his work, effectively cutting off whatever else the doctor was going to say.

Turning away from him in disgust, I caught the look of pity in my doctor's eyes before she nodded at the nurse. "We need to get you into surgery now, Ms. Webster."

"O-okay," I tripped over my words and my nerves took complete control of my body, causing it to shake uncontrollably.

"It'll be okay, sweetheart," the kind nurse leaned in to whisper as they began moving me from the room. "We'll take good care of you, then you'll have two precious babies to love when it's all over."

"Thank you." I tried so hard not to cry. It was supposed to be a happy day, a blessing. I was finally going to meet my babies after so many months of pregnancy. I hated that I was letting Lance take that joy away from me.

It wasn't until I heard Cameron's shrill cry in the delivery room that my tears turned from those of sadness to happiness. From that moment forward, I'd finally have two people in my life to love me as unconditionally as I loved them.

FOUR DAYS HAD PASSED since the twins were born, and each passing day was another that Lance couldn't be bothered to come to the hospital to see us. After briefly checking on me in recovery, he'd gone to the nursery to see the babies. He'd stayed for an hour, tops, before leaving to go home and get some sleep.

Every time I called, he was either too busy or too tired to come up and visit. I was heartbroken. Finally, on the fourth day, the doctor released us to go home. The discharge papers had been completed, the babies' diaper bags had been stocked, and we were ready to go. All that was left to do was wait for Lance to show up.

I held the phone to my ear as the call when to voicemail yet again.

"Hey, it's me. The doctor released us to go home two hours ago. Could you please come get us? I know you're busy, but if I have to stay in this hospital any longer, I'm going to lose my mind. Please call me back."

It wasn't like I could have just called a cab to come pick us up. I had two babies and no car seats. Lance was our only way home and he couldn't even be bothered to answer the phone. Another four hours passed before he finally graced us with his presence, and by that time, I had already worked myself up so much that I couldn't contain my anger when he walked through the hospital room door.

"Where were you?" I demanded as I rocked a fussy Cameron in my arms. Callie slept peacefully in the hospital's little basinet, but Cameron had proven to be a difficult sleeper. I'd spent the last three nights rocking and singing to him to try and get him to relax, but nothing seemed to work. I was exhausted and angry.

"I was at work," he answered coldly, staring me down with his icy blue eyes.

"I've been calling you all fucking day! They released us this morning, Lance. Is it too much to ask for my *fiancé*, the father of my children, to show the hell up when he's supposed to? You haven't even been here!"

"Well, I'm here now," he hissed through clenched teeth. "So let's fucking go. I need to get back to the office after I drop you off."

"*Are you kidding me?*" I shouted, startling a cry from Cameron. I hadn't meant to yell like that, but I was just so damn furious. "You've been working the entire time we've been here! Can't you take a goddamned day off? I could really use your help!"

"Let's. Go." That was all he had to say.

A nurse arrived with a wheelchair to help me down to the car. I kept both babies perched in my lap the whole way down since their own father couldn't be bothered to carry either of them. Once we had them properly buckled up, I slowly climbed into the passenger's seat, still unable to move comfortably due to the C-section. Lance walked around the front and climbed into the driver side as I leaned my head back and closed my eyes, exhaustion tugging at me incessantly.

"Mackenzie," Lance said, drawing my attention to him.

The vicious slap he landed across my cheek the moment I turned my attention to him startled a pained yelp from me, and tears instantly welled up in my eyes. He grabbed hold of my chin and jerked my face back toward his.

"If you *ever* talk to me like that again, I'll make you fucking pay. You understand me?"

All I could do was nod as my stinging tears broke free, running down my already swelling cheek.

We drove from the hospital to the house in utter silence. Once there, he helped me get the twins and all their stuff from the car. As I expected, he couldn't be bothered to make sure we were settled before he was out the door again.

As I spent the rest of the night trying my best to take care of two children all on my own just days after their birth, I kept asking myself how it was possible that I'd allowed my life to become so horrible.

CHAPTER THIRTY

KENZIE

PRESENT

"BEAUTY," Brett said in a rush the second I answered the phone.

"What's wrong?"

"Just got the call; Emmy's in labor. I'm on my way to the house to pick you up."

I looked from the stove where I had dinner cooking over to where the kids sat, watching *Tangled*.

"We can't take the twins to the hospital, Brett. Odds are it's going to take a while. They'll get antsy. Why don't you just head straight to the hospital and I'll try and find a sitter. Hopefully, I can meet you there in a few hours."

"Already got it covered, baby. Jeremy's mom is on her way over there now. She offered to watch the twins for us."

There was that melty feeling again.

"Honey, you didn't have to do that."

He chuckled through the phone line. "You're my family, baby. A man takes care of his family. That's our job."

"Emmy and Luke are your family too, you need to be there for them."

"And I will be, just as soon as I get my kids squared away and my woman in my jeep."

Every time... every single time the man opened his mouth, he turned me into a puddle of goo. "Good Lord, I love you."

"Right back at you. Now get your sexy ass moving. We got a baby to meet."

I was at the stove, trying to finish dinner when the doorbell rang.

"Hey, there sweetie," Jeremy's mother, Kathy greeted with a beaming smile as soon as I opened the door.

"Thank you so much for watching the twins. I can't tell you how much I appreciate this."

"No problem," she offered with a wave of her hand as she made her way into the living room where Callie and Cam sat, still transfixed on the TV. "I've got a whole mess load of grandbabies. These two will be a cakewalk. Believe me."

Just then, Brett came rushing through the door like his ass was on fire. "We ready to roll?"

"Yep, just a second." I turned back to Kathy and the kids. "Dinner's in the oven. It just needs a few more minutes to cook." Leaning down, I planted a kiss on the twins' heads. "Be good for Ms. Kathy. We'll be back soon, okay?"

"Okay," they answered as Brett stepped up to give them each a kiss as well.

"Love you, Mommy," Callie said, followed closely by, "Love you, Daddy," from Cam.

Kathy and I both pulled in a gasp as we turned our wide eyes to Brett. My son had just called him Daddy.

Brett's chest was puffed out, his smile so wide I was scared it might crack his face. It was obvious that hearing my son refer to him that way had just made Brett's entire year.

"Love y'all, too, my precious rugrats."

Kathy shot me a knowing grin as Brett placed a kiss on her head, as well. Then we were out the door.

"I'M NEVER HAVING SEX AGAIN!" Emmy wailed from her seat in the wheelchair.

Brett and I ran into the hospital just in time to see the nurse begin to wheel Emmy to the back.

"It'll be all right, baby girl," Luke cooed, running a hand over her hair lovingly.

She used both of her hands to slap at him. "Don't touch me! Don't you touch me! This is all your fault, you asshole. I'm going to kill you."

That, of course, was followed by a long groan as she hunched over in pain while another contraction took over. Yeah, I so didn't miss those.

"Can someone please get her the fucking drugs?" Luke shouted, his eyes dancing from nurse to nurse frantically.

I could see that the nurse who answered was trying hard no to roll her eyes at Emmy and Luke's dramatics. "Sir, we need to get her in a room and see how far along she is first."

"I'M FAR ENOUGH! Give me the drugs or I'll murder everyone!"

Another long groan.

"Is this normal?" Brett leaned in to whisper to me as Emmy and Luke disappeared around the corner.

"Yep," I answered as we made our way into the waiting room. Our friends were already in there, along with Luke's mother.

Savannah sat, wringing her hands in front of her as Jeremy tried to calm his clearly worried wife.

"Hey, it's going to be just fine," I told her, taking a seat in the empty chair to her left and wrapping her in a tight hug. "Everything is okay. She's exactly where she needs to be."

As I looked around the room, I saw the same sullen expressions on everyone's faces. They were all concerned about Emmy. After what had happened the last time, our little group was waiting with baited breath, praying this delivery would have a different outcome.

I did what I could to try and keep the spirits up. I made coffee runs, offered to go grab dinner for everyone, anything I could to try and keep their minds off the negative. But the mood in the waiting room remained grim until Luke finally walked in three hours after they'd taken Emmy back.

Savannah immediately jumped from her chair and scurried over to him. "Is she okay? Is he here? How'd it go?"

"Slow your roll, killer," Luke chuckled. She wasn't as far along as we'd hoped when they took her back. She's only just now getting close, but I wanted to update y'all. The doctor's seen our girl and it's all systems go."

I could practically feel the tension in the room melt away.

"So she's doing okay?" Savannah asked, still concerned for her best friend.

"Well, she hated my ass up until they gave her that epidural thingy, but now it's all good. I'll come back as soon as the little guy's here." Luke leaned over and planted a kiss on Savannah's head before taking off back in the direction he'd come from.

With that little reassurance, everyone was finally able to feel the excitement that the day warranted.

"JESUS," Brett grumbled two hours later. "Does it always take this long?" he asked me. "I mean, this can't be normal. This isn't normal, right? Shouldn't we have heard something by now?"

I continued to flip through the year-old magazine I'd found in the waiting room, having already answered that particular question three times. "Yes, honey," I replied, not once taking my eyes off the magazine. "It's totally normal."

He opened his mouth to argue just as Luke came flying into the waiting room.

"I'M A DADDY!" he shouted at the top of his lungs, fists held high in the air. Everybody jumped up to take their turn giving hugs, but it wasn't until Luke's mother stepped up to him, eyes bright with tears as the smile wobbled on her lips, and whispered, "So proud of you, baby. I love you so much," that he finally broke down. Wrapping his tiny mother in a tight embrace, he cried against her shoulder, so overwhelmed by his love for his new son. It was one of the most moving things I'd ever seen in my life. It was *exactly* how a man should react to welcoming his baby into the world.

"Can we see her? Can we see her?" Savannah jumped up and down as soon as Luke pulled himself together, anxious to get to her bestie.

"Yeah. We want everyone to come on back and meet our little guy."

Walking into the hospital room, hand in hand with Brett, I tried my best to stay back, giving everyone else a chance to ooh and aww over Emmy and the new baby. I desperately wanted to hold the little guy, but I knew everyone else was more important. I was new to the group; they all needed their turns first.

"Come on," Brett tried to coax me into moving closer, but I just released his hand with a smile and waved him on.

"You go ahead. I'll see him. I'm just going to wait until y'all are done."

"Beauty." His brow furrowed as he stepped closer to me.

"You know you're a part of this family, right? You're just as important to us as everyone else is."

I opened my mouth to respond, but no words came. He truly meant that. These people who had life-long bonds had accepted me as a part of their family without so much as blinking.

Just as I took a step toward Brett, Emmy called out, "Kenzie! Oh thank god."

I rushed over to the side of the bed and looked down at her anxious face. "What's the matter, sweetie?"

"I don't..." she sniffed. "I don't know what I'm doing!" Then the waterworks began. "I don't know the first thing about being a mom. What if I mess up? What if I do something wrong? What if *I break him*?"

I rubbed a hand over her hair. "Aw, honey, it's all going to be okay."

"I need you. You're the only one of us who's done this before." Her eyes were so full of panic as she looked up at me that I felt a tug at my heart. I understood that fear all too well. I'd felt the exact same thing when the twins were born. Fortunately for Emmy, she had something I never did. She had a solid foundation of people who loved her, Luke, and this new baby. Where I was alone, she had people who would do the best they could, even if they weren't sure what it was they were supposed to do. But I couldn't deny the fact that it felt really damn good to be needed.

"I'm here, Em. I'm only ever a phone call away. Don't ever hesitate to call me if you have any questions. I'll always be there to help."

Her chest rose and fell with a deep breath of relief and I couldn't put into words how good that made me feel. *I* had been able to calm her. I was the one to offer her assurance.

"You want to meet little Matthew?" she asked me, her face

splitting into the brightest, most beautiful grin as her gray eyes danced with happiness.

"I'd love to." I reached down and took the snuggly little bundle from Emmy's hands, holding him tightly to my chest as I leaned down to press my lips to his downy head. I wanted this again. I knew I'd been toying with the idea of having more children with Brett, but in that very moment, holding Matthew Allen in my arms, I knew without a doubt I wanted this very thing again. And I wanted it with the man who was staring at me from across the hospital room like I was his whole world.

CHAPTER THIRTY-ONE

KENZIE

"SERIOUSLY, WOMAN," Lizzy declared as I finished up my last appointment of the day. She was still going on about the same thing we'd been discussing all day. "You didn't see his face. You were too busy sniffing on baby Matthew to notice—"

"Hey, in my defense," I interrupted, "babies smell awesome! It's like a new car smell but a thousand times better. Don't act like you don't know what I'm talking about."

"All right, I'll give you that. But I'm telling you, the man looked like he wanted to push to you the ground and impregnate you right there in front of everybody."

My head fell back in a laugh at her description of how Brett had been looking at me in Emmy's hospital room as I held the baby, gently rocking him to sleep.

"Oh, he did not!"

"Yuh huh! Swear to god. Brett's got some serious plans in that head of his. I could see the wheels spinning. He wants to make a billion little Brenzies with you."

I looked up from where I was cleaning my station and arched a brow at her. "Brenzies?"

"Yeah, like Brett plus Mackenzie. It was the best I could

come up with. Y'all's names suck combined together."

"Whatever," I giggled. "There will be no *Brenzies* being made any time soon."

Lizzy gave me a knowing grin as she stated, "But you're not ruling it out."

"No," I admitted. "I'm not ruling it out. We've actually talked about it."

The squeal she emitted was almost loud enough to shatter glass. "You've talked about making babies?"

She plopped down in the chair opposite me at my little table, and I leaned in to tell her, "Yeah, we've talked about all that stuff. Honestly, Liz, I really feel like he's the one, you know? He's just so freaking wonderful. He loves Cameron and Callie so damn much..."

"He loves you too, sweetie."

"I know," I replied with a happy sigh. "Did I tell you Cameron called him Daddy the other day? You should have seen his face. He looked like he was about to explode; he was so damn happy."

"Aww, that's so cute!"

"And he told me he was going to propose one day, and that I was going to say yes. I never saw this coming, Lizzy. I swear, I never thought I'd ever meet a man who loved me the way he does, let alone love my kids so fiercely. He actually told me that, even though they weren't his by blood, Cameron and Callie were *his* in every way that matters."

"Oh my god," she breathed, her bright green eyes misting over with tears. She quickly reached across the table and grabbed my hands in hers. "Sweetie, I'm so happy for you. You deserve someone who makes you happy like this. You're such an amazing person. I can't tell you how excited I am for you and those rugrats."

"I love you," I told her, feeling myself starting to choke up a little. "I love all of you. Moving here was the best decision I've ever made."

"We all love you, too, honey. You're one of us, you and those kiddos. You're family."

I gave her a watery smile before brushing a few stray tears from my cheeks. "Speaking of kiddos, I need to go get them from daycare. I'll see you at Luke and Emmy's tomorrow."

Emmy and Matthew had been released from the hospital earlier that day, and there was going to be a small welcome home party for the new mommy and baby. Luke had been absolutely beside himself, so excited to get his family back under their roof. Poor Emmy had actually called Savannah earlier, complaining about how he was trying to order the hospital staff around like they were at some five-star resort. She said that if he tried to tell one more nurse how to do their job properly before finally just trying to take over and do it himself, she was afraid they were going to mutiny and kick him out for good. He even went so far as to try and tell Emmy how to breastfeed. That ended in her telling him that unless he grew boobs to nourish their child with, he could keep his damn mouth shut or she'd shut it for him. I was pretty sure there was also the threat of never letting Luke near her boobs again if he didn't shut the hell up.

"See you there, babe. Have a great night."

"You, too."

I made my way to the break room and grabbed my purse from the lockers Lizzy had put in for us. As I headed out to the staff parking lot back behind the building, I pulled my cell phone from my purse to check for any messages. There were several missed calls from an unknown number. Dread began to set in as I scrolled through my call log. There were ten in all, all made within the last few hours. The only people who had my number were the people I'd met in Cloverleaf. I made sure to get a new phone and number after leaving Lance, so whoever had been calling over and over wasn't someone I was in regular contact with.

Fear twisted my stomach into knots at the thought of who it could be. There were no voicemails or texts, but I had only ever known one person to call so incessantly. And the thought that he had somehow gotten my number caused bile to rise in my throat as panic set in.

No, it couldn't be. He had no way of getting my new number. Lance didn't know where we were. We were safe in Cloverleaf...we had to be. But no matter how much I kept repeating that to myself, my gut was saying otherwise. A sense of foreboding was blanketing me, telling me my time was up.

The crunch of gravel behind me had me spinning around in fright, and a sob broke free at the sight of him standing only feet away.

"Hello, Mackenzie. Have you missed me?"

No. *No, no, no, no, no!*

"W-what are you doing here, Lance?" I choked out, so many emotions bombarding me all at once. But the one that stood at the forefront was anger—anger that he'd found me, anger that he'd come to ruin my perfect little world.

"I've come to take back what's mine. You and the kids have been gone long enough. It's time to come home."

The man was delusional if he thought for one second that I was just going to walk away from my new life, the life I'd built for my babies, just because he'd told me to. I wasn't the same weak, scared little girl I'd been before I left him.

"How did you find me?" I demanded.

The sound of his laugh was so sinister. "You stupid bitch. You really think I didn't know where you've been hiding all along? I've known about this little piece of shit town since I met you."

Oh god. I was going to be sick.

"That's right. Public records, baby. Your father still owns that shack your grandmother died in. It only took me a matter of hours to track you down. There isn't a place on this fucking planet where you can hide from me. The only reason you've been here for so long is because I've allowed it. I've been enjoying my freedom while you've been fucking that stupid hillbilly. But now I'm done playing around. I want what's mine. You and those kids are *mine*."

Despite the terror coursing through my veins, I lifted my chin and stared him down. "No. I told you what would happen if you came looking for us, Lance. If you don't leave now and forget you ever saw me, I'll leak every single thing I have on you."

"You fucking cunt!" he growled as he charged me. I flinched as his face came within an inch of mine. "You have no fucking clue what I'm capable of. Do you have any idea how many connections I have? You really think that goddamn file you're keeping on me will do you any good? That I didn't do damage control after your little threat? There's nothing left, Mackenzie, not a single goddamned piece of evidence that can link me to any of it. You're file against me is useless. Especially since someone else has already gone down for all that shit. Fired and disbarred, what a shame. A man's career down the drain because he was morally corrupt. It's astounding what a person will do for money, isn't it?" he ended on a laugh.

My heart plummeted from my chest at his admission. I had nothing. Everything I thought I held against him to keep me and my children safe was useless now. He'd framed someone else for everything he'd done. I should have known. After living a decade in hell with him, I should have known just what he was capable of. But I underestimated him.

"I can take those kids from you in the blink of an eye. I can make it to where no judge in his right mind would see you as fit to raise them. After all, I'm a powerful, successful attorney with an outstanding reputation. You're the woman who kidnapped my children and kept them from me for over a year. Who do you think a judge would side with?"

"You're an asshole!" I shouted as I reared back and slapped him with everything I had. All my fear was forgotten at the threat against my children. I'd die before I ever let him take them away from me. As soon as my palm connected with his face, I saw the fury take over. Lance's eyes darkened to an almost unnatural color before his arm pulled back. He brought it forward and punched me in the face so hard I went flying back into my car door. The back of my head hit the car window with such force the glass cracked and splintered in a million directions like a spider web.

He hit me again, and the well-placed shot to my stomach expelling all the air from my lungs. My knees hit the ground, but I barely registered the sharp pain of the gravel jabbing into my skin before he kicked me, again and again. I'd seen Lance's fury on multiple occasions, but never to this extent. The look in his eyes was absolutely murderous. He'd finally snapped. For the first time in all the years I'd known him, he'd lost complete control.

And in doing so, he had made a grave mistake. He couldn't cover up the beating this time. I knew it the moment I heard the voices.

"Hey, stop! What the hell are you doing? Get away from her!"

Thank god.

The sound of a scuffle ensued just as the darkness started closing in.

My last thought was of Brett, Cameron, and Callie just seconds before everything went black.

CHAPTER THIRTY-TWO

BRETT

"HELLO?" I answered my cell in confusion when I saw the number to the twins' daycare pop up on the screen.

"Hi Brett, this is Lori."

"Hey, Lori. What's going on?"

Silence passed through the line before she spoke again. "Well, I'm calling because Kenzie hasn't shown up to pick up Callie and Cameron. We're closing in fifteen minutes and she's never been late before."

My stomach dropped to my feet as I took in what she's said. She was right; Kenzie would never be late picking up the kids. Not unless something had happened.

"I'll be there as soon as I can."

"Thank you, Brett."

I left the work site and ran to my Jeep, disconnecting the call so I could make another one. "Lizzy," I blurted out as soon as she answered. "Kenzie with you?"

"No, she left a little while ago to get the rugrats. Why? What's wrong?"

Shit. "She hasn't shown up at the daycare. Can you see if her car's still in the parking lot?"

"Yeah, hang on just a second." I could hear the click of her shoes against the tile floor as she made her way to the back lot. The sound of the heavy metal door being opened echoed through the phone. But it was the two words Lizzy cried out that made my blood run cold.

"Oh god!" she gasped just before I heard a man's deep voice shout out. "Hey stop! What the hell are you doing? Get away from her!"

"What the fuck is going on?" I shouted through the line as Lizzy yelled out for someone to call nine-one-one. "Lizzy! Goddamn it, tell me what the fuck is happening!"

"She's here." Her voice broke on a sob, causing me to slam the gas pedal down. "Her ex...it's bad...get here now."

No, no, no, no. I couldn't believe this was happening. I couldn't lose her. I just *couldn't*.

"The kids," I whispered into the phone, remembering they still needed to be picked up.

"I'll call Savannah. She's on the list. Just get here."

Throwing the phone onto the passenger seat, I pushed the Jeep as fast as it would go, finally squealing into the lot of Elegant Nails five minutes later. That had been the longest drive of my life. As I jumped from the cab of my car, I could hear the sound of sirens in the distance, alerting me that help was on the way. But I was unable to focus on anything but Kenzie lying motionless on the gravel.

"Oh god. Beauty, wake up," I begged as I pushed past the people who surrounded her, falling to my knees over her body. Blood poured from gaping cuts on her lips and cheeks, bruises marred her beautiful face. "Come on, baby. Wake up for me," I pleaded, feeling completely helpless as I cradled her limp body. "I need you to wake up. Please, baby."

The loud shout of, "Get the fuck off me!" pulled my attention over to where three men were struggling to hold on to another one. Through eyes bleary with tears, I was able to make out the dark haired, blue-eyed man, and my gut told me it was him. It was Lance struggling to get away from the men restraining him.

"*Motherfucker!*" Jumping to my feet, red clouded my vision as I charged him, visions of Kenzie lying hurt and bleeding ran through my mind. He'd done that to her. He'd caused her that pain.

And he was going to fucking pay.

"I'll fucking kill you!" As if my body had detached from my brain, I planted my shoulder in his gut, taking him down to the ground in a heap. It was his goddamned turn to bleed. I got several good punches in, getting a sick pleasure from the sound of his nose breaking before someone was pulling me off him.

"Brett, man, you have to calm down," Luke spoke in my ear as I fought against him. "Calm the fuck down! I don't want to have to arrest you, too."

At the threat of not being able to stay with Kenzie, I finally relaxed against his hold. I'd been so consumed with rage that I hadn't even noticed the police cars and ambulance pull into the parking lot.

"Paramedics are loading Kenzie in the ambulance now, brother," Luke told me. "Let me handle this piece of shit. Go take care of your girl."

Rushing back over to Kenzie, I took her hand in mine, grasping tightly as the paramedics wheeled her gurney into the ambulance. After jumping in, I turned back before the doors closed to call out to Lizzy. She stood there waiting for us to pull away, tears rushing down her cheeks, her hands over her mouth as she cried for my girl.

"Call Savannah," I said. "Make sure there's someone to keep the kids. Do *not* let them find out about this."

Her head bobbed up and down, "Yeah, okay. I'll handle it

and meet you at the hospital. Take care of her, Brett," she ended on an anguished whisper.

"With my life, Lizzy-Lu."

I turned my attention back to Kenzie, taking in her mangled face as the doors were slammed shut and we drove away. Right then and there, I prayed to God that if he made sure she was all right, I'd spend the rest of my life protecting her.

———

"THE MOTHERFUCKER HASN'T SAID a word since we dragged his ass in."

I barely registered what Luke said as I paced the waiting room, anxious for news on Kenzie. She'd woken up halfway to the hospital, sobbing hysterically and talking about having to take the kids and run. Lance had found her and her flight instinct had kicked in hard. I couldn't let that happen. I'd be damned if I let that son of a bitch take them away from me.

"I swear to god, Luke, if I get my fucking hands on him, I'll kill him."

"He's in lockup, man. Just focus on your girl for now. You have any idea how he tracked her down?"

I raked my hands through my hair as I collapsed into one of the hard plastic chairs. "No idea. When she woke up in the ambulance, all she'd say was that she needed to leave. That she needed to get the kids and they needed to take off. She wants to run again, man. I can't let her do that. I can't lose them."

"Shit," he muttered.

"Yeah."

"What are you going to do?"

My head dropped in defeat as I admitted, "I don't have a damn clue. Right now, I just need to know she's okay."

WORTH THE WAIT   231

As if God was answering my prayers, the doctor came walking into the waiting room. "You're family of Ms. Webster?"

"Yeah, that's me," I rushed out as I hurried over to where he stood. "Is she okay? Can I see her?"

"She's going to be fine.

At that, I could finally breathe again. Knowing she was going to be okay was the biggest relief I'd ever felt.

The doctor continued speaking. "She has a concussion and a few fractured ribs. Lost of bruising. The cuts on her lip were mainly superficial, but we had to stitch up the one on her cheek. She'll be in pain for a while, but nothing she won't heal from." He briefly turned his eyes to Luke, fury laced through his words as he said, "I've made sure to photograph and document each and every one of the injuries. *Including* the shoe prints on her ribs and back.

I had to push down my rage. I couldn't hunt that bastard down and kill him when Kenzie needed me. "Can I go see her?"

"Yes, I'll take you back there now."

I didn't even bother glancing back at Luke as I headed down the hall; my only focus was on the woman who was sole my reason for living. I just needed to get to her and everything would be okay.

KENZIE

I TRIED to argue with the doctor when he told me he was keeping me overnight for observation. I needed to get out of the damned hospital. I needed to get to my kids and get out of Cloverleaf. I had no idea where we'd go, but I just knew I had to get them away before Lance got out, which he undoubtedly would.

I'd tried my hardest to fight the effects of the pain meds they'd given me, but it was no use. Sleep eventually took over.

By the time I'd opened my eyes again, it was already daytime. The sun was shining so bright, the sky a perfect, cloudless blue. It was beautiful outside. So beautiful that the weight currently sitting on my chest slowly suffocating me, felt out of place. It shouldn't have been possible for bad things to happen on such pretty days. With the dread I was feeling, it would have been more appropriate for the skies to be dark gray, rain falling in sheets as lightning and thunder cut through the air. Looking out the window to see birds chirping and the breeze gently blowing felt like a slap in the face.

My room was full as all of my friends, my new family, had come to give me their support, but as they argued over how the situation with Lance should be handled, all I could do was stare out that window, cursing myself for ever thinking I was clever enough to outsmart him. I should have known he wouldn't let me go. Even with everything I had on him, it still hadn't been enough.

"Beauty," Brett whispered from beside me, stroking my hair and pulling my attention away from the window to those expressive, dark eyes of his. "Running isn't the answer. You need to stay and fight. Don't let him win, baby."

"I *can't* fight him, Brett," I stated firmly. "Don't you get it? I'm a fucking nail tech. He's a partner at a big time law firm. He has the money and the connections to take everything away from me. He's going to take my babies." My voice broke as tears fell down my bruised cheeks. "My babies, Brett. He threatened to take my babies from me," I finished on a pained sob.

He leaned over the bed rail and pulled me into an embrace,

mindful of my sore ribs. "But what about that stuff you threatened him with? You said you hacked into his accounts. Can't we use that against him?"

A dry, sarcastic laugh bubbled up in my throat. "It's useless. He covered it all up after I threatened him. I've got nothing."

"What information did you have, Kenzie?" Luke asked, stepping away from Emmy to come to the other side of my bed. When I'd woken up that morning, I'd been shocked to see everyone I cared about in the room with me. Brett, Emmy and Luke, Savannah and Jeremy, Lizzy and Trevor, Gavin and Stacia, Ben and Mickey. They were all there. Jeremy's mother had once again offered to babysit the twins, who had been told that Mommy was in an accident but was doing just fine and would be home soon. They'd all come to try and find a way to help me out of my mess. The men tried to think of different ways to make Lance suffer painfully, while the women talked about places to hide the body. My chest warmed with love for all of them, even though I knew it was pointless.

"He'd been taking bribes for years. Destroying evidence in cases against the people he was prosecuting in exchange for payoffs. I'm talking hundreds of thousands of dollars. Prostitutes, drugs, you name it. He framed another lawyer at Spaulding, Jefferies, & Dunn. An innocent person lost everything because I thought I was smarter than Lance."

"Jesus Christ," Luke muttered.

"Yeah, so you understand what I'm dealing with now. If he's capable of doing that to someone, I have no doubt he'd do everything in his power to take my kids away, just to make me suffer."

"Wait," Savannah interrupted. "You said Spaulding, Jefferies & Dunn?"

"Yeah, why?" I questioned.

Her forehead wrinkled in deep thought for several seconds

as we all stared at her. Then she turned to look at Ben. The two of them communicated silently with each other from across the room, keeping the rest of us in the dark. I was just about to ask what was going on when she finally spoke again.

"I think I have an idea."

CHAPTER THIRTY-THREE

KENZIE

EVERYONE EVENTUALLY CLEARED out not too long after Savannah and Ben left to go put whatever insane idea she had in her head into motion. With promises to stop by Brett's house later that night once I was released, they left me and Brett alone in my hospital room, curled up in the tiny bed together. Neither of us had said a word for hours as we lay together.

Finally, having had enough of the silent tension that filled the room, Brett spoke. "I can't lose you, beauty," he said quietly against my neck. The agony in his voice caused my silent tears to fall even faster. I wanted so desperately to tell him that he wasn't going to, but I couldn't force the lie past my lips. Because that's exactly what it would have been. A lie. If whatever hare-brained scheme Savannah was working up fell through, I knew exactly what I would do. I would take my kids and run. I'd leave behind the life and people I'd come to love if it meant keeping them safe.

"I love you," was the only response I was able to give him. "No matter what, Brett, I will *always* love you."

There was a soft knock on the door before another word

could be said. Savannah came through, pulling us both out of the depressing thoughts running through our heads.

"Hey, sweets, how you feeling?"

"I've been better, but I'll be great if this plan of yours works."

She graced me with a small smile before pushing the door all the way open. Ben walked through, quickly followed by a short, older man. If I had to guess, I would have put him in his late sixties, early seventies. He had a gentle disposition and a kind face. With his white hair and round belly, it felt like I was meeting the real life Santa Claus.

"Kenzie, Brett, this is our boss, Bradford Pruett. He's the founding partner of Pruett & Carter."

"The law firm here in town?" I asked in confusion.

"Yeah, I'm a paralegal there and Ben's an associate. We specialize in handling family law cases."

"Oh, dear girl," Mr. Pruett said softly as he walked up to my bed and extended his hand. "It's a pleasure to meet you. I just wish it could have been under different circumstances."

I sat up in the bed as Brett moved to the chair next to it to give me room, and shook his hand. "Nice to meet you, too."

"When you told us the name of the law firm Lance works for earlier, I knew it sounded familiar, but it took me a moment to figure out where I'd heard that name before. Then it hit me."

"You see, Ms. Webster," Mr. Pruett chimed in. "My cousin is Reginald Spaulding." When I continued to look at him in confusion, he pressed forward. "The *Spaulding* in Spaulding, Jefferies, & Dunn and the managing partner of the firm."

My eyes grew wide and my mouth dropped as I tried to wrap my brain around what he'd just said. Unable to form an intelligible sentence, I was struck mute as Brett spoke an excited, "No shit?" from beside me.

"That's right. Our family founded that firm years and years

ago. It was actually where I started my career before deciding something smaller was more my pace. I moved here and started up my practice, but I've remained close with all of my relatives in Ohio. I make an effort to travel there at least twice a year. Funny thing, that six degrees of separation, isn't it?"

"Mr. Pruett, please forgive me, but I'm not sure I see how this pertains to my situation."

Ben stepped forward and placed his hand on the old man's shoulder. "We did some digging into your allegations against Lance. We wanted to make absolutely certain there wasn't anything left out there that could lead back to him being the one accepting bribes."

Hope burst in my chest as Ben talked. "Were you able to find anything?"

"Our highly skilled, very well paid private detective was able to track something down," Mr. Pruett answered.

The grin that spread across Savannah's face was positively beaming. "Apparently, the dude turns into a talker after he gets off. He had a little thing on the side he'd spill all his dirty little secrets to after they had sex. Only problem was, he didn't take into account how pissed off she might be when he up and left her to come track you down. Turns out, she had his bun cooking in her oven when he bailed. The woman's all too happy to spill every last dirty detail as revenge for being knocked up and ditched."

"You're kidding me," I gasped.

"It's also been discovered that he enjoyed videotaping some of his more...illicit adventures. My guess is he didn't expect Baby Mama to make copies of her own as a failsafe. He'd know all of this if he bothered to return any of her calls."

"Oh my god!" I laughed. "Never underestimate a woman scorned."

"No matter how smart a man is, it's guaranteed their dicks

will always make them stupid in the end."

The three men in the room all turned to glower at Savannah.

"What?" she asked with a shrug. "Don't act like it's not the truth."

Ben chuckled and shook his head. "Anyway, it would appear the asshole thinks he's so untouchable that he managed to let this slide past his radar."

"So what now?" Brett asked.

Mr. Pruett's gaze bounced between the two of us. "Well, I think that with this, paired with the assault charges for what he did to Ms. Webster, it's safe to say his career will be coming to an abrupt end."

"And jail time?" I cut in.

"Well, he'll have to go to trial for the assault. Charges will undoubtedly be pressed for the bribery, not to mention that he framed a colleague. At the very least he'll be looking at two to five years behind bars."

"Two to five years? *That's it?*" Brett hissed. I could see the muscle ticking in his jaw as his hands clenched into fists by his sides. He looked like he was ready to blow. He was out for blood where Lance was concerned. Anything less than hard time wasn't going to cut it for him.

But I had other plans. The last thing I wanted was to sit through a trial. I didn't want to have to see Lance every single day or testify against him. I just wanted it to go away. I wanted *him* to go away. I wanted the chance to get back to the life I'd built. I wanted to live happily, knowing that I never had to look over my shoulder again, and that my children were always safe.

"I'm not pressing charges," I stated firmly, catching everyone's undivided attention.

"What? Are you kidding me?" Brett shouted, shooting up from his chair and leaning over me. "Beauty, you can't let him get away with this. He needs to pay."

"Honey," I said softly, stroking his cheek covered in stubble from a few days of missed shaves. "I don't care about vengeance or making him pay. None of that matters to me. The only thing that matters is that he's out of our lives for good. Don't you see? With this information, we can make that happen."

"How do you plan on doing that?" I could see the uncertainty in his eyes. He honestly believed that unless Lance was in jail, there was no escaping him. But I knew otherwise.

"I know Lance. The only way to really get to him is to hit him where it hurts. His career and reputation are all that's ever mattered to him. That's why I thought I was safe when I took the twins and ran the first time. But now I have indisputable evidence. He can't slither his way out of it this time. This can work, baby. You have to trust me."

Releasing a frustrated breath, Brett sat on the corner of the bed and ran his hands through his hair. The room remained deathly silent as everyone waited for his reaction. After a few minutes, he finally looked back at me. "Are you sure about this, baby?"

"I'm positive," I smiled.

"All right. What's the plan?"

It took a lot of convincing to get Brett on board, but after an hour of talking, Savannah, Ben and Mr. Pruett left my hospital room having agreed that, in the end, what I wanted to do would garner the best outcome for me and my babies.

"I can't believe we're just going to let that fucker walk," Brett grumbled once everyone was gone. He climbed back into the bed with me and wrapped me in his arms, planting a gentle kiss on my lips, mindful of the split from Lance's attack.

"It's all going to work out for the best. I promise."

"I hope you're right," he sighed.

I looked up at him with a grin. "I am. Now take me home. I want to be back under the same roof with my family."

His dark eyes shined brightly as he smiled back at me. "Whatever you want, beauty."

CHAPTER THIRTY-FOUR

KENZIE

"YOU DON'T HAVE to go in there with me," I told Brett as we stood with Mr. Pruett inside the Sheriff's department. He stood rigid, his eyes laser-focused on the door we were about to walk through.

"Like fuck I'm letting you in there with that man by yourself."

"I'm not going to be alone. Mr. Pruett's going to be there with me."

I had to bite the inside of my cheek to keep from laughing at the frown Brett shot me. He'd been anxious all morning long, wanting to put the meeting off until I was healed. But I was finished with waiting. When we left the hospital the day before, my entire body felt lighter, like the thousand pound weight I'd been carrying on my shoulders all those years had finally lifted. I knew my plan was going to work; I felt it in my bones. My mood finally matched the beauty of the day. I was walking on cloud nine until we arrived home.

I hadn't been prepared for the tears in my babies' eyes when they took in the bruises on my face.

"Mommy!" Callie cried out, running over to me. I tried to suppress the wince as she barreled into me, but the jarring of my ribs sent a shockwave of pain through me. "I'm sorry," she whimpered as she pulled back, afraid of hurting me any worse.

"It's okay, honey pot." I took her hand and led her to the couch, Brett and Cameron following after me. When I was seated somewhat comfortably, I opened my arms so she could climb up into my lap. Once she settled, I wrapped my arms around her and hugged my little girl tightly.

"Brett said you was in a assident."

"That's right, baby. But Mommy's okay now. Just a few bumps and bruises."

I looked over to where Cam sat with Brett, his head hanging low as he clutched on to Brett's arm like a vise.

"What's the matter, bubs?" I asked, reaching over to lift his chin. One loan tear trailed down his cheek from those hazel eyes. "Oh, honey. I'm going to be all right. Don't be sad."

"Was it Daddy?" he asked in a huffed voice. His words were quiet but the impact of them hit me like a two-ton car.

Brett's entire body went solid as he looked over at me. "What?" I asked my son.

"Did Daddy give you all those boo-boos? He always yelled and gave you boo-boos when we lived with him. I don't like him. He's a meanie and I never wanna see him again."

Pain sliced through my chest. I'd failed at protecting them from Lance's violence. I thought I'd kept them away from it, not allowing them to see what their own father had been capable of, but I'd let them down. Never again. If it took the rest of my life, I would make sure I never *ever* had to see the pained expression in my children's eyes that I was seeing right then. I would make it up to them. I would make it right.

"You don't have to worry about him anymore, sweetie. He's gone. It's just us now, okay?"

"Can Brett be our new daddy?" Callie looked up into my eyes and asked so sincerely, so earnestly.

"Yeah," Cameron shouted. "I want Brett to be my new daddy! I love him and he's nice and he always buys us presents and makes us burritos at night."

My gaze wandered over to Brett to see his own eyes were glistening with unshed tears. When he looked at me in question, I gave him a small nod, letting him know it was okay.

"I'd love nothing more than to be y'all's daddy," Brett told my kids, his voice raspy as he tried to hold back his tears. "I'll spend forever being nice and buying you presents and making you into burritos, if that's what you guys want."

"*Yay!*" they both yelled, jumping from our laps in excitement, and just like that, all the negativity was gone. Our family was together, strong and happy, just as it should be.

I was determined to keep my promise to them, which was why I didn't want to wait. I had to see Lance right away. I had to finish this.

Cupping his bristly cheek, I gave Brett a kiss and spoke against his lips, "The sooner we get this done, the sooner it ends."

"Then let's do this," he huffed. "But you'll have to cross over my dead fucking body if you think I'm not going in there with you."

"Fine," I relented. "But you have to keep your cool, Brett. Promise me."

"I promise, beauty."

With one last kiss, we turned to face the door.

"You ready?" Mr. Pruett asked with his hand on the knob. I gave a curt nod and steeled my spine. There was no way in hell I was going to show Lance an ounce of weakness.

I paused for just a moment after crossing the threshold into the room. I knew Brett had gotten a hold of Lance in that parking lot. I just had no idea how much damage he'd done. But I'd have been lying if I said I felt even one ounce of sympathy as I looked at his pummeled face. He looked a thousand times worse than I did. I had to lock down the craving to launch myself at Brett and kiss him to death as I took in the damage inflicted on the across from me.

"You look like shit," I told him as I took a seat in one of the chairs on the other side of the table. Mr. Pruett sat down next to me as Brett stood in the corner, arms crossed over his massive chest, a menacing stare directed right at Lance. I got immense pleasure out of seeing him flinch when he caught Brett's glare.

"You don't look so good yourself," he sneered.

"Talk to her like that again and I'll re-break your nose, fucker. Maybe a cheekbone or jaw this time, too."

I hadn't thought it was possible, but I actually saw Lance's complexion pale under all those bruises at the sound of Brett's gravelly threat.

"What are you doing here, Mackenzie?" He asked with an air of boredom, like taking time away from his cell for our little chat was an inconvenience to him.

"I'm here because of this," I said, slapping the folder I'd gotten from Mr. Pruett onto the metal table and sliding it across to him. "Oh, and this is just a sample of everything I have on you." I grinned as he opened the folder. "I also have flash drives, videos, voice recordings, you name it. So just in case you think you can cover all this shit up *this time*, you might want to reconsider."

"And who's this guy?" Lance asked with a chin lift in Mr. Pruett's direction, still trying to act nonchalant even as he flipped through page after page of all his dirty little secrets.

"Oh, I'm so sorry," I laughed. "I forgot to introduce you. Mr. Pruett, this is my ex, the woman beater. Lance, this is Bradford

Pruett, my attorney." He blanched at the mention of his name, and right then, I knew he was aware of exactly who Mr. Pruett was. "I'm sure you've heard of him. He's Reginald Spaulding's cousin. You know, your boss? They're very close. Mr. Pruett also has copies of all of this, as well. So you see, this is no longer your word against mine. It's your word against his," I said with a flick of my thumb in my attorney's direction. I had to swallow down my laughter at the finger wave Mr. Pruett gave to Lance.

"Who do you think everyone at Spaulding, Jefferies, & Dunn would believe?" Lance scoffed with false bravado.

"Trust me, boy, my connections make yours look like child's play," the old man said. "Don't let the small town fool you. For every high-up official you think you have in your corner, I have four more who are even higher. I am *not* a man you want to go up against."

Wow! In the short amount of time I'd known Mr. Pruett I'd started to think of him as a kind, softly spoken man. I never thought he was capable of being so intimidating. I was happily proven wrong.

Lance's throat bobbed as he swallowed audibly, the tension finally beginning to show on his face as he turned back to me. "What do you want?"

Leaning forward, I braced my hands on the cold metal table and stared him down. I would never cower to this man again. "I want you to disappear from my life and my children's lives for good. I want you to go back to Ohio and leave us alone. Don't call. Don't write. Don't *ever* show up in Cloverleaf again. If I even so much as *think* you could be lurking around, I'm going to your boss and the police with everything I have, and I do mean *everything*. That includes Mr. Pruett's unwavering support."

"Unwavering," Mr. Pruett emphasized.

"If you leave me and the kids alone, not only will all of this go away," I told him, waving my hand at the folder in front of him, "but I won't press charges against you for the attack in the parking lot of my work. You'll get to leave here no worse for the wear. Well...I mean, aside from the broken nose and fucked-up face. But your life will still be perfectly intact."

Lance leaned back in his chair and clasped his cuffed hands in front of him. "And what about you?"

"What about me?"

"What are you getting from all of this?"

A huge, beaming grin stretched across my lips. "I get to go home knowing I never have to see your face again. I get to enjoy the fact that you have a pregnant woman out there, hell bent on destroying you for leaving her."

At that, his eyes grew to the size of salad plates.

"That's right. You know Gloria? The woman who kindly gave me all this stellar information? She's knocked up. Oh, and she's out for blood, Lance, so you might want to watch your back. Looks like you found your match with that one. I hope you two will be happy together."

"Gloria. That fucking slut," Lance hissed to himself through clenched teeth.

"There's one more thing I want from you before I go."

"Oh?" he asked sarcastically. "And what the hell could that be?"

I pulled the document from my bag, along with a pen and slid them over to him. "Sign it."

He scanned the papers before looking back up to me. "Are you fucking kidding me? They're *my* kids. I'm not signing over my rights!"

Placing my hands on the table, I calmly stood until I was leaning over, hissing in his face.

"You *will* sign over your rights to those children. Don't sit here and act like you give a shit about either of them, because we both know you don't. Give them a chance at a good life, Lance."

"So, what?" he sneered. "You want that fucking redneck back there to play daddy to *my* kids? I don't think so."

I slapped my hand down on the table so hard it echoed loudly through the room, startling a jump from him. "Goddamn it, Lance! For once in your pathetic fucking life, do something for someone else! If you don't sign those papers, I'll make sure to rain fucking *Hell* down on you so hard you'd wish you'd never crossed my path. I'm not the same woman I was when I was with you. I let you off easy. If you don't do this for me, I swear to every god in existence, I *will* make you pay for everything you've done to me and those children. Do. Not. Test. Me," I ground out so harshly spittle flew from my mouth, hitting him in the face.

I sat back in my chair slowly as Lance cowered away from me. The moment my butt hit the cold metal, Brett's soothing hand appeared on my shoulder. For just one second, Lance's eyes bounced back and forth between Brett and me, and I saw something flicker in the icy-blue depths, something that looked awfully close to regret. But as quickly as it was there, it was gone. He reached for the pen on the table and scribbled his signature on all the proper pages.

That was all it took. Thirty seconds and my children and I were finally free. I wanted to cry in relief as he pushed the pen and papers back toward me.

Grabbing both, I stuffed them in my purse and stood. "You can keep those," I said, pointing to the folder. "As soon as I walk out of this room they won't matter."

"What's that supposed to mean?" Lance asked.

The air in the room grew thick with tension as Brett looked at me with confusion in his eyes. Only Mr. Pruett knew what I was about to say. After all my talk about not wanting revenge, the kindly old man had helped me see the error of my ways.

"I told you *I* wouldn't leak that info to your bosses. But I didn't say anything about Gloria not doing it. I had a good, long chat with her last night. She's *really* upset with you, Lance." I gave him my best attempt at a sympathetic face.

Brett's jaw dropped as Lance started to sputter. "B-but... But, you said this would go away if I signed away my rights!"

"Yeah," I nodded. "*That* copy. But I had Mr. Pruett send everything we had to Gloria, along with all the photos and my doctor's statement from the hospital a few days ago." I glanced down at my watch. "Your bosses, and every other employee at your firm, should be receiving an email any second now. Looks like I don't have to press charges to see your ass behind bars after all."

"You vindictive bitch!" Lance tried to stand, but it was pointless. He was cuffed to the table, so there was no chance of his getting to me.

"You took everything from me," I whispered, staring him right in the eyes, letting every ounce of my hate for him shine through. "Other than my babies I had nothing. Now I'm going to take everything from you. Did you really think I was just going to let you walk away without paying for everything you did to me? How stupid are you?"

"I'll make you pay, Kenzie! I swear to Christ."

"I'm not too worried about that," I said with a shrug. "If I were you I'd concentrate on watching your back. Something tells me the guys in prison are a lot harder to beat up on than defenseless women." With that, I was finished. I walked away without so much as a backward glance. The second that door closed behind me I collapsed into Brett's arms and proceeded to sob like a baby.

"Beauty," he whispered in my ear after several minutes.

"You're starting to freak me out, here. Isn't this supposed to be a happy moment?"

"H-happy t-tears," I stuttered, wiping my nose against the soft cotton of his shirt. "S-so happy!"

Brett's entire body shook with laughter as he squeezed me tighter. "Christ, baby. I can't even begin to tell you how proud I am right now. That was fucking amazing to watch."

"Thanks," I whispered against his chest. "It felt pretty fucking amazing." When I finally pulled away, I was surprised to see all of my friends standing there.

"Well?" Lizzy asked, wringing her hands in front of her nervously. I knew exactly what she was asking.

"It's over," I whispered, trying to push back another wave of emotion trying to come to the surface. "It's finally over."

They all erupted in cheers as the women ran to engulf me in a gentle hug, mindful of my soar ribs and bruises. Once that was done, each man took their turn until I'd finally made it back to Brett.

"What are you guys doing here?" I asked, wiping more happy tears from my cheeks.

"You're family, babe," Emmy answered. "And we always support our family."

Family. I never knew it was possible to love so many people at one time. These people took me in when I had no one, and accepted me, scars and all. If I lived to be a million years old, I'd never find a more loving, caring group of people. I was blessed to have them in my life.

"Who's got the kids?"

Emmy answered, "Luke's mom has Matthew and Kathy's at your place with the twins."

"I'm seriously starting to worry that Mom's going to kidnap your kids and keep them as her own," Jeremy told me with a laugh.

As I smiled at everyone standing around me, Brett leaned down and whispered in my ear. "Let's head back to our rugrats, beauty."

My smile was positively beaming as I looked up at the love of my life. "Yeah," I breathed. "Let's go home."

EPILOGUE 1

BRETT

THREE MONTHS later

I'D NEVER GET USED to how Kenzie stole my breath each and every time I looked at her. I stood at the bar with a beer in my hand, watching her from where she sat, three-month-old Matthew in her arms as she chatted away with all the girls. My gaze wandered a little farther behind her to find Cameron and Callie running and laughing, blowing bubbles at each other. No doubt, they were going to be a soapy, sticky mess when we got home. Whoever had the genius idea to set bubbles out on the tables for all the wedding guests should have been strung up by the short hairs.

"Yeah, that's a pussy whipped expression if I've ever seen one," Trevor teased as he, Luke, Gavin, Jeremy, and Ben made their way over to where I was standing.

"Like any of you assholes have room to talk. Y'all stare at your women the exact same fucking way."

"Yeah," Jeremy sighed like a lovesick puppy as he gazed adoringly at his wife. He and Savannah dropped the bomb on us not too long ago that she was four months pregnant. They'd been keeping it on the down low until she was in her second trimester, but considering her tiny little belly was poking out of all her clothes, they wouldn't have been able to hide it anyway.

Loud laughter drew all of our attention to our girls. Emmy sat next to Kenzie, leaning in and laughing at something Savvy said as Kenzie rubbed on her tiny baby belly. Mickey, Stacia and Lizzy all surrounded them, each woman with a different expression of bliss on her face.

If you'd have told me a year ago that this was how my life was going to turn out, I'd have laughed in your face. But now I couldn't help but wonder how I ever functioned before Kenzie, Cameron and Callie came into my life. I woke up every morning with my woman curled up in my arms, thanking the Lord above for bringing those three into my life.

Yeah, they made me whole.

"So tonight's the night?" Trevor asked, giving my shoulder a nudge.

"Hell yeah," I grinned. I couldn't fucking wait.

Just then, the DJ's voice echoed through the dimly light room.

"It's that time, folks. Let's get the bride and groom out here for their first dance as husband and wife!"

Everyone in the packed ballroom broke out in applause.

"If you'll excuse me, assholes," Luke said with a shit-eating grin. "I need to take my wife for a spin on the dance floor."

Luke dragged a beaming Emmy to the floor as the rest of us took our seats.

"Hey there, beauty," I whispered into Kenzie's ear as I pulled my chair close to her.

"Hey, handsome, have I told you how sexy you look in a tux?"

My lips tipped up in a cocky smirk, and I gave her a wink.

Yeah, she wanted me bad. "That so? Well, play your cards right and I may just drag you into the coat closet before the night's out."

"Promises, promises," she teased, making me laugh.

"*Daddy! Daddy!*" Callie yelled as she and Cameron came running over to us. That was another thing I was never *ever* going to get tired of. After everything that had happened with Lance, and me telling them that I'd love nothing more than to be their father, they'd quickly taken to calling me Daddy. Every time that word slipped from one of their mouths, my heart jumped. I never thought it was possible to love anyone as much as I loved those two.

"Look it! I can make the biggest bubble in the world!"

"Mines is bigger!" Cameron insisted, trying to shove his sister out of the way.

"Hey, you two, no fighting," Kenzie scolded as she gently rocked a sleeping Matthew, still tucked comfortably in her arms.

I turned to them and leaned forward. "Tell you what, rugrats. If you promise not to fight for the rest of the night, I'll make sure you both get *two* pieces of cake! And wedding cake's the best cake in the universe."

"*Yay!*" they shouted with more enthusiasm and energy than I thought two little people were capable of having. Then they were off like a shot, running around and blowing bubbles like nothing had even happened.

When I turned back to Kenzie, she was passing the baby off to Luke's mom, Ilene.

"You're dealing with them when they're in the middle of their sugar high, you know that, right?"

"Wouldn't have it any other way," I told her, leaning in to steal a kiss. We turned back to the dance floor to watch as Emmy and Luke danced to some song about loving someone for a thousand years. I'd never admit it out loud, because it would make me sound like a pussy, but I was thrilled those two finally made their way back to each other.

"They look so happy, don't they?" Kenzie asked as she leaned back against me, resting her head on my shoulder.

"Yeah, beauty, they do." And I decided right there, that it was time. The moment was perfect. Reaching into the pocket of my tuxedo pants, I pulled out the ring I'd been carrying around for months, just waiting for this moment. "How'd you like to be that happy?"

"Already am, honey," she told me as she snuggled back, eyes still to the happy couple.

I held the ring up in front of her so she could see. "So you'll marry me then?"

Her gorgeous hazel eyes were wide, shining with tears as she spun around to look at me. "Really?"

"Really. I told you I was going to ask you to marry me, didn't I?"

She nodded enthusiastically, a few tears breaking free to flow down her cheeks. "Yes. You also told me I'd say yes."

The grin that stretched across my face was so wide it hurt my cheeks. "Well? Get to saying it then."

Her head fell back on a laugh before she lunged at me, wrapping her arms around my neck and kissing me for all she was worth. "Yes," she whispered against my lips. "Yes, I'll marry you."

"That's my girl," I spoke before taking the kiss deeper, slipping my tongue passed her lips. When we finally pulled ourselves away from each other, her breathing was erratic and there was a sexy flush on her cheeks and neck.

I'd just finished slipping the ring on her finger when she told me, "I got something for you, too?"

"Oh, yeah? Is it something that'll require us heading to the coat closet?" I asked with a wiggle of my brows.

"Ha! No. But I'm hoping you'll like it just as much." She grabbed her tiny purse off the table and opened it, pulling out a bunch of folded up papers. Her hands shook slightly as she handed them over.

As soon as I unfolded the document, my jaw dropped. Tears burned the back of my eyes as I read the first page over.

"Adoption papers? Are you serious?"

"Yeah, I'm very serious. I mean, only if this is what you want."

"Hell yeah, beauty!" I shouted, jumping from my chair and dragging her with me. "Hell yeah, I want this." I dipped her backwards and kissed the shit out of her. My girl just made my day. Hell, she'd just made my entire life.

"So you're happy?" she asked me once the kiss was broken.

"Ecstatic, baby. Never been so happy in all my life."

"I love you, Brett."

"Love you, too, beauty."

Life was perfect. I had my soon-to-be wife in my arms and we'd be going home later to tuck our kids into bed. I was living the dream.

And it was totally worth the wait.

EPILOGUE 2

THE CLOVERLEAF GANG

FIVE YEARS later

"OH, FOR THE LOVE OF..." Emmy muttered from her perch at the picnic table. "Matthew, stop pulling Everly's hair!"

"But, Momma! She started it!"

"I'll get him," Luke stated, planting a kiss on his wife's cheek before he stood to pull his son off Savannah and Jeremy's daughter.

"I swear," Savvy huffed. "Those two are going kill each other before the hit puberty."

"Nah," Stacia chirped. "I'm putting my money on those two getting married one day. Just you wait."

"Like hell, Jeremy grumbled as he took a pull of his beer.

"You saying my kid's not good enough for yours?" Luke asked defensively as he made his way back to the table.

"No, what I'm saying is Everly's never dating *anyone*. *Ever*."

Mickey let out a laugh as Jeremy glared in her direction. "Good luck with that. She's already a hardcore flirt, just like her mom."

Savannah gave Mickey a playful shove before stating, "Well then, she comes by it honestly. And like you have room to talk. With you and Ben as his parents, Conner's destined to be a tatted-up lawyer when he grows up." She gave a nod in the direction of Ben and Mickey's three-year-old son. "He's already doodling on his arms with sharpies."

"Dad!" Cameron called as he and Callie ran over to where their parents sat with all their aunts and uncles. "Uncle Trevor's hogging the ball again."

Everyone laughed as Lizzy let out a frustrated breath. "Every damn time," she complained as she passed her one-year-old baby girl, Maggie, over to Stacia so she could try to wrangle her husband. Maggie was their second child. They had a four-year-old boy who Trevor insisted be named Merle. After five months of silent treatment and no sex whatsoever, he finally broke down and agreed to name their unborn son Rick.

"Are we going to have to ban flag football from our Sunday family day?" Gavin shouted after her as he bounced his and Stacia's eight-month-old daughter, Blaire, on his knee."

"Wouldn't do any good," she yelled back as she made her way over to where Trevor stood with the rest of the kids. "He'd find a way to act like a big-ass child no matter what!"

The gang burst into laughter at the sound of Trevor's whiny, "What'd I do now?" from across the park.

"They kicking a lot today?" Callie asked, rubbing on her mother's protruding belly as Kenzie leaned back in Brett's arms with her feet resting on the bench. It was her third pregnancy. Only about a year after getting married four and a half years ago, Brett and Kenzie welcomed their son, Cole, into the world. The third pregnancy was unexpected, but no less welcome. And when they discovered they'd be having twins, they were on cloud nine. They were also done. Five kids was more than enough. Kenzie had even gone as far as to threaten Brett with bodily harm if he ever tried to knock her up again.

"Like soccer players, honey pot," Kenzie answered her daughter.

"I can't wait to meet them," Callie said in awe, smiling up at her mom and dad.

"You're such a great big sister, ladybug," Brett told her, kissing her on the top of her head.

"Thanks, Daddy." She grinned lovingly at Brett before she and Cam took off to play football with—a hopefully better behaved—Trevor.

As the gang watched their little ones run around the park, all giggling and happy, each one sent up a prayer of thanks for the life they'd been granted. They each had it all. Friends who had become their family in the quaint little town of Cloverleaf.

Life had thrown some serious curve balls, each of them going through their own ups and downs, but they'd all managed to pull through it with the love and help of each other.

Yeah, life was great for the Cloverleaf gang.

And every day was better than the last.

The End

*meet the ladies of Girl Talk in **Seducing Lola***

Seducing Lola

I'VE HAD my fair share of bad relationships. I've dated liars, cheaters, shoe fetishists, and everything in between. Sure, these

experiences would make any woman cynical when it comes to dipping her toe back into the dating pool, but I used my past for good and made a career out of helping other women avoid going down the same paths I had.

And I was damn good at it.

Until a random act of fate set my life on a course I'd been avoiding for years, and put me in the crosshairs of a man that made me feel things I swore to never feel again.

Now I'm in his sights and it seems like he'll stop at nothing to seduce the hell out of me. He might hold my career in the palm of his hands, but if Grayson Lockhart thinks he can black-mail me into submission with his sexy voice and sexy hands and sexy everything, then he's...probably right.

Turn the page for a sneak peek

SEDUCING LOLA EXCERPT

Prologue

IF YOU'D HAVE ASKED my twenty-year-old self what I saw in my future ten years down the road, I probably would've answered the same way as every other naïve co-ed living the college dream on Sorority Row.

I'd be married to the love of my life, raising our two perfect children in the suburbs—because the city is no place to bring up a family, obviously—and driving a top-of-the-line SUV that all the minivan moms would envy because I had *way* too much style to ever be caught dead driving a minivan.

Clearly, my twenty-year-old self was an idiot.

It was she who forgave—then was subsequently dumped by —my college sweetheart after finding him pile-driving my sorority sister from behind on the handmade quilt I'd spent countless hours creating out of his old high school football T-shirts as a birthday present. His brilliant excuse? "You're just not adventurous enough, Lola. She's willing to try things in bed that you aren't."

Apparently refusing to allow him to film us having sex and entering it into a contest on a porn site was just too *vanilla* for him. Last I heard, he was making a killing on the amateur scene.

Unfortunately, my twenty-one and twenty-two-year-old selves weren't all that smart either.

It was my twenty-one-year-old self who discovered I'd unwittingly been made a beard by Brad, the guy I had dated for six months, because his evangelical parents just "wouldn't understand."

BTW, Brad and Phillip's wedding was a really lovely affair. He asked me to stand as his best *woman*—since he considered our relationship the reason he finally made his way out of the closet—but I turned down the honor, choosing instead to get annihilated on mojitos at the open bar.

My twenty-two-year-old self thought I had finally found a decent guy. That was until I came home to find him doing something I'll never be able to unsee to a pair of Louboutins I'd spent the better part of a year saving up for.

The saddest part? I hadn't even had a chance to wear them before his defilement. I didn't have the heart to throw them in the trash, so I let him take them with him when I kicked his ass out.

I should've known better, honestly. It wasn't like I'd grown up in a home with my very own personal June and Ward Cleaver. Oh no, my parents split when I was only six years old. And it was anything but amicable. My mom never kept her hatred for my father secret. And dear old Dad never hid the string of women he kept on tap, one for whatever mood he may've been in. It was shocking that I hadn't grown bitter at an even younger age, having to deal with their drama, but I was in my early twenties and still a believer in happily ever afters.

Like I said, I was an idiot.

Now I know what you're thinking. After three miserable failures, I was probably a jaded cynic who was convinced true love didn't exist.

Well, you'd only be half right. See, I believed in love, sure... as long as it was happening to anyone other than me. I'd been the fateful target of that bastard Cupid's stupid-ass arrow three times already; I had no desire to go for a fourth. I wasn't anti-relationship when it came to *other people*. To each their own and all that jazz. And I didn't *hate* men. I just didn't believe they were of any use to me for anything other than a few hours of fun that eventually led to a—hopeful—mutual release before I sent them on their way.

I learned from my mistakes, grown wise as the years passed. I knew exactly what I wanted out of my life, and believe me, there wasn't a shitty picket fence in sight. If the suburbs were for families, then the city was exactly where I was meant to be. I was a successful, accomplished thirty-two-year-old woman who'd gotten where I was in life by hard work, perseverance, and the cluelessness of women all around the world.

My name was known in households all throughout Washington State. I, along with my two best friends, hosted Seattle's most successful female-based talk radio show, aptly titled *Girl Talk*. I'd managed to make more money in the past ten years by offering relationship advice to helpless women than I'd ever know what to do with.

It was safe to say the rose-colored glasses were off. I lived in the real world where men cheated and women drowned their sorrows in vats of Ben & Jerry's.

Sure, I wasn't living the future I saw for myself when I was twenty, but then again, at twenty, I still thought Brad Pitt and Jennifer Aniston were *meant to be*, that *Wedding Crashers* was cinematic brilliance, and that the whole Tom Cruise/Oprah couch jumping "I'm in love with Katie Holmes" thing was actually romantic. What the hell did I know back then?

A lot had changed over the years. And as I gazed out the floor-to-ceiling windows of my penthouse apartment, overlooking the Puget Sound, I could honestly say without a shred of doubt that I wouldn't have it any other way.

Chapter 1

Lola

"And you won't *believe* what that asshole you call a father did this time!" My mother's voice echoed through the receiver, drowning out the honking cars and the clicking of my five-inch Gucci heels on the pavement as I crossed 7th Avenue. The typical bustling city sounds were lost as Elise Abbatelli ranted and raved through my cell phone.

"No telling, Ma," I answered with a roll of my eyes.

"Well I'll tell you!" she continued. "He showed up at The Met with that... that... *woman*! It was like he wasn't the slightest bit embarrassed to have a *call girl* on his arm during the mayor's birthday celebration! I tell you, Lola, that man has no shame whatsoever. It's humiliating to know we run in the same circles."

I let out a deep sigh as I shoved open the glass door of the Starbucks near my building and joined the line of customers, all of us in desperate need of a morning pick-me-up. I inhaled the rich scent of brewing coffee and the sweetness of the pastries as I searched for my calm. Talking to my mother had a tendency to drive me a little batshit. Then again, I came by it honestly, seeing as my own mother was more than just a little crazy.

"For the last time, Ma, Chelsea isn't a call girl. She's a gold digger. Contrary to popular belief, there really is a difference. And you wouldn't run in the same circles if you'd just stop attending all the events you know Dad's going to be at. The only one you're torturing is yourself. Hell, no one would even know you two had been married once if you'd quit going around and announcing it to all of Manhattan."

"Don't you sass me, Lola Arianna Abbatelli!"

The irony that my father's surname stood for "little priest" in Italian wasn't lost on me. The last thing Roberto Abbatelli could ever be compared to was a priest. The man was toeing the line of sixty and *still* couldn't keep his dick in his pants. But then again, why would he? He built his investment firm from the ground up, eventually earning so much success he'd been listed in *Forbes* more times than I could count. With money and power like his, fidelity and commitment were a joke.

"I'm not sassing you, Ma." I sighed again, moving up another step as the long line shuffled forward. "I'm just stating facts. You've been divorced for over two decades. With the money you got from that settlement, you could go anywhere, yet you *insist* on staying in Manhattan where you know you'll run into Dad constantly. What's the point? Move to the Caribbean or something! Find a smokin' hot cabana boy to fill your free time." I heard a masculine snort of laughter come from behind me but was too entrenched in my mother's rantings to give it any thought.

"I *have* a life," she insisted haughtily. If I'd been standing in front of her, I had no doubt her chin would have been tilted up, nose in the air. "I have friends—"

"You have acquaintances. And I've met most of them, Ma. Believe me, you wouldn't be missing out by shirking them off first chance you get."

She didn't argue with that, knowing good and well most of those so-called friends were nothing but bloodsucking leeches. "I have my work."

I let out an indelicate snort. "You don't work!"

"I'll have you know I'm on the boards of many very influential charities."

Another eye roll. "You can write a check from the beaches of Barbados."

"Well... I have your brother!"

There was no way I could suppress my eye roll just then. "That's just sad, Ma. Dom's a grown man. You should've cut the cord a long time ago. You're making excuses."

"I am not!"

I lowered my voice, making sure to keep my tone soft as I said, "I get it, Ma. I do. Dad was the love of your life and it sucks having to let him go, but you're never going to move on if you're constantly bumping into each other. And I'm tired of seeing you get your heart broken. You deserve better than anything he could ever give you."

The line was silent for several seconds before she finally declared, "I'm happy with my life, thank you very much."

My shoulders slumped ever so slightly. It wasn't the first time we'd had that particular conversation, but it didn't hurt any less. My mother was in pain and refused to do anything about it. I tried to be understanding, but it was just so damned frustrating. It was like beating a dead horse, then turning around and banging my head against a brick wall. Trying to make her see reason was pointless.

"If you say so," I told her as the line shuffled again. "But it's your loss. There's probably a young guy named Marco on one of those islands just waiting for you to come and show him what it means to be a *real* man."

"So scandalous," she chided, but I could hear the smile in her voice. "If you're really concerned with making me happy, you'd quit this nonsense and give me the grandbabies I've been dying for."

I finally reached the front of the line, holding my phone to my chest and placing my order before moving to the side and lifting the receiver back to my ear.

"Hate to break it to you, Ma, but if you want grandbabies, you need to start annoying Dom about it. Odds are he's got at least one illegitimate kid out there anyway. He is his father's son, after all."

Mom gasped loudly, the very definition of scandalized. She was probably clutching her pearls just then. "You watch your mouth, young lady!"

I ignored her chastisement. It had always been like that. As far as she was concerned, Dominic would always be her "perfect little boy," philandering man-whore and all.

"As it stands, if some guy's spunk manages to break through the condom I'll definitely be making him wear *and* my birth control pills, we have some serious problems of the biblical variety."

"Language, Lola!" my mother admonished at the same time someone let out a choked cough from behind me.

I chanced a quick glance over my shoulder, my face drawing in the "sorry, didn't mean for you to hear me" look I seemed to have to paste on my face every time I was out in public. That filter most people were born with, you know, the one that kept them from spewing totally inappropriate things when in crowded places? Yeah, I so didn't have that. And it wasn't something that had ever embarrassed me. Maybe it was the Italian in me, but I'd always said exactly what was on my mind right when I thought it, eavesdroppers be damned. I mainly apologized because it was the politically correct thing to do.

The man who'd just heard me trying to convince my mom to get her groove back *Stella* style while shooting down her hope for future grandbabies all in the same conversation was standing two feet away, hands in his front pockets and a knowing smile stretched across his picture-worthy face.

"Sorry," I mouthed as I did a quick scan of his body. In just those few moments, I was able to tell his suit was high quality, no doubt designer. And judging from the broad expanse of his shoulders, tailored to fit his body. And what a body it was. Slightly disheveled chocolate brown hair, amazing green eyes, a square, chiseled jaw, and a nose that was just crooked enough to make him appear rugged without going Owen Wilson overboard wrapped up the insanely hot package. The dude was most definitely spank bank material.

I'd made an art out of reading men over the past decade, and this guy, with his expensive suit and casual confidence, screamed money and power. Both of those attributes, while hot as hell, were something I stayed far, *far* away from when it came to the opposite sex.

I tended to go for middle-of-the-line good guys who didn't take life too seriously. I found they were the easiest to scrape off whenever the sex became monotonous or I just got bored and wanted to move on. Men who wielded power in their professional lives had a tendency to think they could carry that over into the personal side—including the bedroom. And when it came to sex, I *always* had the power. I didn't allow it any other way. Losing power only led to heartbreak, and despite what my career would lead people to believe, I was of the firm opinion that heartbreak was for suckers.

So, despite the fact that the man behind me was the type to rev my engine, sadly, it wasn't meant to be.

"Lola? Lola, you there?"

I spun back around at my mother's voice, determined to put Mr. Power Suit out of my mind. "I'm here."

"You know, there's nothing wrong with settling down," she told me, the same line she used every single time we talked.

I snorted—*loudly*. "There's nothing right with it either."

"Lola Arianna—"

"Abbatelli, I raised you better than that," I interrupted, imitating her nasally, put-out tone as I finished her trademark sentence for her.

"I do *not* sound like that," she harrumphed, causing me to smile.

"How about this. You don't push me for marriage and babies, and I won't push you for hot, sweaty island sex. Deal?"

"What did I do," she started, undoubtedly looking at her ceiling as she spoke to God—yet another thing I'd grown accustomed to seeing during my life, "to deserve such a crass, uncouth daughter?"

"Just lucky, I guess," I answered snidely as the barista called my name and sat my drink on the counter. "Now I have to go," I told her as I pushed through the morning crowd, trying to get to that big cup of caffeinated goodness. "I need to get to the station and I haven't had coffee. I'll call you back tonight and we can talk shit about Dad for your allotted thirty minutes."

"I do not talk *shit*, Lola," she said, as if the very thought were beneath her. "I simply express my exasperation at his childish antics."

"Tomato, to-mah-to." I shrugged, even though she couldn't see. "Gotta go. Love you, Ma."

"Love you too, sweet pea. Talk soon."

I disconnected the call and slid my cell back into my red Kate Spade bag before reaching for my venti white mocha. "Mmm," I hummed, eyes closed in delight as I sucked down that first necessary sip. That first hit was always the best. And yes, I was aware that comparison made me sound like a crack addict, but whatevs. I was a hardcore coffee addict and wasn't the slightest bit repentant.

"If that conversation I heard a few minutes ago wasn't intriguing enough to catch my attention, that noise you just made certainly would've done it."

I opened my eyes and landed on a pair of slightly familiar grassy green ones. "And if a lame attempt at a pickup line like that were enough to catch my attention, I'd have to shoot myself," I replied with a sweet smile as I blatantly looked Mr. Power Suit up and down. *Damn, what a shame.*

"Grayson!" the barista called, setting a drink on the counter behind me. "I have a venti Americano at the counter for Grayson Lockhart!"

"I take it you're Grayson Lockhart?" I asked, quirking an eyebrow as he stepped closer and reached past me to grab his coffee, paying extra attention to brush the sleeve of his jacket against my arm as he kept his stare focused on mine. I had to give it to him—he was good. His eyes never once deviated past my chin, and I was rocking some pretty sweet cleavage if I did say so myself. Not slutty cleavage, mind you. Classy cleavage. I was a professional woman, after all, but I'd also been blessed with the Abbatelli curves. I might've only been five feet, two inches tall, but I rocked a full C-cup, had a teeny waist, a J-Lo booty, and what my nonna lovingly referred to as "child-bearing hips."

Even if I wanted to cover up what God gave me, I wouldn't have been able to. At present, the short-sleeve, boatneck red and black Versace dress I was wearing hugged my curves and bared a modest half inch of décolletage. It wasn't too much, just enough to hint at the more that lay beneath, but Mr. Power Suit made a conscious effort not to look. I was impressed.

"And you're venti nonfat, no-whip white mocha for Lola," he said with a devastatingly handsome smile. A smile that would make any woman—other than me—shudder with need.

"You got it, Suit." I sidestepped, prepared to go around him when he spoke up again.

"I'm clearly at a disadvantage here. See, you have my full name, but I only have your first name and drink preference."

I scrunched my face in mock speculation as I tapped my chin. "That's quite the conundrum you got there, Grayson Lockhart. Hope you get it straightened out." I patted his chest and moved around him, heading for the door.

"You're really not going to give me your name?" he asked, a bewildered smile on his face that said with his good looks he was used to getting what he wanted. Unfortunately for him, so was I, and he wasn't currently on my list of wants.

"I'm really not. Stings, I know. But I have no doubt your pride will bounce back, someone as handsome as you and all."

"So you think I'm handsome?" he called out, shamelessly watching my hips as I sauntered toward the exit, his lips turned up in a seductive grin.

"I might not be interested, but I'm not blind," I scoffed, one corner of my mouth tilting into a smirk as I turned and walked backward to continue our banter.

"Not interested, huh?"

I shrugged nonchalantly as I pushed the glass door open with my shoulder. "I've made it a habit never to date someone prettier than me. See ya around, Lockhart."

The door closed on his hearty laugh as I headed back out into the gray Seattle morning.

Nothing like a little harmless flirting to brighten a girl's day.

OTHER TITLES FROM THE LADIES OF GIRL TALK

Tempting Sophia

HAVING my heart broken once was enough to make me give up on the idea of love all together. Instead of searching for The One I decided to embrace variety and turn my back on monogamy. I made a living convincing women they didn't need a man to feel complete.

And I totally rocked at it.

Until the man who shattered my happily ever after came waltzing back into my life, determined to make me fall for him all over again.

He claims that I'm the love of his life. He wants a second chance, and it seems like he'll stop at nothing to tempt the hell out of me. But if Dominic Abbatelli thinks he can win me back with his puppy dog eyes, heartfelt apologies, and declarations of love then he's...probably right.

Enticing Daphne

IT'S easy to stop believing in happily ever afters when the man you thought you'd spend the rest of your life with abandons you right before your wedding day. After that disastrous event I decided that commitment was for suckers. I was young, successful, and in the prime of my life.

I didn't need a man to make me happy.

Then an unexpected blast from the past came waltzing into my studio and decided I was a challenge he was more than willing to accept. The only problem is that he doesn't remember he's met me before.

He's the ultimate playboy, determined to stop at nothing until he entices the hell out of me. But if Caleb McMannus thinks he can lure me in with his sinful looks and silver tongue, then he's... probably right.

Charming Fiona
coming March 7th

Click here for more information

DISCOVER OTHER BOOKS BY JESSICA

THE PICKING UP THE PIECES SERIES:

Picking up the Pieces

Rising from the Ashes

Pushing the Boundaries

Worth the Wait

THE COLORS NOVELS:

Scattered Colors

Shrinking Violet

Love Hate Relationship

Wildflower

THE LOCKLAINE BOYS (a LOVE HATE RELATIONSHIP spinoff):

Fire & Ice

Opposites Attract

Almost Perfect

THE PEMBROOKE SERIES (a WILDFLOWER spinoff):

Sweet Sunshine

Coming Full Circle

A Broken Soul

ABOUT THE AUTHOR

Born and raised around Houston, Jessica is a self proclaimed caffeine addict, connoisseur of inexpensive wine, and the worst driver in the state of Texas. In addition to being all of these things, she's first and foremost a wife and mom.

Growing up, she shared her mom and grandmother's love of reading. But where they leaned toward murder mysteries, Jessica was obsessed with all things romance.

When she's not nose deep in her next manuscript, you can usually find her with her kindle in hand.

Connect with Jessica now
Website: www.authorjessicaprince.com
Jessica's Princesses Reader Group
Newsletter
Facebook
Twitter
Instagram
authorjessicaprince@gmail.com